THREAT
LEVEL

THREAT LEVEL

WILLIAM CHRISTIE

PINNACLE BOOKS
Kensington Publishing Corp.
http://www.kensingtonbooks.com

For Beth, of course

PINNACLE BOOKS are published by

Kensington Publishing Corp.
850 Third Avenue
New York, NY 10022

All Kensington Titles, Imprints, and Distributed Lines are available at special quantity discounts for bulk purchases for sales promotions, premiums, fund-raising, and educational or institutional use. Special book excerpts or customized printings can also be created to fit specific needs. For details, write or phone the office of the Kensington special sales manager: Kensington Publishing Corp., 850 Third Avenue, New York, NY 10022, attn: Special Sales Department, Phone: 1-800-221-2647.

Pinnacle and the P logo Reg. U.S. Pat. & TM Off.

First Pinnacle Printing: October 2005

0-7860-1707-4

10 9 8 7 6 5 4 3 2 1

Printed in the United States of America

"Do we need a new organization?"

Secretary of Defense Donald Rumsfeld.
Memo to his aides and the Joint Chiefs
of Staff; Subject: Global War on Terrorism.

"Rumsfeld has long been enamored of the idea of expanding the role of Special Operations forces in fighting terrorists. He has dramatically boosted the budget of the forces and last year ordered the Special Operations Command to draft a strategy to send hunter-killer teams after terrorist cells."

Gregory L. Vistica, the *Washington Post*,
January 5, 2004.

"All men dream: but not equally. Those who dream by night in the dusty recesses of the mind wake in the day to find that it was vanity: but the dreamers of the day are dangerous men, for they may act out their dream with open eyes, to make it possible.

T.E. Lawrence, *Seven Pillars of Wisdom*.

ACKNOWLEDGMENTS

I'd like to publicly thank the members of the military and law enforcement communities who helped me out, but of course I can't. They have my gratitude, and my respect for not telling me anything I really couldn't have found in open source material.

Then there are my friends, who mean more to me than I can say. Some are still serving or otherwise prone to embarrassment, so first names will have to suffice for all. The Bull and Joan. Jad and Peg. The Zooman. Erich and Vicki. Rick and Melissa, Ské and Guia. Dan and Sonita.

Jim and Beth, as always, for everything. My promise is now kept. Anne and Howard, my second set of parents.

Jason and Valerie, Phillip and Sally, Lee, Kimberly, Neil, and Will.

John and Shirley.

Hope, Anne, Jackie. Hobe, and now Gwynn. By all means, Mary.

My family of course.

Gary Goldstein, the editor of this book. A total pro and an absolute pleasure to work with. I don't get to say that about editors very often. Thanks for the act of faith, Gary.

My agent, Richard Curtis of Richard Curtis Associates. The man who kicked everything off. I've said it before and I'll say it again: one of the good guys. A thank you doesn't seem at all sufficient, Richard, but it's yours anyway.

And finally my mother, who both made me and made me a writer.

I can be contacted at christieauthor@yahoo.com.

1

The fading moonlight glistened across the Shit River. Which was what generations of sailors had called the wide drainage channel that separated the former U.S. Naval Base of Subic Bay from the Philippine town of Olongapo City.

When the U.S military left in 1991, the Philippine Armed Forces had looted nearby Clark Air Force Base right down to the office coffeepots. When they tried to do the same at Subic they were met at the gates by the civilian workforce brandishing hammers and wrenches. This had spared one of the finest deepwater ports and ship repair facilities in Asia. Now Subic was a special economic zone, the port handling traffic for nearby Japanese factories. The bars and clubs of Olongapo, whose very memory was enough to still raise a smile on the faces of middle-aged men across America, now serviced sex tourists from all over the world.

The violet predawn light slowly revealed darker thunderheads building up over the South China Sea across the bay. The tropical air was heavy and damp; it smelled of everything from rotting jungle and raw sewage to cooking smells foreign to the Western sense memory.

"Smell that?" Sergeant First Class Enrique Silva asked Master Sergeant Edwin Storey.

Storey was making sure he still had all the luggage he'd come off the plane with. He was inventorying it by touch. Gas mask, pistol, Racal multiband walkie-talkie radio, stun grenades, blast strips, rifle and pistol magazines. Preoccupied with his task, he muttered back, "Smell what?"

"The P.I., man," said Silva. "The P.I. I did J.E.S.T. here when I was with the First Group on Okie."

Translated from army-speak, Silva had traveled to the Philippine Islands while stationed with the First Special Forces Group on Okinawa. The legendary Jungle Environment Survival Training course had been run by native Negrito Indians under contract by the navy.

Dawn broke as they turned onto Magsaysay Drive. Storey's eyes flashed down the street, checking off landmarks. And not failing to notice the gritty storefront establishments with loud signs and garish lighting. Sidewalks still teeming at that hour. "Okay, more bars per square foot than any other place I've been in my life. I'm assuming you got laid."

"Laid!" Silva exclaimed. "Laid? Laid doesn't even begin to describe it. The women in this town are pros, but they *love* their work. This is Disneyland for adults, my man. Our boy ain't the only Arab in town, but if he hadn't been the only Arab in town *not* getting laid, we probably wouldn't have found him."

"You've got to live your cover," Storey said in agreement.

For the hundredth time, Silva checked the chamber of his rifle to make sure a round of ammunition was loaded. It was one of his partner's little tics that Storey was accustomed to. His own rifle was propped between his knees, barrel pointed down. It was the CQB, or Close Quarters Battle, version of the M-4 Enhanced Carbine, used exclusively by the U.S. military's Tier-1 counterterrorist units: the army's Combat Applications Group, still informally known by its original name, Delta Force; and the Navy SEAL Special Warfare Development Group, which had originally been called SEAL Team Six. Special operations units tended to change their names whenever one of their number wrote a tell-all book about them.

The CQB rifle was an M-16 carbine with sliding stock, very short ten-inch barrel, and beefy plastic front hand guards. The rest of the special operations community still used the previous generation M-4A1 carbine with the 14.5-inch barrel. But the weight of all the equipment Delta and DevGroup habitually hung on the front of their rifles—sound suppressors, laser sights, grenade launchers, etc.—actually bent the barrel once it got a little warm from firing, seriously affecting accuracy and reliability. The CQB rifles were hand-built by the Naval Weapons Station at Crane, Indiana.

As if to prove the point, both Silva's and Storey's rifles had Picatinny Lightweight Shotguns mounted under the front hand guards. This was just a naked twelve-gauge shotgun barrel, simple action, and five-round magazine. The shotgun was mainly used to blow the locks off doors. Also mounted to the rifles were Surefire tactical flashlights and Aimpoint Comp M red-dot sights.

"I've gone in every way from helo to horse," Storey told Silva. "But this has gotta be a first."

Silva nodded. They were traveling in a jeepney, basic Filipino public transportation. A four-wheeled, open-sided bus/taxi, usually painted in the brightest of colors, resplendent in chrome, and hung with more lights than a redneck's front yard at Christmastime.

Storey actually thought the jeepney was a brilliant idea. Olongapo never really slept, even during afternoon siesta. The usual dark-colored SUVs with tinted glass roaring down the street would have put the town into an uproar before they even got near their target.

The idea had come from the men seated behind them in the jeepney, quietly chattering in Tagalog. An assault group from the Anti-Terrorist Unit of the Philippine National Police Special Action Force.

"Coming up," said Silva. They'd carefully studied street maps and photos taken by the technical intelligence team. He and Storey pulled green balaclavas made from fireproof Nomex fabric over their heads and strapped on helmets. "You're gonna get shot in the head."

Unlike the others, who were all wearing Kevlar ballistic helmets, Storey had insisted on the old black plastic Pro-Tec helmet that all of Delta Force used to wear on assaults. The only protection it provided was against low doorways and falling debris, but it was light and Storey valued being able to move his head quickly over bullet protection. "So you keep telling me."

The two had worked together in strange places and very close quarters all over the world, lending them something of the quality of an old married couple.

"Here we go," said Silva. "Hotel California. Great name for a skivvie house. By the hour or by the day."

"You can check out any time you like," Storey said in a monotone, "but you can never leave."

"Wel-come to the Hot-el Cal-i-for-nia!" came bursting out in full song from the assault group behind them, seriously startling Silva and Storey, who both fell over laughing before leaning over the seat to deal out high fives that were muffled by everyone's green Nomex gloves.

"The boys are loose," Silva whispered to his partner.

"Shit, they do this for real more often than we do," Storey replied quietly, pulling the ballistic goggles down over his eyes.

"Let's hope they do it well," said Silva. They'd had less

than a day to practice with the Filipinos, always an iffy proposition.

Storey made a series of radio calls to check that everyone was in position: the assault team hitting the rear, and the snipers on the building across the street.

The jeepney squealed to a halt in front of the hotel, and the group piled out. Gunfire not being unknown on the streets of Olongapo, pedestrians were already beginning to scatter.

Through the front door and pounding up the stairs. The sight of a line of men in green Nomex assault jumpsuits, helmets, and thick bulletproof vests bulging with deadly toys caused the desk clerk to immediately drop to the floor and curl up into a ball under his desk.

The second floor and a dog was barking frantically nearby. Down a hallway smelling of urine not fully masked by industrial cleanser. Storey was out in front. They were moving slower now, and much more quietly. Storey confirmed the room number and exposed the adhesive on a strip of foam rubber loaded with a three-hundred-grain-per-foot explosive cutting charge, sticking it onto the hinge side of the door lengthwise. It was a light charge. Third World buildings were made from cardboard and tissue paper, and it would be professionally embarrassing to bring down the entire building, with you inside, while trying to blow in a single door.

The top-tier antiterrorist units all relied on explosive for the initial door breach. Battering rams, Halligan pry bars, and hydraulic doorjamb spreaders all might work on the first try, but if they didn't, then the element of surprise was lost and the target alerted. Likewise Hatton or Shoklock rounds fired from a shotgun to blow off locks or hinges. The lock or hinge might come off, but then again it might not. Shotgun rounds were better suited for use after the first shot had been fired. Explosives were surer.

Storey backed away from the door, unrolling the

blasting wire. The explosive was fired by an electric
match, like a model rocket though much more reliable. Storey ducked behind the Kevlar breacher's blanket held up by one of the Filipinos to protect them
from back fragmentation: wood splinters and pieces of
hinge and lock. The rest of the team was stacked up
behind them.

Storey raised his hand, and starting from the back,
each man slapped the shoulder of the one in front to
indicate he was ready. When Storey felt Silva's hand on
his shoulder, he released the lever on the firing box in
his left hand, sending an electrical charge down the wire.

At the sound of the explosion the hotel power went
out, killed from outside. The door disappeared in a
rush of dark smoke. Already up, Storey threw a stun
grenade, or flash-bang as it was always known in the
trade, hard through the open doorway. A second later
it blew with a five-pound-per-square-inch shock wave, 175
decibels of sound, and two million candlepower of
white light.

Storey went through the doorway, fast, and turned
right, hugging the wall. An instant behind him, Silva
went left. It was impossible to watch movement in opposite directions, so anyone in the room who hadn't
been deafened, blinded, or stunned by the flash-bang
still couldn't keep up with what was going on. Both
men had the white-light tactical flashlights attached to
their rifles switched on.

In the smoky haze a figure was raised half up from the
bed, as if caught in indecision. Storey fired his shotgun.
A shot-bag round, lead shot in a cloth bag that hit like
a bucking mule, but nonlethal.

It knocked the figure back onto the bed, he grabbed
his chest in pain, and that was enough to close the distance. Storey grabbed the man by the neck and threw
him onto the floor. His full weight was on the man's neck
while the flexible plastic handcuffs, like electric cable

ties, went on. Storey felt paternal pride as the Filipino number-three man glided smoothly past him to cover Silva, who popped another flash-bang and cleared the bathroom. The number-four man came up to cover Storey as he handled the prisoner.

The prisoner was only wearing underwear, which made the search easier. Storey rolled him over and shone his light across the Arab face. It was their man.

"Clear," came Silva's voice over Storey's earphone.

"White, Bravo, Seven—clear," Storey radioed out, giving the room code number. "Target secured." Always intensely self-critical, he thought that had gone fairly smoothly. He flicked the pillows off the bed, revealing a SIG 9mm pistol and a Russian RGD-5 hand grenade.

As Storey bent over to pick up the weapons, a burst of incoming fire stitched the air above his head. Dropping to the floor, he looked up through the mist of plaster dust and saw the line of bullet holes that had been fired through the wall at them. "Taking automatic fire from Red Eight," he radioed instinctively. "Single AK." Silva was all right, on the floor and crawling toward the door to the adjoining room. One of the Filipinos was down, and was being attended to by the other.

There wasn't supposed to be more than one target in the building, but this wouldn't be the first time faulty intelligence had jammed itself up his ass.

Storey radioed his backup team to stay out in the hall and cover the door to the next room in case someone came out. He removed a Blast Strip from his vest. A thirteen-by-four-inch strip, only two millimeters thick and made from the same explosive material as a stun grenade. Designed to be slipped under doors.

Hours of practice made their timing perfect. Storey pushed the Blast Strip under the door and detonated it. Silva simultaneously fired a Hatton round at the doorknob and kicked the door. The Hatton round blew off the whole doorknob and a chunk of door, then dissipated into a harmless powder.

They entered as before, crisscrossing quickly through the lethal funnel of the doorway. The room was empty but for a pile of expended cartridge cases on the carpet. But there was the door to the next room, and the sound of furniture being thrown up against it. Expecting it, Storey and Silva were already low when the next burst of gunfire came through the wall. Along with the sound of a man yelling and a woman screaming. Hostages.

"We can't wait for the fucker to decide to blow hisself up," said Storey. The only noticeable indicator of his stress level was when rural West Virginia came back into his voice.

Then a bellow came through the wall. "I want to negotiate! I want to negotiate!"

"He wants to negotiate," Silva said to Storey.

"Good," Storey replied. "He won't be shooting while he wants to negotiate."

"Fucker sounds American," said Silva.

Neither of them had the slightest desire to begin hour upon hour of negotiations, helped along by Arab ambassadors and the Philippine press, no doubt. Silva aimed his thumb at the bulging load-bearing pouch on the back of his vest. Storey pulled out and unrolled the three-by-four-foot light wall-breaching charge. It looked a lot like a rubber bathtub mat, except in this case the ridges were explosives.

They taped it to the wall, very quietly, trying to avoid the burst of fire that any scratching would have provoked. Storey unraveled the wire while making a very quiet radio call describing what they were going to do. In response to a question he replied curtly, "We've got it on this end." Silva tipped the bed over on its side, aiming the mattress toward the charge.

As they crouched behind the bed, Silva said, "Hope it's not a load-bearing wall."

"You pay your money, you take your chances," Storey replied.

He detonated the charge. Even with earplugs, open mouths, and a lot of practice standing near things that went bang, it was still like getting hit with a cast-iron frying pan—an experience he remembered vividly from his youth.

To give them more time to get through the hole, Silva threw in a multiblast flash-bang. Popping the fuse ejected seven separate submunitions from the grenade body, sending them bouncing all over the room. These exploded separately over a random three-second period.

Storey had been trained to ignore them, and as he came through the hole he acquired a figure holding a woman out in front of him, AK-47 jammed into her neck. Each blast lit up the room like a photographer's strobe, then darkened to the two flashlight beams. Like a football player so focused he cannot hear the crowd, Storey saw lips moving but registered no sound.

Storey's target was the side of the man's face, only about three inches of which were exposed. Thousands of hours and literally hundreds of thousands of rounds fired in the killing house at Fort Bragg didn't make it easy, but it made it possible. It had made the process part of his instinctive muscle memory, so he did not have to consciously think about it. In the duration of a second his breathing was controlled, the luminous red dot of the sight floated onto the aim point, and his fingertip slapped the trigger twice.

Storey could tell by the way the body fell back that it was dead, but the additional "double tap" of two more rounds to the chest was standard procedure. Terrorists were not protected by the Geneva Conventions, so everyone was shooting hollow-point ammunition.

Storey and Silva didn't let themselves become fixated on the target that was down. They continued their deadly dance through the room, flashlight beams sweeping around overturned furniture. There was one more man in there, but he was no terrorist. A fat middle-aged blond, bare-ass naked, crying in German. No terrorist, but experience had taught Storey to make no assumptions, so he handcuffed the man anyway.

The woman was a Filipino, also naked, but silent, with eyes widened into two dark tunnels. Silva grabbed her and pulled her down to the floor, telling her she was all right and to stay there.

Waiting for his partner had held Storey up before moving on to the bathroom. But his flashlight beam was trained on the door, and picked up the dark object sailing out.

"Grenade!" Storey shouted, dropping flat onto the carpet.

It was a high-explosive fragmentation, not a stun grenade, and therefore much more powerful. The blast lifted the ceiling of the room right off its flimsy supports. Gravity did the rest, bringing it and the contents of the upstairs room back down on top of everyone.

Storey's bell was well and truly rung, but the adrenaline and willpower were both roaring, like with a badly hurt accident victim who still has to be held down. As soon as he tried to move he realized that his right leg was pinned. Wiggling around until his back made contact with something solid, he tried to use his left leg to push away whatever was holding him. It didn't budge on the first try, but then he put all his power into it. With his abdominal muscles feeling as if they were about to give, wood cracked and moved, and he was able to pull his leg free. With debris over his head, Storey looked around for an open space to pull himself up to. The windows and drapes had been blown out by the explosion, and sunlight was now streaming into the room.

Storey could hear someone moving around. He hoped it was Silva, but on the chance it wasn't he stayed silent and pushed himself through a gap in some timbers. Halted midway, he quickly realized that his rifle was pinned under the debris, and the sling was yanking him back like a leash. His fingers found the folding knife clipped to his vest and cut it.

Big chunks of ceiling were lying on top of the hotel room furniture, which amazingly hadn't collapsed under the weight. More furniture, from the upstairs room, was lying on top of that, but there were spaces and openings everywhere.

Storey pulled himself up through one and emerged onto the top of the debris field. And found himself face-to-face with a Filipino crawling over the ceiling pieces, heading for the window, a pistol in his hand.

At the sight of Storey he stopped and the pistol came around. Storey went for the .45 on his thigh holster, with a gunfighter's melancholy realization that he was going to be the loser. The pistol was swinging right at his head; he might not even be able to take the bastard with him.

While his hand moved Storey focused on the two brown eyes, hoping they'd hesitate or freeze. They didn't even blink. Storey himself was blinking rapidly to fight off the adrenaline that was tunneling his vision. He couldn't even pop off a last-ditch hip shot—he had to get the pistol up and over all the wood in front of his chest.

Then, still focused on those eyes, Storey saw the hair on the side of the head puff up. The eyes changed, and with a crack that he first thought was the pistol though he quickly realized it wasn't, a red mist clouded the air.

His adversary's body lurched back and then began spasming violently. Storey recognized the action. Brain shot. The destroyed brain was firing off a few last frantic, incoherent commands to the body.

Storey looked out through the gaping hole of the window. That shot had to have come from the sniper team across the street. Well, he was buying the drinks.

Storey climbed atop the debris and tried his radio. Dead; smashed, most likely. He called out, "Ricky, you all right?"

The room began to fill up with Filipino Special Forces wielding pry bars and dragging in a Jaws of Life. Which was actually standard hostage rescue equipment.

The German tourist was found under a desk, totally uninjured, though in deep shock. And still pink and naked and handcuffed.

It took the Jaws of Life and six very strong men to get the beam off Silva's back. The Filipino whore was underneath him, protected by his body, weeping quietly.

Silva was conscious, and Storey was right next to his ear as the beam came off. "How you doin', hombre?"

"Can't feel my legs, bro," Silva replied. The words turned Storey's stomach to ice. Silva's eyes turned down to the girl. "But I may just have a hard-on right now."

Storey wanted to say a few other things, but what came out was, "We can all step outside if you don't want to waste that woody."

"Nah." Silva looked down at the girl again. "But make sure you get her phone number for me."

Doc Smith, the Delta medic and leader of the team that had covered the rear of the hotel, placed a plastic cervical collar on Silva and secured him to a backboard with straps and inflatable bags. Only then did they lift Silva up, turn him over, and take him off the girl. Doc Smitty started a bag of intravenous fluid and injected drugs to minimize swelling of the spinal cord.

A chain of operators passed Silva out into the hallway. As they went down the stairs the girl, now wrapped up in a Mylar space blanket, broke away from her protectors and walked along with the backboard, her palm on Silva's forearm.

"You think we could get her back home without a visa?" Silva asked Storey. "Maybe I could adopt her or something?"

"We'll send for her later," Storey suggested. "She'll be a big help with your rehab."

As usual with these types of scenes in the Third World,

the building quickly filled up with cops of all descriptions and various official and semiofficial rubberneckers. All of whom seemed to have their own press contingent to document their involvement. The Americans pulled their balaclavas up over their faces and hurried to clear the area.

At the bottom of the stairs Storey ran into the intelligence team, who were carrying a big bag of material they'd gleaned from the hotel rooms. Storey was carrying his mangled rifle in one hand. "Good work, you two," he said in the calm easy tone that made it even harder to take. "This is one guy." He held up a single finger. "And this is three." Three fingers went up. "You step out for a quick blow job and lose count?"

They made no reply.

What looked to be the local police chief, who had definitely not been informed of the raid for fear that he'd find someone to sell the information to, was shouting angrily at the Special Action Force commander. What looked to be the hotel owner began shouting at both of them, until a cop gave him a hard "mind your manners" slap on the back of the head.

There was quite a crowd gathered on the street, and a lot more reporters and photographers. The thunderheads had arrived overhead and it was raining hard, a tropical downpour. The Americans piled into a van with tinted windows. Their prisoner was already inside, a cloth bag over his head.

The Special Action Force Anti-Terrorist Unit boarded their own vehicles, leaving the scene cleanup to the locals.

TV crews filmed them all the way to the Subic Bay gate, where they were left behind to argue with the guards.

The vans followed Argonaut Highway around to the far side of the bay, to the Subic Bay International Airport. Or what had once been the Cubi Point Naval Air Station.

Waiting on the tarmac was a U.S. Air Force C-130

transport to take the Special Action Force and their vehicles back to Manila. And two Gulfstream business jets, in air force livery. One to take the prisoner, along with a CIA team, to the interrogation center at Bagram Air Base in Afghanistan.

Storey collared Doc Smith. "We taking Ricky to Manila?"

Smith shook his head. "Kadena."

"You sure?"

"Ed, you know Bin Laden could walk into a Manila hospital and shoot him in the head, and no one would even notice. He can make it to Kadena."

Storey hoped so, even though he understood the reasons.

The sniper team, two DevGroup SEALs Storey had never worked with before, were unloading their rifle cases from the van.

"Great shot," he told them.

They both grinned.

"Who took it?" he asked.

The younger of the two, black with a baby face that made him look even younger, raised his hand.

Storey shook it. "*Really* great fucking shot."

"Yeah," the SEAL replied. "I know."

Storey liked that. "If you're drinking, I'm buying."

"Oh, we're drinking," the sniper said.

Before the Filipinos boarded their aircraft, Storey passed among them shaking ha..ds and passing out envelopes. Inside each was a crisp new hundred-dollar bill. The man in his team who'd been hit was all right. His vest had stopped the round, and he was proudly showing off the angry purple bruise. He got two envelopes.

Inside a nearby parked car the unit commander was receiving a much thicker envelope from the CIA chief of station. An agent in the front seat surreptitiously took a photo of the exchange with his picture phone, just in case the future relationship ran into any snags. It was the way things were done in these parts.

Storey's envelopes were because the troops would never see any of that cash. Rank had its privileges. Once they got a peek inside, the operators pressed around Storey, giving him their phone numbers in case he needed them again. He dutifully entered every one into his PDA. You never knew when they might come in handy.

The rain stopped with tropical abruptness, and the Gulfstream took off for Okinawa. Silva was laid on the cabin deck.

When Storey emerged from the bathroom, Doc Smith motioned him over to the seat beside him. Storey sat down heavily, with an audible groan.

"How you feeling?" Smith asked him.

"Old, Smitty. Really fucking old."

"Ed, you're thirty-four."

"Yeah," Storey said, with feeling. "I sure am."

2

It was just after 9:00 PM on the other side of the world. Roseville, Virginia, to be exact. A suburban development. The kind where all the houses looked the same at night, and anyone unfamiliar with the streets might end up driving in circles for hours.

Two people walked down the sidewalk, occasionally detouring around a poorly placed lawn sprinkler. One was much shorter than the other. They were wearing dark clothing and hats, possibly baseball caps. And sneakers, because their feet made no sound on the concrete. The only streetlights were at the intersections. Otherwise it was just front door lights and flickering TVs through living room windows.

The two walkers abruptly disappeared from sight, having turned down a short driveway. There was the sound of a garage door opening. A sound absolutely no one in the suburbs paid any attention to.

To keep thieves from driving down a street, recording the radio codes of automatic garage door openers, and then simply playing them back whenever they wanted to break in, the door manufacturers used a simple encryption system that changed the code every time the door was opened. But all these systems had one thing in common. A resynchronization mode when the remote and the opener got out of sync. Universal remotes were available that used the resynchronization mode every time.

The pair disappeared into the darkness of the garage, and the door rumbled closed behind them. Inching their way through was easy enough without turning on a light, since there was a car missing. A faint glow came from a small keypad mounted on the wall next to the door leading into the house.

Most people enter and leave their homes through the garage, so that was where burglar alarm installers tended to mount the controller.

Contrary to popular belief, burglars do not use hand-held computers that randomly generate numbers until the alarm PIN is entered. Why go to such trouble when the typical home owners leave their garage door open when they enter their PIN, not knowing they're being watched through binoculars?

There were even easier methods, but this had dropped into the pair's laps the first day they cased the house.

And instead of the usual technique of prying the door open with a crowbar, the shorter one produced an electric lock pick that looked just like a small battery-operated screwdriver. The pick and tension wrench were inserted into the keyhole of the very fine Yale dead bolt lock. The unit was turned on briefly, and it vibrated the pick needle like an electric toothbrush. This struck all the lock pins at the same time, causing them to jump into the air and become aligned. The split second that happened, a twist of the wrist turned the tension wrench and opened the lock.

As soon as the pick gun had been turned on, there was a pounding of feet on stairs, fast-moving nails clicking on hardwood floor, and the wild, deep-throated barking of a very large dog on the other side of the door. The pair seemed neither surprised nor concerned. The tall one got a good grip high up on the door. He opened it quickly. The broad snarling head of a rottweiler lunged through. The door was pulled shut, hard, catching the dog's neck between the door and the door frame like a cow in a chute. Even such a powerful animal could gain no leverage that would allow it to escape.

The typical burglar would have hit the dog on the head with a hammer, but this pair was more benevolent. The short one produced a syringe pole, removing the plastic cap from the needle end. Around forty dollars from any Internet veterinary supply firm, the pole was basically a sixteen-inch stick with a disposable hypodermic syringe on one end. The pressure of the pole being jabbed into the animal's front shoulder injected the drug. In this case two milligrams of Butorphanol, a synthetic opiate used to sedate both pets and people. In less than two minutes the dog was immobilized but not totally unconscious.

The two stepped cautiously into the house. Both of them together couldn't carry nearly two hundred pounds of deadweight very far, so they dragged the animal through the hardwood-floored entryway and into the kitchen, where there were no carpets to produce unneeded drag. They left the dog there, its eyes fluttering at half-mast and its stomach heaving up and down at every breath.

Then they got to work. No lights were turned on. The tall one went upstairs. The short one passed by the TV and stereo without a glance. The computer was in a small study off the living room. The shorter intruder sat down in front of it. A tiny flashlight with a blue lens held between the teeth provided sufficient light. Blue rather than white preserved night vision.

Paper clips were set down to mark the exact position of the computer keyboard on the desk before the unit was turned over and the screws removed with an actual battery-powered screwdriver. A great deal of care was taken to keep the small screws together. Then a box the size of a man's thumb was inserted into the keyboard housing, a plastic clip snapping it onto the outgoing cable. The unit was screwed back together.

The keyboard was returned to its original location, and the paper clips pocketed.

Next a sheet of plastic was spread on the floor to catch any debris, and the louvered grate unscrewed from one of the central air ducts in the ceiling. Double-sided tape attached a black plastic box slightly larger than a pack of cigarettes to the metal side of the ductwork, far enough back to be out of immediate sight. The grate was screwed back into position. Then plastic objects roughly the size of thick dimes were carefully salted throughout the room. Mainly inside the upholstered furniture.

Working deep within the guts of an overturned arm-chair, the short intruder suddenly stopped and straightened up, pressing a finger to one ear. A voice crackled through the walkie-talkie earphone, "Get out. Get out."

The tall one came flying down the stairs, but both were halted by another radio call, "Coming down the street. Get out fast."

It was too late to exit through the garage. The tall one seemed to waver, but the short one pointed toward the kitchen, mimicking the plunging action of a hypodermic.

The tall one followed the instructions. In the kitchen the dozing rottweiler was injected with 1.5 milligrams of Narcan, a drug used to treat overdoses. It quickly reversed the narcotic effect of opiates.

The short one dashed for the garage entry, opening the door, reactivating the alarm, and ducking back into the house. The door was shut just as the garage door began to open.

A cool and careful walk through the living room to make sure everything was back in its original position, then to the kitchen. Every alarm system had a delay before it armed, and with a big dog roaming the house there wouldn't be motion sensors in the rooms. Only the doors and windows would be wired.

The pair stood still as statues in the kitchen. The rottweiler was shaking its head groggily, beginning to regain consciousness.

The garage door closed, and the dog was trying to get up.

More time passed, marked by the ticking of the kitchen clock and low growling from the dog.

The dog suddenly sat up on its front legs, head rolling about as if unable to focus. The tall intruder brandished a can of pepper spray that the short one immediately pushed away.

The dog got fully up, staggering slightly, and began to turn toward them. A key scraped in the lock, which meant the alarm was off. The kitchen door was opened, quickly but quietly. The pair slid out, the short one closing it just as the home owner came into the entry. The electric pick did its job again, and the tension wrench turned the dead bolt very slowly so it wouldn't snap.

They ran through the backyard. The neighbor's dog was barking; the reason they hadn't come in that way.

Over the back fence, then another yard and onto the next street over. Back to walking normally down the sidewalk.

A car pulled up behind them. The pair got in. The interior lights had been disabled.

The tall one collapsed back onto the rear seat, unzipping his windbreaker and pulling up the bottom of his T-shirt to wipe the sweat off his face. "Jesus Christ, Beth!"

The shorter one took off her baseball cap, and shoulder-length hair cascaded down. "Well, what else were we going to do—have tea ready when he came in?"

"We could have gotten out."

"And left the doors open, the burglar alarm off, and a drugged dog snoozing on the kitchen floor? I'm sure he never would have suspected a thing. You're all right, Paul. You did okay."

The tall one just shook his head, totally drained by the experience.

The man in the front seat said to the woman, "I'm assuming you want to see Timmins right now?"

"Damn right I do. Was that you allegedly tailing our guy?"

"Not us, Beth, so keep your shiv put away."

A pickup truck with a camper on the bed was parked a quarter of a mile away. Beth blasted out of the car and into the back of the camper.

Two technicians were watching laptop computer screens while two other men in suits, one obviously in charge, watched them.

Special Agent Elizabeth Royale of the Federal Bureau of Investigation had shed her jacket and burglar tools and charged in wearing black jeans and T-shirt. She wasn't heavy but she was well packed, with pronounced curves. As a matter of fact, she was being surreptitiously eyed from the rear by one of the technicians with a mixture of both longing and fear at being caught in the act. Fine auburn hair that flew recklessly around her shoulders. High cheekbones, a cute little nose, and a light spray of freckles. Eyes that people tended to stare at longer than strictly necessary because they were unexpectedly brown rather than blue. She kicked the camper door shut with a backward strike of the foot.

Supervisory Special Agent Benjamin Timmins, somewhat contrary to the image of an FBI boss, began by trying to put the pin back into the grenade. "The Royal Beth," he exclaimed. "Nice piece of work in there."

No matter what his hopes were, the compliment didn't cool Beth Royale down one bit. "Yeah. Thanks for all the advance warning, Ben. 'Get out,' and then two seconds later he's coming down the street. What kind of bullshit surveillance is that?"

"You know we haven't got his car spiked yet," Timmins

replied calmly. He *was* in charge of the operation, but just about the last thing anyone ever wanted to do was tell Beth Royale to calm down—especially when she was right. "We couldn't tail him too close, and he came home a different way. But what about you? You couldn't have left when you were told to? If only to preserve the lining of my stomach?"

"Not without compromising the operation, Ben." Having made her point, she stacked up two plastic crates that had held electronic equipment and sat down on them, hard.

"Well, you've certainly got the nerves of a cat burglar," Timmins said. He paused at that. "Hey, wait a minute. The Cat. I like that."

"Ben . . ." It came out like a warning.

"Hey, it worked for Cary Grant in *To Catch a Thief.* He was 'the Cat.'"

"At least it's better than '*Betch*,'" she said.

At that the other agent almost came unmoored from his chair. Beth smiled at him sweetly. "Didn't think I knew that one, did you, Pete?" And then, without turning around, "You through checking out my ass, Johnny?"

The technician flushed red and almost broke his neck getting it back to the computer screen. The other technician stifled a chuckle.

"Now, if we're through," said Beth, "could someone please tell me that all the equipment is up and running?"

Timmins folded his hands behind his head and smiled triumphantly. "The bugs are all working fine. His wife is bitching at him with no interference. Right now he's on the computer doing a Google search to find out what you do when your rottweiler is acting sluggish."

Her mood completely changed by the news, Beth clapped her hands together delightedly and treated them all to a wild, raucous laugh. "We'll know for sure when Salem sends his next e-mail to Detroit."

The FBI already knew that the Roseville home owner,

Salem Awar, was buying low-tax southern cigarettes in bulk and smuggling them up to high-tax Michigan with his cousin Gasim.

What else, they weren't sure of, since they couldn't read Salem's e-mails. Usually this was not a problem, since phone lines were easily tapped. And cable was even easier, as the line streamed in every porn site the entire neighborhood was surfing.

But Salem sent his e-mail encrypted with the freeware program Pretty Good Privacy. Which was why the FBI had conducted what they formally called a surreptitious entry into the premises to install listening devices and a keystroke logger.

The keystroke logger was the hardware Beth had inserted into the computer keyboard. Working from induction on the outgoing cable, a flash memory chip recorded every keyboard stroke before it made it into the computer to be encrypted. The chip could store up to a year's worth of typing, but long before that its contents would be transmitted to the camper.

Likewise, all the small, low-powered listening devices scattered throughout the house transmitted to the longer-ranged base station hidden in the ductwork, which would then pass along every sound.

All the devices could be switched on and off remotely from the camper, so anyone scanning the house for bugs would discover no detectable electronic emissions. The bugs were digital and encrypted, and their transmissions hopped through a broad band of frequencies, so no one in the vicinity with a scanner could pick them up. And microwave instead of VHF or UHF radio frequencies also meant that they wouldn't inadvertently reveal their presence by interfering with the household electronics.

"How did Paul work out?" Timmins asked, referring to Beth's tall partner in crime.

"Real good," she said protectively. "He'll be even better when he gets a few more black bag jobs under his belt."

"You know, Beth, I always suspected it was every lawyer's dream to do some breaking and entering."

"No, Ben. It's every lawyer's dream to do B and E with a warrant from a federal judge making it legal."

3

Drivers on the Washington, D.C., Beltway tend to notice office buildings the same way travelers through Indiana notice barns, thinking: didn't I see that same one a mile back? Stand-alone office buildings, office parks, even office strip malls. The real estate business was good in northern Virginia/southern Maryland, but if the government ever stopped renting, the market would probably collapse.

The reasons were twofold. Most of the headquarters buildings were bulging at the seams; the Pentagon in particular was an ant farm. But the other was secrecy. An otherwise nondescript office building might house a navy submarine design team or a Drug Enforcement Administration surveillance training group without anyone being the wiser. The Mylar film over the windows to defeat electronic eavesdropping, or even disguise the fact that the windows had been bricked over for the same reason, didn't look much different from the film applied for energy efficiency. Only the extra security cameras covering the entrances and parking lots were a reliable tip-off. That, and employees more conservatively groomed and much, much more physically buff than the average software designer.

One such building in an office park in Rosslyn, Virginia,

sheltered just such a secretive military unit. On the door was the seal of the Defense Security and Cooperation Agency (DSCA). A real but little-known part of the Pentagon that traveled around the world doing everything from arranging for training in maintaining the F-16 fighter planes the Defense Department loved to sell to reduce its unit cost, to supplying walkie-talkie radios to border guards in Mongolia and teaching them how to use them.

The secretive military unit in question was located, for budgetary reasons, within the DSCA's office of Policy, Plans, and Programs. One thing was certain. No one within DSCA, let alone the office of Policy, Plans, and Programs, knew anything about it. But the receptionist at the front desk had DSCA brochures to hand out, evidence of your tax dollars hard at work. This was how things were hidden in relatively plain sight.

Every administration comes to power in Washington with the foolish assumption that it's actually in charge of the government. At first it issues orders and directives, confidently sits back waiting for its will to be carried out, then blinks in utter disbelief when it isn't.

All bureaucracies, particularly government ones, work under their own imperatives. And there are always plenty of wooden shoes lying around ready to be jammed into the machinery.

For example, buried deep within the corporate memory of the CIA was the conviction that they'd been dragged into too many dubious ventures by too many different administrations, who then danced off and left the company to take the blame for the ensuing disasters. The lesson learned was that whenever the CIA switched from trench coats to guns they were in for trouble. Even in the post-9/11 world this made them very, very cautious about what they took on.

In the Pentagon every civilian political appointee is assigned at least one if not more military aides, who report back to the generals and admirals everything the appointee is even thinking about doing.

And if a particularly activist secretary of defense comes in like a ball of fire to change things, he soon finds his schedule jam-packed with round-the-world trips and mind-numbing conferences. A few months of continuous fourteen-hour days and twenty-hour flights soon take the starch out of him.

Why? A little-known fact is that generals and admirals absolutely *hate* to undertake military operations. Unlike peacetime routine, where officers' careers are advanced by proficiency with PowerPoint briefings, well-landscaped bases, 100 percent participation in charitable contributions, and canned exercises whose mistakes can be buried in five-hundred-page after-action reports that nobody ever reads, in combat things can go *wrong*. Missions fail, reputations are ruined, and careers end.

Except for bombing. Bombing is relatively safe, as long as it's done from a high enough altitude and no one is all that particular about what gets hit.

But with civilian politicians wanting to run raids or snatch terrorists, all kinds of unacceptable things could happen. Like letting the special operations troops out of their cages, and those animals were always much too eager to get blood on their uniforms. So whenever such missions were proposed, all the briefing and Power-Point skills were employed to show why they weren't feasible. And if those thickheaded civilians persisted, the Pentagon or CIA would just blow the operation by leaking it to the press.

The typical newspaper reader would curse the treasonous liberal press, but really it was a just a case of a high-level official—since this was a game only high-level officials dared to play—taking his ball and going home.

The typical secretary of defense usually threw up his hands after this, knowing that an embarrassing leak about himself would probably be next.

The current secretary of defense, however, found

himself fighting a war on terrorism with a military designed to fight huge armies, navies, and air forces. And an intelligence community that knew when the Russian president pulled a muscle playing judo and could listen in to two Chinese colonels talking on the radio in Shanxi Province, but couldn't track down one man living in an apartment in Lahore, Pakistan, who used Internet cafés to communicate.

The secretary initially turned to Joint Special Operations Command and the soldiers of Delta Force and the SEALs of DevGroup. And they did well in Afghanistan. But in more covert operations around the world they still had to brief their chain of command, the generals and admirals, who refused to give their blessing until the lawyers had all signed off and unanimity was reached to cover everyone's ass. Even if JSOC was capable of pulling off a mission in hours, that didn't matter if it took days to get permission. Worse, the special operators also had to obtain prior approval from the American ambassadors of the countries they operated in, whose first priority was not getting their turf soiled and the locals upset. And even in the rare event that wasn't the case, the operators found themselves saddled with an ambassador with his or her heart set on playing military proconsul in the best Vietnam tradition.

Frustrated by the sluggishness, lack of imagination, and obstructionism, the secretary of defense took matters into his own hands and formed his own unit. An experienced Washington infighter, he moved like lightning, snagging off sixteen highly experienced operators each from Delta Force and the SEALs, along with technical specialists from all the services.

He made it into a Special Access Program, the same level of security as Cold War projects like stealth aircraft. This reduced the number of people cleared to know about it to such a small number that none of them dared leak.

Even though the president was periodically briefed, the

command system was two individuals: the secretary of defense and the national security adviser. So a mission could be approved with two thumbs up and the transmission of a code word to the troops in the field.

The unit was designed to send small teams, usually as small as two individuals, around the world to hunt terrorists. These teams would operate either undercover in unfriendly countries, or liaise with the special forces and intelligence units of friendly ones. If the target was small enough they would capture or kill the terrorist themselves. Otherwise they would do the necessary groundwork and then call in and guide a larger unit to do the job. The larger unit might be anything from a sixteen-man Delta Force troop or Navy SEAL platoon, up to a six-hundred-man Army Ranger battalion.

The military hated everything about it, especially Special Operations Command, which was transforming itself from an administrative entity to an operational warfighting command and didn't want to give up control of any assets.

In the interest of operational security the new unit wasn't even given a name, just an alphanumeric code and a task force number that changed so often that no one but the admin people bothered to keep track of it. So everyone on the inside just called it "the office." Careerists avoided new secret units like the plague, because they might be forgotten come promotion time, so the trailblazers were always snake eaters who hated administration. Therefore the unit, with a strength of around fifty total, was broken down with a bluntness uncharacteristic of today's military into the three subsets of the classic raid mission: assault, security, and support.

Support was the technical specialists in surveillance of all types: physical, electronic, and photographic.

Security was the backup for the assault teams: medical specialists, snipers, and operators being groomed for the assault teams.

Assault was the elite: the two-person teams of undercover

operators, all former members of either Delta Force or SEAL Team Six.

And in that Rosslyn office building on a Monday morning, Master Sergeant Ed Storey was meeting with the unit's senior enlisted man, Navy SEAL Command Master Chief Petty Officer Peter Goldbrook.

And Goldbrook wasn't exactly thrilled by what Storey was proposing. "I dunno, Ed. We've never had a mixed army-navy assault team before."

Storey had been a soldier too long to get excited by resistance of any kind. "The unit's less than a year old, Pete. We're not talking five-hundred-year-old regimental traditions here. Everyone in assault is already teamed up. Support? Well, they're outstanding techies but they're not shooters. Security? Half the guys in security couldn't operate covertly unless there was a power lifting competition in the country they were going to."

Goldbrook took that as a subtle dig at many of the SEALs, whose highly developed upper bodies made them well suited to climbing up the sides of ships and oil rigs, but not for masquerading as computer salesmen. "So you want Troy."

"He saved my ass," said Storey. "It wasn't just that he was good enough to make an amazing shot, it was that he had the balls to take it in the first place."

"Balls he's got. You want him, Ed, you got him."

"Just one question: is he an evangelical?"

It took a lot to throw a master chief, but Storey managed. "How the fuck should I know?" Goldbrook blurted out. "I guess he's a Christian. You got something against evangelicals?"

"Not hardly. They're first-class killers. They just get all twitchy when they have to bribe someone. And in assault Troy'll have to bribe more people than he kills."

"I can find out for you."

"No, that's okay. If you don't know I'll find out for myself."

Goldbrook shook his head. "Evangelical is out . . . black is okay?"

"Hell yes. He can go places I can't."

Reluctantly, Goldbrook said, "There's probably something I'd better mention."

"Oh?"

"Troy is kind of weird."

Storey didn't bat an eye. "He's a SEAL, Pete. He's a sniper. Define weird."

"I don't want to put anything in your head, Ed. The kid's just a little weird."

"He's not a serious boozer, is he? Or a shitbird who just happens to be a brilliant shot? That's definitely not what I want."

"No, no, no," Goldbrook assured him. "He's a damn fine SEAL. He's just a little . . . weird."

"Someone SEALs think is weird," Storey said, amused. "I can't wait to talk to him."

But before the master chief let that happen, he had his own little talk with Petty Officer First Class Lee Troy.

"We've never had a mixed army-navy team," Goldbrook informed him. "So everyone wants this to work, you read me?"

"Yes, Master Chief." Troy had learned early in his career that there was only one acceptable response when the command master chief was giving you the word.

"Don't get fooled by Ed Storey," Goldbrook warned. "A lot of people hear that down-home accent and take him for a dumb shit kicker. And he likes people to do that. But he's got a master's in psychology. All done at night, when he was with operational units."

"Is he going to mind-fuck me?" Troy asked.

"Only if you *need* to be mind-fucked," Goldbrook said, hoping he was making his point.

"Okay. I read you, Master Chief." Troy paused. "All

those Delta guys are real smart." The SEALs regarded Delta as the Poindexters of the special operations community, while Delta paid the SEALs the hollow compliment of being "real studs," implying they were more endowed with brawn than brains.

"Don't get fooled by that, either," said Goldbrook. "Storey did Desert Storm and Panama as a young troop with the First Ranger Battalion. Then the Fifth Special Forces Group before he got invited to Delta selection. He's been to every dance except Mogadishu, and did a three-year exchange tour with the British Special Air Service. When he got selected he was the youngest master sergeant in the army." He paused for emphasis. "There's a lot of good operators around. But there's no one better at low-visibility operations and low-visibility infiltration than Storey. The CIA makes him an offer every year. Keep your eyes and ears open, and you won't get a better learning opportunity. You still reading me?"

"Yes, Master Chief."

If Goldbrook had any reservations about how a black SEAL with a down-easter Yankee accent was going to get along with a southern redneck soldier, he didn't express them. "Just one more thing, Troy."

"Yes, Master Chief?"

"Try not to act too weird."

Troy didn't seem surprised to be hearing that. "Yes, Master Chief."

Storey was waiting outside Goldbrook's office. Troy understood why he was Mr. Low Visibility. The kind of unremarkable face that didn't stick in your mind. Brown hair that was running to salt and pepper. Just shy of six feet tall and lean. Average. As they shook hands, Troy said, "Good to see you again, Top." Military slang for a master sergeant.

Not inappropriate, especially since, like the elite military special operations units, no one worked in a uniform. Jeans, khakis, polo shirts, and short-sleeve shirts were the order of the day. But Storey replied firmly, "Ed."

"Okay, Ed," said Troy, pleased by the informality.

"You get used to calling me Top, you're going to call me that at the wrong time. So don't use it again."

Troy halted their walk across the office. "*Men in Black*, right? You're Tommy Lee Jones, and I'm Will Smith?"

Storey didn't change expression. "Who's Will Smith?"

They stared at each other for a moment; then Troy said, "Okay, Ed."

The only clue to Storey's mood was a slight crinkling of amusement at the corners of his eyes. You never had to kick a special operator in the ass. You usually had to hold him back by the belt. He liked a little attitude. And Troy had just the right look. A SEAL who didn't look like a SEAL, just what the doctor ordered. About five feet eight and that baby face, he even looked a little soft, though Storey knew there was no such thing as a soft SEAL.

They continued across the office. The cubicles, desks, chairs, computers, and phones were all out of the government supply catalog. Other than the occasional family photo on a desk, there were few traces of individuality anywhere. Which wasn't unusual for military offices. In that culture everyone moved on to a different job every three years—everything you packed in and put up only had to be taken down and packed out. And this office in particular was one that people didn't expect to be spending too much time in.

They ended up at a back room that had been converted to equipment storage.

"Just a few assault-specific items to add to your issue kit," said Storey.

"All right," Troy said. "The James Bond shit."

The technician had it all ready, along with the custody card for Troy to initial and sign.

Troy picked up the Iridium satellite phone and began playing with it. "No encryption package?"

"Businessmen carry satellite phones," said Storey. "They don't carry satellite phones with encryption sleeves."

Troy moved on to a top-of-the-line Personal Data Assistant. "Metal-cutting laser?"

"Nope, just a GPS, and a better camera in case you need to snap some documents. You'll keep cover files and a fake address book—but with real numbers in it—so cops and customs can take a look at them. But if anyone tries to access your secure files and programs without your password, the whole unit wipes itself clean. This has the crypto on it. Serial cable links it to the phone."

"What crypto?" Troy asked.

"Pretty Good Privacy."

"Really?"

"We don't want the NSA reading our traffic either." The National Security Agency, the communications interceptors and code breakers of the intelligence community, supplied all communications encryption equipment to the government and military. They also added back doors to everything so *they* could listen in. "That PDA is your most important piece of gear."

"No notebook computer?"

"You can't carry a notebook around with you all the time," said Storey. "And wherever you leave it, someone can get at it, crack it, or slip a bug inside. The phone and PDA never leave your body."

Troy locked back the slide of the Glock Model 26 pistol and peered into the chamber. The entire handgun nearly fit into the palm of his hand. "I thought you D-boys were queer for .45s."

"We are, but it's hard to find .45 ammo in the rest of the world. Nine millimeter is everywhere."

"You think you could walk into a store in Egypt and buy yourself a box of ammo?"

"No," said Storey. "I think you could hit a cop in the back of the head with your pistol and take his rounds. If worse comes to worse."

"Get some," Troy muttered. He picked up a small

black cylinder, only three inches long. "Look at this little baby."

"Gemtech Aurora sound suppressor. Uses urethane wipes, like washers. A lot less messy than grease as a silencing medium. You change to a new pack of wipes after every two magazines."

"Quiet?" said Troy, screwing the little can onto the specially threaded barrel of his Glock.

"Very." Storey handed him a package. "Null USH shoulder holster. The best. Wear it under your shirt—the holster won't print through, and the polymer material won't soak up your sweat. I've got a tailor who'll alter the cut on all your shirts and put Velcro on, so you can rip them open without losing all your buttons."

Troy tried the holster. The Glock slid neatly into the polymer pocket, which also covered the trigger. But the pistol wouldn't come out. "Okay, I give up."

"Get a sold grip, twist, then pull."

"Sweet."

"Try not to shoot a hole in your armpit," said Storey. "I'd never hear the end of that, would I?"

"No, you wouldn't." Storey continued, "When we're at the tailor we'll also get you a couple of business suits."

"Black?"

"Or dark blue or gray."

"Sunglasses?"

Storey allowed himself his first small smile. "Like businessmen wear. Number-one rule: always live your cover. You'll draw passports, documents, and credit cards according to the mission. Diplomatic for overt, fake for covert. Not even the diplomatic will have your real name."

"That's it?"

Storey put emphasis into his statement. "All you really need is your brain."

"I'll bring it."

As they moved Troy into the small, two-desk cubicle, Storey reached into one of his drawers and pulled something out. "There's always one more thing." He handed

Troy a coffee mug. "Everyone in assault has one. Sergeant First Class Green's daughter is a potter."

Troy checked out the mug. Two clean-cut young Americans in business suits—both white, Troy instantly noted—standing on the front steps of a house. A worried-looking Arab wearing a kaffiyeh headdress over his face in terrorist fashion was peering at them from around his door. "The Missionaries?"

"Just a little in-house nickname. We travel around the world spreading the good word."

"And what good word is that?" Troy asked.

"Don't fuck with Uncle Sam. By the way, the mug doesn't leave the building."

"What's next?"

"We'll get you familiar with the PDA and the rest of the equipment first. Then we'll work on tactics. We won't get much time before we have to go operational."

"Storey's Rules," said Troy.

"You heard about them, eh?" Storey said, annoyed. "People have big mouths."

"How many rules are there?"

"A few."

"They work?"

"I'm still here."

The PDA took most of the morning. Storey was relieved to find that he never had to repeat anything.

Then they turned to the desktop computers and Intelink, the intelligence community's own highly classified and highly secure Internet. After, that is, Troy signed more security declarations than he'd ever seen at one time.

"Whenever you start thinking about how much fun it would be to do some surfing with this," said Storey, "your next thought ought to be how much fun Leavenworth would be."

"I figured they log everyone who uses this."

"Yeah, but you know how it is. If you were spying for the Russians they'd never find you. But if you were just fucking around they'd squash you like a bug. It's almost worthless when it comes to current intelligence. But the research is where you make your money."

"What's next?"

Storey liked that. He glanced at his watch. "Lunch. I'll give you three choices. We can eat, PT, or go to the Secret Service range and try out your new *pistole*."

"Let's go to the range. I like to PT after work, to cool myself down."

Storey was examining him again. "So do I."

They were just getting up when Storey's phone rang. He listened, and said, "Great, thanks." Then to Troy, "This is good. You needed to meet Beth Royale, and she's on her way up."

"Who's Beth Royale?"

"FBI. Counterterrorism Division."

"Great. One of those."

"Beth's not your typical special agent."

"That'll be a change."

"Be patient when she sits down. She's going to want to talk about Rick Silva first."

Troy gave him a questioning look, but Storey was already standing up. Initially puzzled, Troy looked around for officers before a hard glance from Storey put him on his feet.

Beth was wearing a dark suit, flats, and her hair back. "Hi, Ed."

Storey said, "Beth, I want you to meet my new partner, Lee Troy."

They shook hands. "Nice to meet you, Lee."

"Likewise."

"Maine?" she said.

"That's right. Little town near Camden."

"Just outside of Boston," said Beth.

They both smiled at each other.

As they were sitting down, Beth said, "Ed, how's Ricky doing?"

Troy's head whipped around to look at Storey, who

ignored him. "He's paralyzed from the waist down, Beth. It's permanent."

Troy was expecting tears, but all she did was let out some breath in the form of a grunt and say, "I was afraid of that."

Storey said, "His first thing he wanted to know from the physical therapist was sex techniques for the paraplegic."

"That's the Enrique I know."

"He wanted me to tell you he liked your chocolate truffles a hell of a lot more than everyone else's flowers."

"Ricky's not a flower guy."

Troy was sitting through this exchange feeling like the outsider.

Storey picked up on that, getting back to business. "What brings you over in person, Beth?"

"The dead guy in Olongapo."

Storey's only reaction was to ask, "Which one?"

"The hostage taker," said Beth. Then, after a hitch, "The black male."

A glance at Troy. Troy wasn't exactly unfamiliar with white people getting uncomfortable around him. That was their problem; he wasn't in the habit of offering any reassurance to make them feel better. But something made him look over at Storey. Storey didn't look uncomfortable. Storey didn't look like anything. Storey was watching *him.*

Beth flipped through some papers. "In your report you said his accent was American."

"That's right," said Storey.

"Well, he was," said Beth. "Karim Abdul-Amin, formerly Kenneth Livingston of Detroit."

"That's not good," said Storey. Terrorist networks using non-Arab Muslim converts were the universal nightmare.

Troy broke in. "Ex-con?"

"That's right," said Beth. "Burglary, drugs, assault. Filipino wife, lots of trips back and forth."

"Abu Sayyaf?" said Storey. "Or Jemaah Islamiya?"

The first was a native Filipino terrorist group. Founded in the early 1990s with the help of Osama Bin Laden and the goal of creating an Islamic state in the Philippines. The group lost its religious focus once they found out just how profitable it was to kidnap for ransom and hire out as general-purpose thugs. Lately they'd rediscovered their faith after being ordered by Al Qaeda to stop kidnapping foreigners because it brought down too much American military heat.

Jemaah Islamiya was an Indonesian-based terrorist group that acted as Al Qaeda's surrogate in Asia. They also ran training camps in the southern Philippines.

"Neither," said Beth. "The Rajah Solaiman Movement."

"The what?" said Troy.

"Got me on that one, too," said Storey.

"Formed in 2002," said Beth. "Unlike the Moros or Sayyaf they want the whole country to be Islamic, not just Mindanao."

"I'd think there are a few too many Catholics for that," said Troy.

"When God gets dragged in it doesn't have to make sense," said Storey.

"They claim the whole Philippines was Moslem before the Spanish arrived," said Beth. "They recruit Christians, then turn them into militants."

"How many Moslem converts can there be in the P.I.?" Troy asked.

Beth turned some more pages. "Quarter of a million or so. Mostly men who worked as migrant laborers in the Middle East, then came home."

"Where's this group's money come from?" Storey asked.

"Abu Sayyaf," said Beth. "Saudi charities. We're working a case in Detroit, and we're looking for possible connections. The prisoner you took is caught up in the interrogation backlog at Bagram. We'd like to get him bumped up to the head of the line."

"I'll talk to the colonel and see if we can create some pressure from our end," said Storey.

"Thanks, Ed," said Beth.

"President's making a trip to Asia in the fall," Storey remarked.

Troy took note of how he just threw it out into the air like that, then added, "That may end up being as smart as going to Dallas in 1963."

"It's on everyone's mind," said Beth. "Ed, if we find any links I'll let you know."

"I know you will, Beth."

"I owe you another one," she said.

Troy also took note of Storey's shy smile, because it was so out of character.

"I'll put it in my little book," Storey told her.

Beth rose and shook Troy's hand. "Nice to meet you, Lee."

"Same here," Troy replied. He then watched Storey's eyes follow her from the office. "Not your usual FBI: act like insurance salesmen; take but don't give."

"Beth takes no shit, so I'd advise you not to give her any. Smart, too. Columbia Law School."

"What's she doing in the Bureau, then?"

"Looking for a little action, I guess. Why did you want to be a SEAL?"

"It wasn't because the law bored me."

Changing the subject, Storey said, "Where did you say you grew up?"

"Ogansquogg, Maine."

"You like it?"

"No."

"Joined the navy to get out of there?"

"That's right," said Troy, hardening up a little because he couldn't see where the conversation was going. In the military, that usually meant you were about to take some shit.

"Ever going back?"

"No."

Storey paused. "Well, I grew up in that same town in West Virginia."

Troy cracked a smile, but changed the subject right back. "Beth's a pretty good-looking woman. If you like redheads. Little too much booty for me, though."

Storey rose to the bait. "You're crazy. She's built like a real woman."

"Go for it," Troy said triumphantly.

If Storey was annoyed at being trapped, it only surfaced in the look of respect he gave Troy. "Right now I need another relationship like I need another marriage."

"How many you had?"

"Marriages? Two."

"Nothing wrong with that, if you're into marriage."

"Yeah, well, I need another one like I need another Purple Heart."

"How many of those you got?"

"Three. I'm better at getting wounded than I am at getting married."

4

A city of fourteen million was easy to hide in. It was even easier if it was the southern port city of Karachi, Pakistan. The fourteen-million figure was just a guess. Fifty years ago Karachi had been home to only a hundred thousand. In 1981 the census came in at five million. In 1994 they figured ten million. The bottom line was that not much urban planning had been done in the interval.

Abdallah Karim Nimri was wandering through Lea Market, checking his back. He'd chosen the market because it was a surveillance nightmare. Spanning whole blocks, both shops and open air, Lea had everything for sale, from automobiles to produce to pushcarts.

Vehicular surveillance was impossible. The roads were a dawn-to-dusk traffic jam. There were the cars of shoppers indulging in the latest fad of curbside purchase without even leaving their vehicles. The trucks of shippers and the buses of the transport operators. Both of whom, following Pakistani custom, would simply pick a spot to use as their terminals and grease the palms of the police to seal the arrangement. A thousand horns blared continuously, in the custom of cities around the world. Something in their DNA leaves human beings positive that if they only lean on their horns long enough and loud enough, the traffic obstruction in front of them will somehow dematerialize.

Anyone trying to surveil a target from a distance with high-powered optics would be confronted by thousands of men who looked almost exactly like Nimri: early thirties, dark hair, moustache, dressed in inexpensive Chinese slacks and long-sleeve dress shirt. More than a few would also be carrying cheap canvas shoulder bags.

The only possible way to trail someone in Lea Market was on foot, and even that was problematic. There was barely room to walk. The vendors had encroached on every bit of open space, again after paying off the police.

Nimri took more than usual care, because his contact had sent him the signal for an emergency meeting. This made him suspicious. Especially since the contact was an army captain from the Directorate for Inter-Services Intelligence, the Pakistani spy agency.

Knowing any surveillance in the teeming market would have to be close-in, Nimri stopped abruptly at a *jadoogar's* shop. No one in front or behind him stopped abruptly, so Nimri shifted his peripheral vision to the magician's wares. The usual snakes and scorpions. A mummified bear cub. And, in pride of place, a moldy stuffed lion that reminded him of the toy animals at a state fair in America.

The proprietor was busy, having just killed a large lizard right before the eyes of an enraptured customer. He then lowered the reptile into a cast-iron caldron filled with boiling oil. After filtering it, the oil would be used by the customer to improve his sexual Shakti.

Hiding his Islamic disapproval, Nimri passed a few rupees to the shop boy and was led into the back storage room. Parts of every dead creature imaginable were in jars, stacked up in piles on shelves, or hanging by cords from the ceiling. The smell inside the shop had been heavily masked by burning incense, but in the storage room it was indescribable. Fearing he would vomit, Nimri held his breath and pushed the boy before him. He didn't take another breath until he was out the back door and in the narrow alley behind the shop. The alley was littered with filth, and someone nearby was burning waste in a fire, but these odors were almost pleasant compared to those of the *jadoogar's* shop. Nimri stood immobile, bent over slightly, until his stomach stopped rolling.

A glance at his watch told him he was running out of time. Turning onto an aisle of produce stalls, Nimri spotted Captain Husain Baloch pretending to evaluate melons while also searching the crowd.

Catching Baloch's eye, Nimri mopped his face with a red handkerchief, the all-clear signal. It was just as well, because he needed it. The heat from all the bodies, stoves, fires, and vehicle exhaust was like a furnace. Baloch nodded imperceptively, and they began pushing through the shoppers toward each other.

Nimri's head throbbed. He knew that one day the wind might shift and Baloch would show up not to pass a message, but to arrest him. Abdallah Karim Nimri had spent two years in prison in his native Egypt, and had no intention of ever again repeating the experience. Especially not at Guantanamo Bay. Taped to his belly was a Chinese Type 82-2 hand grenade, and tucked away in his shoulder bag a Russian Makarov pistol.

This would be a "brush pass." In what would look like accidental contact, Baloch would pass Nimri a written message, then both would continue on their way without a word.

When the two men were shoulder to shoulder, Nimri turned his body inward. He felt the hand touch his shirt, and waited for the pack of cigarettes to be slipped into his pocket. But an unexpected shove from another impatient shopper instead caused the pack to slide down the front of his shirt and bounce off his shoe.

In violation of all tradecraft, Nimri and Baloch both stopped, took a step back, and stared at the cigarette pack lying on the ground between them. As if each waiting for the other to bend down and pick it up.

The decision was made for them. A boy, certainly no more than twelve, flashed between them, snatched up the pack, and broke into a run.

Stunned hesitation overcome by an eruption of rage, Nimri sprinted after the boy, plunging a hand into his bag and yanking out the Makarov.

Street children spent their lives running. For them the stakes were higher than any track meet; natural selection took care of the slow. The boy had started out with a ten-foot lead, and the only thing that kept the race close was him having to push his way through a mostly unyielding public.

None of whom made any move to stop him. People would be more surprised if an hour passed *without* a wallet snatching, and why risk a knife in the stomach? Especially for someone else's wallet.

The boy cut to the right at the end of a row of stalls, and Nimri almost got a hand on him. But the crowd thinned out and another alley loomed ahead.

Knowing the chase was lost, Nimri extended his right arm. One, two, three, four, five shots, the pistol bouncing in his hand. Screams rang out from behind, but still the boy kept running. Now totally consumed by his wrath, Nimri fired again.

The boy stumbled and went down, skidding to a stop. In four strides Nimri was on top of him.

The boy, crying, had one hand pressed to a dark blotch on his hip. The other, outstretched toward Nimri, held the pack of cigarettes. He said nothing, probably not wanting to risk saying the wrong thing, but all his body language was begging for mercy.

Panting heavily, Nimri snatched the pack and jammed it into his trouser pocket. Then, grasping the pistol with both hands to steady it against his breathing, he fired two shots into the boy's face.

He'd actually yanked the trigger three times, but nothing happened on the third. Nimri nearly screamed out his fury before he realized that the Makarov slide was locked to the rear, signifying an empty magazine.

Glancing over his shoulder to confirm what he expected, a crowd silently watching him, Nimri thumbed the release to send the slide home and jammed the pistol back into his bag. He trotted down the alley, away from the mob of onlookers. A few more rupees to calm the proprietor of the shop he entered from the alley, and soon he was again one of the anonymous mass of shoppers.

The audience to the shooting would soon disperse with Karachi cold-bloodedness, leaving the body where it lay. The other part of the story would be the useless questions and time-wasting procedures of the police, whose capriciousness might just as easily result in an innocent witness being dragged off to jail, beaten with an inch of his life to extract a confession, followed by his family being extorted for money for his release. Better to move on.

Nimri caught a bus. A wheezing old Ford, not one of the new Japanese Hinos. Optimistically, the transport company had put up a sign near the entrance: MODEL 2004. Model 1973 would have been more like it, and the fact that it was only the year 2003 did much to water down the impact of the advertising.

When Islamic law had been imposed in the country, Pakistan's buses were fitted with an iron wall to segregate the women's section. Some sportsman had opened a peephole in this particular wall, and a few men were gathered around it, making lewd remarks.

Nimri paid them no mind. The adrenaline draining from his system, he sat with his hands on his knees to stop them both from shaking. He was still furious, this time with himself. He knew he should have let the thief go. The message inside the cigarette pack was in code. Even if the boy, or whomever he sold the cigarettes to, had turned the paper over to the police instead of throwing it away, the police would not have been able to break the code.

He could easily have signaled Baloch to break off the contact. But the captain's urgency in requesting the meeting had put him on edge. And after all the precautions, to have the pass fumbled and the message container dropped at their feet, and then stolen, was simply too much. He had charged off after the boy without even thinking.

And it could have been disastrous. Only by God's will was he not sitting in an interrogation room, an Egyptian with Pakistani identification that would not stand up to close research, the police peering at the coded message, Baloch and the entire network on the run. All due to his rash foolishness.

The bus traveled south down Chakiwara Road, then west into the Saddar district. Nimri got off as soon as he thought it safe. Karachi buses had a tendency to blow up, either due to disagreements of business or politics. He stopped at a news vendor and took a park bench in the shade. Now, for the first time, the cigarette pack was open.

Nimri badly wanted a smoke, but the Prophet, God's blessings upon him, had forbidden the use of tobacco. So he only removed and unfolded the message, groups of numbers on flimsy onionskin paper.

The more times a code is used, the easier it is to break. Especially in the computer age. Ideally, a code should be randomly generated and used only one time. Preferably on a computer of one's own. But Nimri no longer used one. Too many brothers had been captured along with their computers, giving valuable information to the enemy. And the Americans had given the Pakistanis the ability to trace the e-mail messages from Internet cafés, along with mobile phone calls. Nimri communicated either face-to-face or written messages in his favorite book code.

The sender and recipient of a book code used identical volumes. The sender thumbed through and picked out individual words to form a message. The recipient decoded number groups that indicated the proper page, paragraph, line, and finally word.

Book codes could be broken with enough computer power, and if the individual and his volume were captured, all previous messages would also be compromised. But Nimri had added his own twist. His book was a daily newspaper, each edition used only once. Even if a message was delayed, it was a simple matter to visit a library for a back issue.

He and Baloch had chosen the Urdu-language *Daily Jang*, a pro-government paper, with the knowledge that the Americans had precious few Urdu translators.

Nimri now had that very newspaper draped over his knees, the message concealed from view behind it and a pencil at the ready. Until, that is, he realized he was being watched. A thin young man in the traditional *shalwar kameez* of matching pantaloons and knee-length shirt. But with his hair in a most untraditional ponytail.

Nimri searched for the others. Somehow they had followed him. An American tracking device?

The young man seemed to make a decision, and began to approach him. Nimri slid his right hand into his shoulder bag. Only to realize in horror that he'd forgotten to reload his pistol. Another flash of anger, this time at his continued foolishness. His fingers relinquished the plastic grips of the Makarov and passed into his shirtfront to begin rolling the elastic band off the pin of the hand grenade taped to his stomach. The elastic off, he slipped his finger through the pin and took up the slack, muttering quietly to himself, "There is no God but Allah, and Mohammad is his Prophet. God is great." The last words that would speed him to Paradise.

The young man kept looking nervously from side to side as he approached. Nimri applied pressure to the pin.

Then, standing before him, the young man smiled shyly and said, almost whispering, "Oil massage?"

Nimri almost jerked out the pin. "What?" he demanded sharply.

More hesitantly this time. "Oil massage?"

At last finding his wits, Nimri barked, "Be gone!"

The young man departed quickly, before Nimri could call for the police. Something he had absolutely no intention of doing.

Nimri had been so offended by the insult to his manhood that he'd forgotten one more thing. His finger was still inside the grenade pin. His heart thumped even harder when a touch told him that it was halfway out. He carefully pushed the wire back in, them refitted the rubber band around it, checking the work twice before removing his hand from inside his shirt.

The killing at the market had shaken him, but not like this. Rather than dying in holy war against the forces of American imperialism, he'd nearly blown himself to pieces over a homosexual proposition.

The message he decoded didn't improve his mood.

Imram Hasan source for Federal Investigative Agency. Extent of information he provided unknown. Assume everything. Take precautions. Advise.

"Son of a whore!" Nimri exclaimed out loud. The Federal Investigative Agency was the Pakistani police unit with the reputation of being friendliest to the Americans. While Inter-Services Intelligence was thoroughly Islamic. In fact, the creators of the Taliban who had equipped and trained Al Qaeda members to do battle with India over Kashmir.

Imram Hasan was his number two. He had to assume that whatever Hasan knew, the FIA and the Americans did also.

Abdallah Karim Nimri took out a cigarette lighter and burned the decoded message. Then he spent the rest of the day on the park bench, planning what he was going to do. He paused only for prayers.

5

Joseph Oan loved his garden. When he finished work and returned to his home in Manassas, Virginia, he always went directly to his backyard. The roses along the border fence; the grapes spreading across the arbor he'd built himself. He loved sitting at his lawn table, and he loved it when his wife, Yasmin, brought him tea.

Then came the part he didn't love. When his wife had to unburden herself of everything she had been fretting about all day, while he longed for peace and sanctuary. But it was always like this.

"Why won't you take the supervisor's job?" she demanded, as if in exchange for the tea. "Don't you want to wear clean business clothes and work in an office?"

"If I'm a supervisor, I'm not in the union," he explained, trying to be patient with her. "The next time they cut jobs, they could decide they don't need another supervisor and cut my job. But if I drive the truck I'm in the union and my job is safe."

"But you would be home more—"

"Enough," he said.

A pause from her, then, "Steven is being teased at school."

"Again?"

"They call him an Arab terrorist."

Oan was silent.

"You'll speak to the principal," said Yasmin, making it more of a statement than a question.

"No."

"Why no?"

"Because I won't. He has to be a man."

"The principal won't mind."

"I won't complain about my son the same week the FBI questions me about driving a gasoline truck." Women always wanted what was impossible, never considering how, only the wanting.

"Rashid," she said. "It is always about Rashid."

Oan turned on her. "Never speak his name again! I have no brother." And, as always, the expression on her face made him sorry for his temper. "Let me drink my tea."

She went inside. He took a sip and sighed. His tea had cooled. He liked his tea hot. And calling her would only start it again.

The phone rang inside the house. He sighed again, not wanting to get up.

Yasmin appeared, holding the cordless handset. She looked terrified. "Who is it?" he said.

"Them. Again." She was on the verge of tears.

He snatched the phone and waved her away. "Who is this?"

"The brother of your brother," the voice said smoothly. In English, though English was obviously not the man's native tongue. "The blessings of God upon you, Youssif al-Oan."

Oan pronounced his name "Owen." But the caller used the Middle Eastern pronunciation. "What do you want?"

"To help you, of course. In any way we can. As your brother would have wished."

"I need no help. Do not call me again."

The voice lost its soothing lilt. "You will always be part of us."

Oan punched the Talk button, and the red light died. He set the phone down on the table and stared out over his lawn without really focusing on it.

After a while he sighed again, rose, and went into his house. The caller ID on the phone read area code 419. All the others had been overseas calls. He thumbed through the phone book. Toledo, Ohio. They wanted him to know; otherwise they would have blocked the caller ID.

His wife was in the kitchen; he could hear his son tapping away at the computer keyboard. He unearthed the stepladder and carried it up the stairs to his bedroom closet. The trapdoor to the attic crawl space revealed ceiling framing, ductwork, and insulation. It was stifling hot. Peeling back a slab of insulation exposed a fireproof document case.

Oan returned to his backyard, the case under his arm. He removed the lid from the barbecue grill, then unlocked the case.

Photographs of him and his brother, Rashid, when they were children in Lebanon. Then in Virginia. Only letters from the madrasa, the religious school in Pakistan, because by then photographs had become forbidden graven images.

As the eldest he had always worked. It was his fault that his brother had too much free time to never feel at home. His brother hated being teased at school, hated twisting his first name to a Christian-sounding one. Hated that when he did so it made life easier.

So dissatisfied with the world was Rashid that he fell in love with the idea of a perfect world that did not exist, a world that fierce men in beards were going to create. His brother didn't remember enough of Lebanon to remember the perfect world men tried to create there.

For every neighbor who snubbed him after September 11, there were more who sought him out and offered their friendship. And when the FBI agents had interviewed him, the union representative and a union lawyer had sat in the room. In Lebanon they would have tied him to the back of a car and driven until there was nothing left but the bloody rope.

He'd begged his brother to marry. A man couldn't hold his new baby in his arms and think the world an evil and useless place. But by then his brother was under their control. They gave him the feeling of belonging.

He unfolded letters from Afghanistan that contained the wisps of doubt. The people there hated the foreign fighters, hated the new world that the men in beards had created.

Then a last letter, from Pakistan, in the words his brother had used to speak. Rashid was dead, buried by the American bombs that hit his bunker. And then nothing but more words of God and Paradise, God and death to enemies, God and vengeance.

Joseph Oan laid that last letter atop the pile in the grill and touched a match to the edge. When the paper and photographs were nothing but ash he replaced the cover on the grill.

The kitchen window slid open and his wife called that dinner was ready.

6

Pakistani cargo trucks made Filipino jeepneys look drab. Abdallah Karim Nimri was sitting by the side of a road in the Layari neighborhood of Karachi, watching the trucks that had come off the N-25 Highway from Quetta drive by.

He'd been there all morning. Pakistani roads were seldom clear and rarely safe, and Pakistani truck drivers never on schedule. So he waited and watched the trucks. Old British Bedfords; new Japanese Hiros. No two decorated alike, and in brilliant color schemes. The decoration could be anything from Urdu poetry to paintings of the Kaaba and Mosque at Mecca, images of popular Islamic saints, or more secular movie heroes, cricket stars, and idealized representations of desirable women. The chrome was blinding. Even the wheel wells were elaborately painted. The front bumpers were extended to project far out in front, and were of course part of the design. The only common denominator among Pakistani trucks was the built-up caps that towered up to nine feet above the driver's cab, called the *taj* or crown. And the two painted eyes to protect the vehicle against the evil eye.

Finally the truck with the brilliant sapphire-blue and

marble-white color scheme came lumbering down the road, belching diesel smoke. The sides had been blocked out into numerous smaller shadowboxes, each containing ornate Islamic calligraphy.

The trucks were part of a network that reached into the Northwest Tribal Territories and on into Afghanistan. The drivers were devout, but they were also paid. You are free to decline if you wish, they were told when approached. But if they agreed they were liable with their lives, and their families' lives, for the safety of their cargoes.

Which was usually computer disks, cassettes, or videotapes. Wrapped boxes filled with cash. Or heroin. Or the occasional human being. The drivers never knew what the packages contained, or the identities of their passengers. Both were passed along the line from driver to driver, stop to stop. Almost undetectable, and almost never intercepted.

And now this truck squealed to a stop beside Nimri, and a passenger climbed down. A man in his late fifties. The gray had given his beard and hair the color of steel. His *shalwar kameez* was dark brown to hide the grime of the journey, and he wore a knitted *pagris* cap.

He and Nimri greeted formally, touching both cheeks. Nimri led him deeper into the neighborhood. The narrow lanes had no names, and the houses no numbers. The two men stepped carefully over the pools of raw sewage in the streets. Flickering kerosene lamps in windows told that the power was out again. Government employees, even the police, were rare sights in these Karachi neighborhoods.

They came to an apartment house. Poor, peeling; the screams of children bouncing off the walls. Electric lines of all colors crosshatched overhead like spiderwebs, illegally tapping the main lines. Lean, hard young men with empty eyes watched their approach. Nimri and his companion trudged up the stairs of the building, followed by even more eyes.

A third-floor door opened at a single knock. A bearded young man in his midtwenties, glowing with undisguised hero-worship, put his hand over his heart and bowed respectfully. He guided them into the sitting room and left them alone. There was the sound of children being harshly quieted elsewhere in the apartment.

A young wife, covered head to toe in a black burka that revealed only her two large brown eyes, appeared to serve tea and a plate of naan flatbread, olives, and figs. The two guests did not even acknowledge her existence.

The older man was waiting, so Nimri said, politely, "Thanks to God you have arrived safely. You are well?"

"Yes, thank you," said Kasim al-Hariq.

"God be praised," said Nimri. After the older man had done so, he took up his glass of tea and sipped from it. A cosmopolitan Egyptian, he enjoyed long stretches of coffee and conversation as much as any Arab. But these Saudis could sit and drink tea and flatter each other exquisitely for three days without ever coming to the point.

Which was the root of their greatest problem, as far as Nimri was concerned. The sheiks were all sitting up in the mountains, still boasting about the great victories of 2001, while 2002 had belonged to the Americans. Afghanistan was lost and Al Qaeda was on the run.

His method was not to engage in any but the required pleasantries. To listen respectfully while the old men spoke their fill. And remain silent when they paused. Soon they gave up and came to the point. This had earned him a reputation for impatience among the brotherhood.

"And you," said Kasim. "You are well?"

"I am," said Nimri. "Well and strong."

"So I see," said Kasim. "You remind me of your father."

Kasim al-Hariq brought this up every time they met. Nimri always felt it was the older man's way of asserting his authority, and always resented it. But it did require a response. "You are too kind."

Nimri's father had been a member of Egyptian Islamic Jihad. An engineer, and not particularly religious, but he hated the Egyptian government, and the Islamists were the only ones willing to fight. He had been arrested in the mass roundups following the assassination of President Anwar Sadat. The family was told he had died of a heart attack in prison. There were a great many heart attacks in Egyptian prisons.

Another glass of tea, and to Nimri's satisfaction Kasim was now the one becoming impatient. "It has been hard," he stated.

Nimri nodded over his tea. As always, the battering ram of conversational ritual had broken on his wall of silence.

"By God's will, we have survived," said Kasim. "Iraq will be to America what Afghanistan was to the Russians."

All Nimri said was, "Do you see it so?"

"We call the Americans crusaders," Kasim replied. "But in truth they are the new Mongols. Destroyers, yes, but a common enemy to unify our people. Except for Palestine, there are no uprisings. The faithful must be roused to action. American arrogance has split their infidel allies in Europe and their apostate puppets in the Middle East. Iraq will bring us new recruits. Their valuable experience there will be as their older brothers had in Afghanistan. When the Americans leave, as did the Russians, we will have a new base for jihad.

"American power rests upon weak foundations. God willing, an Afghanistan that falls back into chaos. Their Pakistani puppet Musharraf dead, and an Islamic government with nuclear weapons. The Saud royal family drowning in their own fat. The puppets will fall. The Holy Land and its oil will be ours. Jerusalem will be ours. The caliphate will be established, one ruler of one Islamic nation stretching over the world."

Nimri was appalled. Was this what they were truly thinking up in the mountains? Convincing themselves that all they had to do was wait for God to deliver them a great victory? Wishful thinking could not defeat the Americans. They could be defeated in Iraq only if they were incredibly foolish. If they turned the country over to a native puppet government, the way they had in Afghanistan, the Iraqis would soon turn against foreign Muslim fighters the same way they turned against all foreigners.

"Our leadership is intact," Kasim went on. "The young still seek to join us. The faithful continue to contribute. We still have sufficient cadre to conduct operations. Do you not agree?"

Nimri agreed that was putting a brave face on the situation, though he did not express this. "Before God, we have demonstrated our faith and our courage," he said.

Kasim nodded in satisfaction.

Nimri continued, "But you must forgive me when I say that I believe God is testing us. We are faced with many dangerous decisions. First among them is future operations. Allowing the local organizations to control their own operations is more secure, but more dangerous to us. Zarqawi was second rate in Afghanistan—now he acts like the king of Iraq. We could split into different factions like the Palestinians. This would be a disaster. After all, our goal is to unify the world of believers."

"This is true, God be praised," said Kasim.

"Even worse," said Nimri, "the local planners may not have the skills and judgment we have. Explosions in Istanbul and Riyadh will not shake the Americans."

"I agree," said Kasim.

"Many things can go wrong. Here in Pakistan, Musharraf promises the Americans many things but has acted only against our leaders, not our organization. But if we try to destroy him, and fail, he will almost certainly try to destroy us."

Kasim was looking down at his tea, not pleased.

"Before all," said Nimri. "By God, we must strike. If we do not, recruits will seek out those who do. Contributors will not support an inactive organization. We must fight to remain worthy of God, who will give us victory."

"It must be a worthy strike," said Kasim. "Worthy of the operations of the Blessed Tuesday." Which was what Al Qaeda called September 11, 2001.

Nimri was so frustrated he wanted to scream. All new attacks now had to be greater than 2001, for the sake of their prestige. The decision to attack the Americans had been correct. The jihadis, the holy warriors, had attempted to destroy the puppet governments of Algeria, Egypt, and Saudi Arabia, but had been nearly destroyed. Nothing could be done until the Americans left the Middle East. And they had to be forced out, as they were in Lebanon. But after the Blessed Tuesday in 2001, the sheiks did not hit the Americans with more attacks while they were in disarray. Nimri would have sent waves and waves, many smaller attacks after the first massive ones, because the massive ones could only be accomplished with total surprise. But the sheiks had sat back and waited for the Americans to surrender. These Saudis were poisoned by the history of Arabian tribal warfare. They understood raids but not a strategy for a campaign. Now they dreamed of chemicals, germs, radiation weapons, not understanding the practical impossibilities. And there was no reasoning with them.

But what Nimri said was, "The problem is that such an attack may take years to plan and execute, with the Americans on their guard and hunting us. The Americans will not die in a single fire, no matter how large. They will die from ten thousand wasp stings over a hundred years."

Kasim challenged him. "What do *you* believe we must do?"

Nimri took a sip of tea to collect himself. "We must

protect Abu Abdullah." This was Osama Bin Laden's code name. Knowing how badly the Americans wanted him, and how much blood money was on his head, they tried not to even speak his name for fear of betrayal. "He is our inspiration to the world. We must take our losses as a gift from God, to make our organization smaller and more lethal. What was the quantity of our fighters, now will be quality. The same for our hidden sleeper agents in the enemy lands. We may be required to recruit and train them in those lands—trusted brothers calling only on trusted friends, to thwart any infiltrators. Likewise, our funds may be both collected and distributed locally."

Nimri had been choosing his words carefully. Now he took even more care. "Large attacks that kill many Americans hurt them terribly and do us honor by God and the faithful around the world. But unless we can accomplish many of these attacks, one after the other, the Americans absorb the blow and the strikes bring them closer to their government. At this time, we do not have the ability to accomplish continuous attacks. So we must split the Americans from their government. We must attack their leaders. If we can kill only a few, then they must be powerful men whose names go around the world."

He did not use the example of the Assassins of the ninth to the thirteenth centuries, who terrorized nations not by slaughtering populations but by eliminating rulers with the dagger. The Aassassins had been Nizari Ismailis, a sect that all Sunni Muslims regarded as heretic. Nimri knew that any mention of them would throw Kasim into a rage.

"Your views have been heard," Kasim replied.

Intimately familiar with Saudi indirectness, Nimri sipped his tea in silence.

Kasim produced a sheaf of papers from his clothing. "You are to be given command of our most important operation."

Nimri set down his glass. He had been planning the operation for over a year. And been waiting months for them to make up their minds.

Children's voices had been growing louder, and now they were quieted again. Kasim dropped his voice, as if that would foil any eavesdroppers. "Brothers in Chechnya have obtained four Russian shoulder-fired surface-to-air missiles, the latest model."

Nimri had to fight to keep his face expressionless. There were no surface-to-air missiles in his plan.

"These missiles will be shipped from the port of Odessa," said Kasim. "When the American president makes his state visit to the Philippines in October, young brothers, led by you, will shoot his helicopter from the sky."

Nimri could hardly believe it. "All the American security services will be focusing all their attention on the Philippines."

Kasim became animated for the first time. "And all the cameras of the world will film him falling to earth, on fire."

Nimri felt a bundle of papers being thrust into his hand. He heard Kasim saying, "Seventy-five thousand American dollars, brother. Precious now, in this time of scarcity. More precious than before. The account number and the bank in Dubai."

"My plan is not approved," said Nimri, feeling like a fool even as he spoke.

"This is your plan," said Kasim.

There was no persuading them. They were too isolated. Nimri knew he did not yet have the stature to persuade them. The only ones who could, the senior brothers, the real planners, were in the hands of the Americans.

He had to accept the operation. It was either follow their orders or leave. Al Qaeda's genius was in creating a central organization for funding and planning—The Base, the literal translation of its name. But rather than attempt the almost insurmountable task of trying to establish groups all over the world, operatives were sent to existing groups to capture them with funding beyond their dreams, expand their horizons, send their people for training in Afghanistan, then finally direct their operations. The Al Qaeda operative Abu Musab al-Zarqawi had first been sent to the Kurdish group, Ansar al-Islam, in northern Iraq. From there he had formed a network to fight the American occupation in the entire country, and was now attracting funding independent of Al Qaeda. For mutual prestige Al Qaeda still claimed him, but Zarqawi had become important enough to be tempted into independence. Nimri did not know if that was the path he should follow. Forming a new organization was tempting. If Zarqawi could do it, anyone could. But it would take at least another year, and then he would have to be on watch for both the Americans and *them*.

He was not ready to try that, yet. Not when attrition had brought him within reach of the top of Al Qaeda. A successful strike would give him the prestige to move the organization. But the old men were out of touch. Necessary as symbols, but if listened to now, the organization, that glorious organization that reached into every country in the world, would not survive.

Kasim was still talking. When he finished, he said to Nimri, "Well?"

"I must move quickly," Nimri said. "There is little time until October." He forced out a smile. "Rest here. I will send my man Hasan to tend to you."

"And how is Hasan? I knew his father."

"Well," said Nimri. "Very well."

7

Driving down Highway 85 just south of Detroit, Special Agent Paul Moody said to Beth Royale, "I still don't understand why we don't take him down at his house. We have to search it anyway."

Beth was watching the notebook computer on her lap. The screen showed a map of the area, and a lighted cursor was moving slowly down Highway 85. "Because you never know what's going to happen when you kick in someone's door. Sometimes you do it right, everyone's nice and shocked and they give right up. Sometimes you do it wrong, they see you coming and you've got a siege. And sometimes, even if you do it right, you kick in the door and everyone's screaming, someone grabs a gun, even if they didn't want to, because everyone's screaming. You never know who's going to come popping out of a blind corner at you; the kids are trying to bite your ankles; the wife's throwing a hot pot of something off the stove at you; maybe you have to shoot the family dog. We do it that way because that's what FBI agents do: show up at the bad guy's door wearing windbreakers that say FBI on them, carrying shotguns."

"Okay," said Moody, sorry that he'd mentioned it.

"And I grant you," Beth went on, "it's fun to put on your

windbreaker and carry a shotgun. But when ten agents hit a house, you've got neighbors, you've got helicopters overhead, and you're sure as hell going to have press. That's fine in a criminal case, not a terrorism case."

"That's all well and good," said Moody. "But the other four perps are getting their doors kicked in."

"Didn't your mother ever tell you that just because someone jumps off a building, it doesn't mean you have to be an idiot and follow them?"

"Now that you mention it, I seem to remember something to that effect."

"Good, I'm glad you listened. If we grab this guy nice and quiet, lock him up, then show up at his house to serve the warrant, we might just get something more from the wife than if we kicked in her door in and scared her kid. Speed up now. I want a visual on him before he turns off."

The black Trans Am they were driving had been confiscated from a drug dealer. It had the full police package, but you couldn't tell even by looking through the window. The radios were in the glove compartment, the antenna was a cell phone antenna. Even the blue lights were hidden. Moody took it up well over the speed limit, and soon the white Taurus came into sight.

Beth radioed her intentions to the sedan full of agents, all from the Detroit field office, who were following them. Then her cell phone began to vibrate. "Beth Royale. Mom, I can't talk right now—I'll call you back later. What? Is he all right? God. Yes, I know, Mom. Frank's there? Okay, I promise I'll call you later. I know, Mom, I know. Love you, too."

"Everything okay?" said Moody.

"My brother arranged for someone to clean the leaves out of the gutters of my parents' house. So my dad wouldn't be going up the ladder. But of course he went up the ladder anyway, to make sure the guy did a good job. And he slipped."

"Jesus, is he all right?"

"My mom came home from shopping, and the first thing she sees is her husband hanging from the chimney by his fingertips. X-rays are negative, but he'll be taking muscle relaxers and antiinflammatants for the next year or so."

Though he knew he really didn't want to, Moody started laughing.

"Yeah, I know," said Beth. "If it wasn't my dad I'd be laughing my ass off. Tell me, Paul. Why do men go insane when they retire?"

"My dad always says that what we do is what we are. I don't know. I had dinner with my wife and kids ten times last month. And that includes the weekends."

Didn't keep you from volunteering for a career-enhancing assignment like counterterrorism, Beth thought. "I know what you mean. I had to find a new home for my cat. I was boarding him so much he was getting neurotic."

"Yeah, it's practically the same thing."

"I really loved Mr. Puss," said Beth.

"Since we're chatting," said Moody, "we're lucky we're not back at the office, the way you pissed Timmins off."

Beth glanced over at him. "That really bugs you, doesn't it, Paul?"

"You told me if I ever had something on my mind not to hold it in. So I'm not holding it in."

"I'm glad. You know why we're arresting these five guys? So the attorney general and the director can hold a press conference and do some showboating. And that's probably going to screw up our criminal case, if we even manage to bring these guys to trial. Just to show we're doing something post–nine-eleven. These guys are a terrorist cell. They're organized that way so no one has knowledge of any other cells, so we can't bust one and roll up their whole network. Their controller knows about the other cells, and probably only one guy among the five we're going to bust today knows who their controller is. If we followed every one of them around long enough, eventually we'd get the controller. But we're going to arrest them so we can hold a press conference."

"But that's going to happen whether or not you make an issue of it with Timmins. So why do it and piss him off?"

Beth smiled. "Paul, I don't do these things just to work out my personal issues, or because I can't keep my mouth shut. I did it so Timmins would give me what I want, just to get me out of his hair." She pointed a finger at the windshield. "And what I wanted was our guy here. I looked them all over, and I'm betting he's the cell leader. And if he is, he knows who the controller is. Or at least how to contact him."

"If I did what you do I'd be spending my whole career on suspension."

"Well, there's another lesson for you, Paul. If you make your bosses look really good, you'd be amazed by how much they put up with. You've also got to know just how far you can take it with each one of them."

"No, thanks, not for me."

Beth didn't reveal her disappointment. "The way I look at it, you've got three choices. You can be bitter about working in a dysfunctional system. You can resign yourself to working in it. Or you can find ways around it."

"Why do I feel like I'm getting dragged along on number three, whether I want to or not?"

"Don't worry, Paul. I won't get you fired." They were approaching a stoplight. "Okay, here we go."

Beth was holding a plastic box that looked very much like a television remote control. She aimed it through the windshield and pressed a button.

Up ahead, the white Taurus's engine shut off.

Beth tapped the mouse button on her notebook, and Arabic cursing could be heard coming through the speakers.

The light turned green, and Beth pushed another

button on her remote control. The driver finally got the ignition to turn over, and lurched the Taurus through the intersection.

Beth activated the remote again at the next light, and the Taurus died once more. She waited long enough into the green for the horns to begin before repeating the process, giggling the whole time.

"You're a very sick human being," Moody said.

"Well, if you're going to spike a listening device and a tracker in someone's car," said Beth, pronouncing it the New England way with a long *a* and an *r* that only dogs could hear, "it only takes a couple of extra minutes to wire a kill switch into the ignition. This job is fun, Paul. If you don't have fun, you'll get like these old gumshoe special agents who drop dead of a heart attack at fifty."

The Taurus pulled into a shopping center parking lot. Beth activated the remote for the final time, and the car glided to a stop.

The hood was already raised when they pulled in behind.

"I assume you're going to take him," said Moody.

"Yes, but only because it'll pay off in the interrogation later."

"Sure, Beth. Whatever you say."

Moody got out and walked up to the front of the Taurus. "Having some trouble?"

An Arab man in his late twenties was leaning over the exposed engine. His hair was cut short, and he was clean shaven. "Yes," he said in good but accented English. "It will not start."

"You need a jump?" Moody inquired pleasantly, keeping one eye on Beth approaching around the other side of the vehicle.

"I do not think it is the battery," the man replied. "Perhaps the ignition."

"Maybe you've just got a loose wire," Moody suggested,

bending down beside him and directing his attention deeper into the engine.

Thus distracted, the man didn't notice Beth on his blind side.

Eyeing the hand bracing him on the frame as he leaned over the engine, Beth grabbed the wrist and his collar, applying one foot to the back of his knee. With all the leverage she needed, she twisted him around and threw him face-first on the asphalt, the wrist locked behind his back.

All that came out of him was a long, high-pitched, "Ai, ai, ai, ai, ai."

"FBI," Beth told him. She snapped one handcuff on the locked wrist, then ordered, "Put your hand behind your back."

There was no response to this, so she yanked the wrist higher up. More howling, and over this Beth calmly repeating, "Put your right hand behind your back."

The hand shot over, and Beth snapped on the second cuff. She and Moody each took an arm and pulled the suspect to his feet.

Beth flicked her credentials case open in front of his face. "Jabir al-Banri, you're under arrest for violation of Title Eighteen, Section 2342 of the U.S. Code. Receiving contraband cigarettes."

Beth noted with satisfaction the look of relief that swept across his face. He seemed pretty happy to have that as the reason for his arrest.

The backup agents were out of their sedan now, and Beth turned the prisoner over to them. She pulled one agent aside. "Remember, not one word about terrorism in front of this guy. From anyone."

The agent nodded.

Beth said, "Is someone going to stay with the car?" The chain of custody had to be maintained until it was searched.

"Until the tow truck gets here. It's on the way."

"Thanks." She called out louder, "Thanks, guys. Great job."

"Nice takedown," the agent said quietly.

"The problem with these guys is a lack of a strong female influence," Beth replied. "We're going to see about changing that."

Al-Banri's home was in south Detroit. A neighborhood of Arab immigrants, working class. The local stores all had their signs in both English and Arabic.

Beth and Moody parked on the street, along with crime scene teams in two SUVs.

A woman with very pale olive skin answered the door. She was in her early twenties, and wearing a headscarf.

"Mrs. al-Banri, I'm Special Agent Beth Royale of the FBI. May we come in?"

Even frightened nearly out of her wits, she gripped the door firmly and didn't give way. "My husband. Not home." Her English was very poor.

"We know," Beth said gently. "We have a warrant to search your property." She handed over the document, took the woman's arm, and led her into the house while the female contract interpreter began explaining things in Arabic.

There was a frantic rush of almost hysterical Arabic in reply.

Soothingly, Beth said, "Why don't we sit down and talk about this?"

The woman froze in midmovement and twirled all the way around, looking at her living room as if she'd never seen it before. Then seemed to snap back into the moment, leading them into the kitchen and pulling out chairs at the table.

Beth fell back and whispered to the first technician, "Pay close attention to the living room—she doesn't want us in there."

He nodded.

And there was probably nothing in the kitchen, Beth

thought. She took a seat next to the wife, and across from the interpreter. The kitchen was spotless.

"What is your name?" Beth asked.

"Rubina." Said very shyly.

Tea was made. Even under such circumstances, the rules of hospitality were sacrosanct.

A little boy, not quite five, kept straying out into the living room and being called back, fascinated by all the big men with guns and flashlights and bags and rubber gloves.

Making tea had calmed Rubina al-Banri down and brought up her defenses. Her eyes kept darting back and forth between Beth and the interpreter, a recent graduate of the University of Michigan named Jane.

"Mrs. al-Banri," Beth said, in the same tone she'd used since entering the house, "we have reason to believe that your husband and his friends have been dealing in contraband cigarettes."

"This is not true," she said quickly. "What friends?"

"Khalid, Feisal, Isam, and Hamid," said Beth. She didn't mention the two cousins in Virginia.

She took it hard, the information forestalling another denial.

Beth was using the questions to determine the extent of her knowledge. The answers weren't important—the body language was. "Your husband is in a great deal of trouble," she said. "He could spend years in prison for each shipment of cigarettes. And we know he has accepted many, many shipments. If he doesn't cooperate with us, he could be in prison for a very long time."

Her face told Beth that not only was she terrified about what might happen to herself and her son, but she didn't expect her husband to cooperate.

Rubina suddenly sprang out of her chair.

Beth almost moved to grab her before realizing it was exasperation with her straying son. She did follow, though.

Rubina plucked up her boy, who protested in Arabic. The interpreter translated the exchange in Beth's ear.

But Beth was watching Rubina's eyes dart around the room. She remained behind when Rubina and the interpreter went back into the kitchen. The little boy was still wailing his displeasure, carrying the latex glove one of the agents had blown up and tied off for him.

One of the technicians approached Beth. "Big ten-pack box of Zip disks next to the computer, but only one disk in the box and none anywhere else."

Beth's eyes were locked on the wall separating the kitchen from the living room. "Did anyone find a magnet? Maybe with some string tied to it?"

The technician eyed her skeptically.

"Ask them," said Beth.

He polled his colleagues, Beth watching as his eyebrows went up. "They did. In the end table drawer."

"Bring it over," said Beth, walking toward the object of her gaze, a double light switch on the wall.

She was examining it under her flashlight when he returned. "The paint's stripped off the screws," she said. "How often do you take the plate off a light switch?"

Now he was looking at her the same way men probably had looked at suspected witches four hundred years ago.

"Always watch where their eyes go," she said. "Let's open it up."

He dropped an article into her palm, then went to work with a screwdriver.

Beth unwrapped the white household twine that was tied to the U-shaped magnet. Extended, the twine was about four feet long.

The technician had the plate off and was probing in the switch well. "The box isn't attached to a stud. It's not attached to anything, just held in place by the electrical cable." He pushed the box with his finger. It slid into the space between the wall, then slid back when he released it.

"Take a look in there with the endoscope," said Beth. She pointed. "Particularly look down."

He passed the lighted end of the flexible cable into the space and twisted it around and down while looking through the bulkier scope. "There's something down at the bottom of the space. Looks like a metal plate."

Another technician with a video camera had come over, and was now taping them.

"Pull the scope out," said Beth.

When the way was clear, she dropped the magnet into the space, letting it down slowly with the twine. When it hit bottom the line twitched as if a fish had taken it, and there was an audible snap of a magnet attaching itself to metal.

Beth pulled her catch up slowly. The first to appear was a thin metal plate, a couple of inches square. She grabbed it and pulled it through the hole. The plate was attached to a shorter piece of twine, and the twine to a plastic bag containing four Zip computer storage disks.

"Here we go," said Beth. "As soon as I show these to the wife, you'll have to send someone to run these back to the office right now. We'll need to at least skim this material before we go into interrogation with the guy."

"You got it," said the technician. He held the bag in his gloved hand as if weighing it. "I'll remember to watch the eyes. I guess women are more sensitive to that stuff."

"That's a myth," Beth informed him.

"You mean women aren't more sensitive than men?"

"I'll let you in on a little secret," she said. "They are, but most of the time they're only more sensitive to their own stuff, not anyone else's."

Frozen by political correctness, he only managed a goofy smile, as if afraid to say *anything* in response.

Beth was already back to business. "Check all the switches and electric plugs. The tops of the doors: you can drill out a cavity to hide something, put a strip of wood over it, and no one ever looks. Inside the poles in the clothes closets, and the shower curtain rod. The stairs don't have carpet on them. See if any look like they've been pried up recently."

Now she had his full attention.

"If the enemy's going to be thoughtful enough to produce training manuals," said Beth, "the least we can do is read them. Just like us, they have people who do nothing but follow the book."

The technician was smiling now. Respectfully.

Holding it by the string, Beth carried the bag into the kitchen. Rubina turned even paler at the sight of it. Once she'd gotten a good look, Beth handed the bag back to the technician who'd been trailing behind her.

Sitting back down, Beth focused on Rubina, who avoided her gaze.

"I think there is more than contraband cigarettes on these disks," Beth told her, then waited for the translation. "I think your husband and his friends were involved in more than cigarette smuggling." Another pause. "If they were, they will never be leaving prison." Then she put in the shot. "You knew about those disks, and where they were hidden. This makes you an accessory to whatever crimes your husband has committed." A very long pause, and Beth reached over to put her hand on Rubina's arm, with a pointed glance toward the little boy playing with a plastic truck on the kitchen floor. "Who will raise your son if you are in prison?"

Rubina burst into tears. Jane the interpreter was staring at Beth across the table.

Beth opened a pack of tissues and passed them over to Rubina, counting on the fact that everyone felt the same way about their in-laws. "If you answer my questions truthfully, I give you my promise that *you* will raise your son."

8

Gagging on all the cigarette smoke inside the van, Ed Storey wondered idly how hard it would be to sell Pakistanis on chewing tobacco. To pass the time he even started assembling a lesson plan in his head, before abandoning the idea. A van filled with smoke was unpleasant, but nothing compared to novice chewers swallowing their dip by accident and puking all over the place.

Storey thought about how many times and in how many places he'd sat in the predawn darkness, waiting for something to happen. Too many times, and too much time to think. He was only along for the ride on this one, so he didn't have the usual premission preparations to occupy himself with.

The Pakistanis in the black jumpsuits were an assault team from the Army Special Services Group, the special forces regiment. In particular Musa Company, which was the antiterrorist/hostage rescue force. Musa, or Moses, was also an Islamic prophet. Running the operation was the Special Investigation Group of the Federal Investigative Agency, roughly equivalent to the FBI. The Special Investigation Group was carefully screened, meaning polygraphed, and American trained. Pakistan's president acknowledged that he couldn't fully trust his military

Inter-Services Intelligence Directorate to hunt Al Qaeda
with complete enthusiasm. So the intelligence support was
provided by both the United States and the Pakistani Intelligence Bureau, a civilian agency that usually kept an
eye on politicians and political activists.

The two vans were nearly a mile away from the apartment building in the Layari District of Karachi. Any
closer and the word would pass like brushfire through the
neighborhood, and their quarry would be long gone
through the labyrinth of streets.

Storey had to give the Pakistanis credit. Where Americans would have staked out the building using digital
cameras with lenses powerful enough to watch Mars,
thermal imagery, cellular intercepts, and parabolic mi-
crophones, the immeasurably poorer Pakistanis sent a
teenager door to door selling stolen radios. He came
back with the plan of the whole building and a profile
of every apartment. The radios probably had been
stolen, and confiscated—Pakistani cops didn't bring
home a big paycheck. But it was a lesson in resource-
fulness that Storey took to heart.

Lee Troy was sitting with his head halfway out the open
window. Up in front, with the unit commander, was
the SIG liaison, a CIA officer named Jim. Only one
thing was certain—his name was not Jim. He was listening to the radio traffic through an earpiece.

Another Pakistani teenager was hanging out near
the apartment building. He had a simple push-button
beeper in his pocket to pass signals.

Storey hated not being able to read while waiting.
Using night-vision goggles would leave him blind from
eyestrain before the end of the first chapter.

He tapped Troy on the shoulder. Troy squinted to see
what his partner had in his hand. It was a deck of cards.
"Want to play some hearts?" Storey asked.

Troy's laughter rocked the van, drawing puzzled looks

from the Pakistanis and one of general annoyance from Jim the CIA guy.

The two of them had driven up from Washington to Dover Air Force Base in Delaware, catching a C-141 jet transport to Karachi. The plane carried military officers, civilian contractors, and spooks from various intelligence agencies. The Pakistani government insisted that no U.S. military were in the country hunting for Al Qaeda and Bin Laden. Which was true, on its face. The military personnel had all been removed from the active duty rosters, a process known as "sheep-dipping," and were officially working for the CIA or various private contractors that were little more than a post office box, fax number, and e-mail address.

Everyone on the plane was wearing civilian clothes. Storey and Troy blended in among them wearing polo shirts and khakis. Ironically enough, attracting a lot less attention than flying commercial on diplomatic passports. Don't make it more complicated than you have to was one of Storey's rules. On air force planes the seats always face toward the rear. Disconcerting, but safer in case of a crash, something the airlines never publicized. After they buckled themselves in, Storey followed the routine Delta Force had adopted to endure long intercontinental flights and remain fresh on arrival. He donned an eye mask, noise-canceling headphones, and popped a very potent Halcion sleeping pill. As he settled back, Troy tapped him on the shoulder.

"You think this intel's going to be any good?" Troy asked. "Or another dry hole?"

"Rule number one," was all Storey replied. His first rule was that, on operations, you always acted and spoke as if you were under electronic surveillance twenty-four hours a day.

"Okay, okay," said Troy.

He was talking a little too loudly. Probably because the iPod was still plugged into his ears. Storey reached out and plucked the unit off Troy's equipment vest, turning down the volume. While he was doing that he scanned through the playlist for the first time. He kept scanning until his finger got tired, because he couldn't quite believe it. Every song was by the Grateful Dead. A twenty-seven-year-old black Deadhead from Maine. He was starting to get a little handle on why the SEALs thought Troy was weird.

The hearts game had attracted onlookers. "No poker?" said Lieutenant Gauhar, the platoon leader.

"No, sir," said Storey, who had served as the interpreter of American cultural myths before. "Hearts."

"Texas hold-'em!" announced one of the *havildars*, or sergeants, farther back in the van.

"What do you guys know about Texas hold-'em?" Troy demanded.

"From the telly," said Lieutenant Gauhar, in that wonderful pronunciation that was half British and half all its own.

It made Troy think, and not for the first time, that at least half of the USA's problems with the rest of the world were caused by the export of American TV and movies. It was amazing how many foreigners took them seriously. Then, to his annoyance, Storey began dealing poker to the Pakistanis. You could take the guy out of special forces, but you could never take the green beret off the guy—always trying to make friends with the locals. Every SEAL's least favorite mission was Foreign Internal Defense—teaching foreign militaries.

The Pakistanis insisted on p'aying for cigarettes. This forced nonsmoker Troy to throw in all his pocket change, declining to bet the items of his equipment that the Pakistanis shrewdly had their eyes on. He didn't lose much, due to their tendency to go all-in on every hand. He quickly suspected they did it only because they absolutely loved the act of pushing in their stack and the sound of saying, "All-in." After which they'd laugh delightedly.

"Stand by," ordered Major Shaykh, the element commander.

The two vans pulled out, negotiating the narrow streets as fast as possible without risking blowouts on potholes or debris. And there were a lot of potholes and debris.

Everyone was buckling up their helmets. The van side door was opened to allow a quick exit.

At that hour there wasn't a sign of life in the building. Until, that is, the van squealed to a stop and eight men in black pounded up the stairs. The other van covered the back.

The Pakistanis were used to using a battering ram, because explosives cost money. But just as there were walls around every private home in Karachi, every door was made of steel. A ram would have meant that everyone in the apartment would be wide awake long before the door gave in.

Having worked with them before, Storey had brought along a quantity of flexible linear-shaped charge, triangular strips of plastic explosive inside a V-shaped sheathing of soft lead to focus the cutting charge.

The Paks were brave men and handled explosives with Islamic fatalism, putting the matter in God's hands. They'd already primed the charge and hooked up the firing system in the van. But they had too much pride for Storey to ever consider saying anything about it.

He did make sure that he and Troy were around the corner when the door was breached. Both were carrying their SOPMOD carbines just in case everything went to shit and they had to shoot their way out of the neighborhood. They knew the intelligence for the raid had come from an informer. Whether it might be a planned setup to ambush some Pakistani special forces and Americans was anyone's guess.

Storey had a finger pressed against each earplug

when the door blew. They all swept into the apartment in a surreal mosaic of flashlight beams—you could see what was in the path of your light, and then on-and-off strobing views of everyone else's.

No flash-bangs. Storey was moving at a low crouch because the Pakistanis were all carrying AK-47s, and there was little hope the apartment walls would contain those Russian 7.62mm short rounds.

The constant in such situations—a woman screaming. An AK opened up with its distinctive deep *bap, bap, bap.* Storey dropped to the floor and found himself face-to-face with Troy. It was always the same story in combat. If you weren't shooting or being shot at, the sound of gunfire was a mystery that had to be solved. Moving toward the sound might be a mistake, but not moving toward it might also be one. Neither Storey nor Troy moved a muscle except to cover the nearest doorways with their weapons. You were just as dead if your own side shot you by mistake.

Shouting in Urdu. Even the bilingual resorted to their original language under stress. The back-and-forth shouting clarified the situation, and the leaders soon got control of it. Then the call, "Clear, clear, clear," coming from each room.

"If they don't mention it, don't ask about the shooting," Storey said to Troy. The Pakistanis were prideful men.

"Yeah, well, I'm not all that curious either way," Troy muttered.

It turned out that while clearing a room one of the assault team saw shadow and furniture that looked exactly like the outline of a man holding a rifle. Storey was sympathetic. These things happened when the adrenaline was pumping. The Pakistanis didn't have the money to shoot ten thousand rounds of practice ammunition a week, not to mention a multimillion-dollar computerized shooting house to fire it in. These guys

THREAT LEVEL   91

were up against it for real every week, and sometimes it really *was* better to be safe than sorry.

"In here," someone called in English. Illuminated by several flashlight beams, Kasim al-Hariq was lying on the floor, handcuffed in his underwear. One of the assault element was brandishing the pistol he hadn't used.

"Just like a little lamb," Troy said to Storey.

"The older guys all go like that," said Storey. "The young ones die fighting. These bastards just send the kids out to die."

They were soon backed up by the two truckloads of regular Pakistani police who'd been assigned the mission of securing the area. All of them held under virtual guard so no one would be tempted to make a phone call and earn himself some extra money.

The Special Investigation Group agents had a very thorough search technique. They ripped out all the walls, ceiling, and floor, and broke up every piece of furniture. The commandoes left right away with their prisoner, Storey and Troy with them. The tenant, his wife, and three small children, all Pakistani citizens, were left in the custody of the Special Investigation Group.

A sullen crowd had gathered outside, held back by the police, so everyone pulled his balaclava over his face. Kasim al-Hariq would be taken to a nearby military base, the headquarters of the Pakistani Army's Fifth Corps. A brief hearing would be held to confirm that he was not, in fact, a citizen of Pakistan. And then he'd be given a quick heave-ho into the arms of the CIA.

They were granted entry to the base after crashing British-style salutes from immaculately uniformed gate guards. Just the sight of them did Storey's military heart good.

But waiting outside the headquarters building were about twenty Pakistanis in civilian clothes carrying AK-47s. Civilian clothes but military bearing.

"Uh-oh," said Troy, retrieving his rifle from under his seat and automatically checking the chamber.

Major Shaykh was looking concerned. Jim the CIA man said, "What the hell . . . ?"

"Inter-Services Intelligence," said Storey.

Major Shaykh turned in his seat, and Jim said, "How do you know?"

"I've met that guy before," said Storey, pointing out the obvious leader, the only one not carrying a weapon. "Colonel Khan."

"Know him good?" Jim asked warily. "Or know him bad?"

"Well, not good," said Storey.

"Stay in the van," Jim ordered, as he and Major Shaykh got out to deal with the situation.

The commandoes, sensing the situation as all good soldiers did, also got out to back up their officer.

"Not good, eh?" said Troy.

"We had a little run-in," said Storey. "The 'full cooperation' he was giving us was bullshit. We kept getting sent out on wild-goose chases."

From his tone, Troy could tell a lesson was coming.

"The question always is," said Storey, "is the intel bad or are you getting fed bad intel? And is the guy feeding you bad intel on his own, or is he carrying out policy? You almost never, ever learn the answers to those questions. So Ricky Silva and I ignored Colonel Khan's intelligence and cut loose from the boys he had minding us. He didn't like it. Tried to get us thrown out of the country, and *he* ended up getting spanked."

"What was the mission?" Troy asked.

"Rule number one," said Storey, glancing down at Kasim al-Hariq handcuffed, gagged, and blindfolded on the floor of the van.

"Okay," said Troy, "so you're not on his Ramadan card list."

"Not hardly."

The discussion going on outside the van was obviously heated, though they couldn't hear it. Jim the CIA man was gesturing angrily, and Colonel Khan had a cold little smile on his face.

"ISI wants our prisoner," said Troy.

"Good," said Storey. "Now tell me why."

"ISI runs guerrillas into Kashmir to fight the Indians," said Troy. "Where do you get radical Islamic fundamentalists willing to die fighting jihad against the infidel Hindus? Al Qaeda. Senior Al Qaeda like this"—he cocked a thumb down at al-Hariq on the floor—"you figure he's dealt with a few ISI agents back in the day. Pretty embarrassing when he starts coughing up his life story to the interrogators." Now he pointed his thumb out the windshield. "So are these guys working for themselves, or the government?"

"You're thinking good," said Storey. "But you're still thinking like an American. These studs aren't working for themselves, not standing up to the CIA and the Special Services Group. ISI is a government unto itself, though the president's trying to get control of it. This could be ISI on its own, or ISI with the support of a faction in the government or military. There's lots of little empires in a country like this. But here's what you do: forget about all that. Leave it to the generals and the politicians. You worry about keeping them from getting your prisoner, because Major Shaykh is a soldier and he's outranked. And they're all blowing off the CIA."

"Imagine that," said Troy.

Jim had broken off from the discussion, and was angrily punching numbers into his cell phone.

"Hook your phone to your PDA," Storey ordered. "When we get close enough, without making a show of it take Colonel Khan's picture and transmit it to the operations center. And then ignore the 'what the fuck?' message they send right back."

"Why am I doing that?" Troy replied. He wouldn't

have asked the question if he hadn't thought Storey had time to answer it.

"Because the general on duty might not have any balls."

"Fair enough. I'm assuming you don't want me to shoot anyone unless you do first."

"You're reading me just fine," said Storey.

On their way over to the argument, Storey put a hand on Jim's shoulder, interrupting his call. "Make the call from the van," he said. "And stay with the prisoner."

Jim immediately opened his mouth to say something, but before that happened Storey very calmly interjected, "I've got it."

Just then, with the kind of timing you can't buy for any amount of money, Jim finally got his connection. He stomped off toward the van, talking at a rapid rate.

Troy was seriously impressed. He'd seen SEAL master chiefs, the very best, who had that gift. A quiet but firm, nonconfrontational way of getting people who outranked them to do exactly what they wanted. You had to have that calm-in-the-storm attitude. And a major reputation as an operator didn't hurt either.

The conversation was being held in Urdu, but it didn't take a linguist to figure out that Colonel Khan was reaming Major Shaykh's ass, and the major was giving him the old "yes, sir, but . . ." every time the colonel paused for breath. The commandoes and ISI were into Mexican standoff mode, each backing up his leader and putting out that "I'm ready" body language. And he and Storey were walking right into the spot Troy would just as soon they'd rather not be, smack dab in the middle between the two sides. If someone fired a round, even by accident, it was going to end like all Mexican standoffs did.

Storey pulled his balaclava back off his head as they came up. His attention attracted, Colonel Khan squinted into the early morning sun. He had a full beard, cut short, and an aquiline nose that was nearly as long and narrow

as his face. It took him a moment; then he made the connection. "Ah, Sergeant Edward, back in Pakistan again.
But without Sergeant Richard, I see." Then the bon-
homie was gone. "This is a Pakistani national matter, on
Pakistani territory. You have no authority here. And you
may tell your young partner that your other colleague is
already calling your consulate for help."

"Oh, he's not calling the consulate, sir," Storey replied,
utterly congenial. "He's just sent your name and pho-
tograph to the Pentagon operations center. And in a
minute or two they're going to be calling the Ministry
of Defense in Islamabad wanting to know what you're
doing."

Troy held up the Personal Digital Assistant to show the
colonel his likeness captured. Not a flattering shot, either.

Colonel Khan wasn't the screaming kind of officer. He
was the type who got icy and cutting when he got mad.
And he was furious. "As I told you, *Sergeant*, this is a Pakistani matter. Your presence is not required here."

"Yes, sir, you did." Storey took out his own satellite
phone. "We'll be over at the United States Government
van, which is United States territory manned by United
States diplomats, keeping Washington briefed on what's
going on. And if you try to take the prisoner we'll have
a major diplomatic incident with both our governments
listening in—in real time."

Storey turned and showed the colonel his back.

The argument rose again behind them.

"We just going to wait here?" Troy asked, knowing that
Storey had seriously exaggerated the speed of the
process. They might very well starve to death before the
U.S. and Pakistani governments resolved the situation.

"Hell no," said Storey. "Give people too much time to
make up their minds, they may not decide things your
way. And Pakistani officers got tons of pride. Even if
Colonel Khan gets ordered to back off, if he thinks his
honor's insulted he may start something anyway just to

satisfy it. We'll make our move while everyone's attention is elsewhere." He hopped into the driver's seat, turned the key, and immediately shifted into reverse.

The sound of the motor diverted shifted Jim's attention from his phone. "What the hell are you doing?" he demanded.

"Leaving," said Storey, backing up very fast.

"Are you fucking crazy?" Jim shouted.

Storey twirled the van around before the ISI men who were running over could block his way. They were brandishing their rifles. He stepped on the gas and gave them a friendly wave, all the while continuing his lecture to Troy. "They'd be expecting this move once negotiations stalled. They're not expecting it now."

Troy kept his rifle at the ready, though out of view of the windows. "People usually start shooting when something unexpected happens."

"Not without orders," said Storey. "Not these guys. And we didn't give Colonel Khan a chance to make up his mind."

"Got right inside the motherfucker's decision cycle," said Troy.

"Couldn't have put it any better myself," said Storey.

Gate guards never stopped vehicles *leaving* a military installation.

Jim kept losing his connection and redialing the Karachi consulate. "Thanks a lot," he told Storey. "You'll be back in the States and I'll be standing in shit so deep I'll need a snorkel to breathe."

"Oh, I don't think it'll be that bad," Storey said pleasantly. "As a matter of fact, I think both sides are going to want to forget about this as soon as possible. Is the plane ready at the airport?"

Jim sat up sharply. "We are *not* going to the airport. We're going to the consulate until I can get this straightened out."

"That's a mistake," Storey told him. "While we were

driving off I had a fine view of Colonel Khan in my rearview mirror. And he was on *his* cell phone."

"Makes no difference," said Jim. "The shit's already up to my waist, and the tide's coming in."

"You know, I feel bad," said Storey.

"Really?" Jim said sarcastically.

"Yeah, I wanted to lay some *baksheesh* on those commandoes." Storey patted the envelopes in his jumpsuit pocket. "Boys did a real fine job."

"Take the next turn," said Jim. "That's back into town."

"You're still making a mistake," said Storey. "But the consulate it is."

The U.S. Consulate in Karachi was as well guarded as you'd expect such a building to be. A short time before, the Pakistani police had defused a van full of explosives that had been parked outside. Pakistani bomb squads got a lot of practice.

As soon as the deputy chief of mission, a career Foreign Service officer, heard that Kasim al-Hariq was on his premises, he began bouncing off the walls. "I want him out of here!" he shouted. "The plane's waiting to fly him out? Fine. Get him on the plane. I want him out of the country *before* I start getting calls from either the host government or Washington."

Al, the CIA chief of station, was also upset—but better at concealing it. "We have some things to discuss," he pointedly told the deputy chief of mission.

The DCM headed for the door. Not that he was averse to listening to some spook talk, but if he was there when any decisions were reached, he'd be a party to them. "Fine," he said. "But I want to be informed the second he's gone."

"You will be," Al said reassuringly. As soon as the door shut, his first statement was directed right at Jim. "This is a real goat-rope."

"I could have settled everything on-site," Jim said defensively, glaring at Storey.

"And lost your man?" said Al. "At least that didn't happen." He turned to Storey. "You think ISI wants this guy free?"

"No," said Storey. "I think they want him dead. I reckon they'd rather have him dead than talking to us."

"You think they'll try again?" Al asked.

"Who knows?" said Storey. "If they do they won't do it themselves. So the quicker we move, the shakier their arrangements are going to be. And the more advantage to us."

"Okay, okay," said Al. "Let's get him to the airport."

"Look," said Storey, "let's at least complicate their planning. Send us out first in an empty vehicle—we'll head straight for the airport. They'll figure we'll be driving him. Twenty minutes later send out one man in a car, a fresh face, with al-Hariq stuffed in the trunk. Head in the opposite direction, make a roundabout trip to the airport."

"Al," Jim said, "we're getting all worked up about nothing here."

"You think so?" said Storey. "Fools die, my friend."

"You calling me a fool?" Jim demanded.

Storey's silence rested his case.

"We'll go with two vehicles," said Al, before Jim could add anything else. Then to Storey, "You want the van?"

Storey shook his head. "Too hard to handle at speed. Flip over when you breathe on them. Besides, they'd be expecting us to use something else. The van would be an obvious decoy."

"I'll take care of it," said Al. "Do you want a convoy?"

"How quick can you put one together?" Storey asked.

"Not before early afternoon."

"We'll go solo then," said Storey.

Troy thought that was a mistake, but held his tongue.

"I'll take care of it," said Al.

"And we don't need Jim," said Storey.

"Fuck you, too," Jim replied.

"You sure?" said Al.

"Tits on a bull," said Storey. "Nothing personal." Meaning, of course, nothing personal to Al.

"When will you be ready to leave?" said Al.

"Half an hour," said Storey.

While they were changing out of their jumpsuits, Troy said, "Did I miss something, or did you just volunteer us to be the bait?"

"I don't know what came over me," Storey said mournfully. "I'm not usually the volunteering type." He busied himself putting on his running shoes. When he finally looked over at an outraged Troy, he broke out laughing.

"I'm glad somebody thinks this is fucking funny," said Troy.

"Ah, a little laughter is always good medicine," said Storey. Another look at Troy and he was back to chuckling. "Look, I don't know whether you realized it or not, but we're burned in Pakistan. Colonel Khan'll see to that. We won't be back here. So we've got to get out of this well-watched consulate sometime. Would you rather do it now, or would you rather put if off until the other side is ready?"

"I'd rather do neither," said Troy. "I'd rather slip out of here one night and sneak out of the country without anyone being the wiser."

It was something they'd both been very well trained to do.

"Well, I suppose that's an option," said Storey. "But we've still got a mission to accomplish. And I've got a pretty good record of doing that, you might say perfect, and I'd like to keep my streak intact."

"Whatever," Troy replied. "I was just saying that since we're not going to be the ones taking the dickhead to the airport, we might as well also *not* be the ones to be the bait. Let's go do it."

Al provided an armored Jeep Cherokee, with untinted windows.

"Do they roll down?" Storey asked. Sometimes they did on armored vehicles, and sometimes the bulletproof glass was so thick it had to be fixed in place.

"Windows roll down," said Al. He'd also provided an incredibly lifelike human dummy to put in the backseat. One from the CIA bag of tricks for countersurveillance work. Turn a corner, drop off an agent, then put up the dummy to make it look like the same number of people in the car.

The dummy was blindfolded, gagged, and seat-belted in.

Storey and Troy were in civilian clothes, but wearing their body armor/assault vests and pistol belts.

A last-minute weapons and communications check, and they were ready to go. A marine guard opened the gate, and they zigzagged through the vehicle barrier.

They headed west. The international airport was just outside the city to the east, but today their destination was Pakistani Air Force Base Masroor, which was less than twenty miles to the west.

Storey was driving. He followed the railway line out of the city, crossing over the Lyari River.

"We're made," Troy announced. "Pair on a motor-cycle. The one in back's trying to hide the walkie-talkie he's yapping into."

Storey checked his mirrors. "Any other bikes?"

"Doesn't look like it."

"Then that's the scout. They're calling it in, and it'll come from somewhere else."

The terrain varied from wooded groves of very small trees to what resembled high desert scrubland. There was plenty of traffic on the two-lane road, and this held every-one's speed down.

"Check out the crossroads coming up on the right," said Storey.

"Yeah, two cars. One silver, one black. Both look like

Mercedeses," said Troy. "They couldn't be any more fucking obvious about being parked and waiting, could they?"

"That's why you want to rush them," said Storey. "Hop into the backseat, you'll probably be shooting out the left side."

Troy scrambled over the front seat. "You know, in situations like this, I always like to ask myself: what would Jerry do?"

"Jerry?"

"Jerry Garcia."

"Shit his pants, I'd expect," said Storey.

"Man, don't put that on Jerry. Motorcycle's coming up."

"They'll probably sit right behind to point us out for everyone," said Storey.

"That's right where they are," Troy replied.

"By the way," said Storey, "you look great."

"What the hell are you talking about?"

"Well, I always heard that SEALs can't go to war unless they've got their shades on and their hair's perfect."

Troy was wearing his high-speed Bollé sunglasses. "You got that right," he said, ostentatiously patting his hair.

As they passed the crossroads, both cars, filled with passengers, pulled onto the road behind them.

"Motorcycle's falling back," Troy reported.

"We'll probably be getting a broadside from the first car as soon as it pulls level," said Storey.

"Here they come," said Troy.

"Buckle up," said Storey. "As soon as they try to pass, I'm making my move." He radioed a contact report to Al at the consulate.

Troy snapped on his seat belt and braced his feet on the front seat.

The black Mercedes didn't have any trouble catching them. It sat behind for a moment, Storey watching to see if anyone with a weapon popped up from the sunroof. Then the Mercedes blinked its lights to pass.

"Windows are all rolled down," said Troy. "Everyone's hands in their lap."

Storey waited until the Mercedes was in the opposite lane. Then he put one foot hard on the brake, cutting the steering wheel to the left. The Cherokee's front bumper hit the Mercedes just behind the right rear wheel. The Mercedes spun completely around, changing lanes.

An AK-47 that was being aimed from a window flew right out of its owner's hands and hit the Cherokee's windshield.

Storey was back on the gas, flooring it. The Mercedes swapped ends right across the front of the Cherokee—Storey passed it in the left lane of oncoming traffic. In the rearview mirror: the Mercedes hitting the sandy shoulder and rolling over at least three times before disappearing in a cloud of dust. Then Storey's eyes back on the road, and a truck coming right at them, leaning on its horn.

Storey couldn't get back into the right lane. He tapped the brake again to lose some speed, then took the Cherokee onto the left shoulder. The SUV almost fishtailed in the sand, but he held it steady. The truck roared by on the right, all horn and onrushing air, seemingly inches away.

A stand of trees was running up alongside the shoulder, leaving them no room and no choice. Storey cut back onto the road, the Cherokee briefly going airborne when the tires slammed into that several-inches-of-elevation difference between the sand and the hard-surface road.

They were still in the wrong lane, and Storey had no choice but to peel all the metal off the side of a little Fiat trying to get out of their way. And now there was also a sound of grinding metal coming from something hanging off the body of the Cherokee.

Cars were flying all over the highway, trying desperately to get out of the way of that big American wrecking ball.

Driving was taking up Storey's full attention, but he knew the silver Mercedes was still with them. He knew this because Troy was firing his weapon out the rear window.

Storey still had the gas pedal on the floor, but top speed was one of the tradeoffs to carrying several hundred pounds of vehicle armor. He wasn't going to be outrunning a Mercedes sedan.

The firing wasn't all one-way. Storey could see both green and white tracer bullets floating over the top and past the sides of the Cherokee.

The windshield was slightly starred from the impact with the AK-47, but the visibility was still good. Good enough for Storey to notice that both lines of traffic were completely stopped less than a mile up ahead, for whatever reason.

"We're running out of road!" he bellowed, trying to get it over the sound of Troy's carbine.

Troy heard it during the brief lull of a magazine change and looked over his shoulder. "Motherfucker!"

Storey didn't have long to make a decision on which shoulder to take. The right seemed to have fewer obstacles. He hit the sand, swerving right around the stopped traffic. There wasn't much room. Someone had left their passenger door open, maybe to step out and take a look, and Storey took it right off the hinges. People who had stepped out to get a better view of the cause of the tie-up were diving out of the way, spurred on both by the Cherokee and the continuing gunfire.

The countryside was opening up. Very soon Storey could shift into four-wheel drive and go off-road over terrain that no Mercedes could negotiate.

A slight rise, but not so slight that a driver could see over it, and all four wheels left the ground. Over the rise, and in front of them a drainage channel that passed *under* the road. Touching ground again, and Storey standing on the brake as the front end of the Cherokee dropped and hit the side of the channel straight on.

White airbags exploded. Total darkness, then light as they deflated. Storey still gripping the steering wheel. Total silence, whether because he was deaf or there really was total silence he had no idea.

In truth only seconds had passed since the crash, but time seemed to stretch out. The seat belt button was jammed. The knife in his vest seemed to fall into Storey's hand, and he slashed the nylon webbing. His rifle was under the dash, the Aimpoint red-dot sight snapped off and gone. Now he could hear the sound of gunfire again, but it was the light chatter of American 5.56mm, not the heavier Russian 7.62mm.

Holy shit—Troy was out in the ditch and already putting down fire. How had the kid managed that? The passenger door was slightly ajar. Storey kicked it open and threw himself out. It only rained during the monsoon, so the ditch was bone dry.

Troy was prone over the lip of the ditch. Blood was running down his face, but Storey knew they didn't have time for first aid. Troy was firing single-shot, very deliberately, enough to keep the opposition from maneuvering toward them, but still conserving ammunition.

Storey knew the sounds of the Russian armory by heart. They were taking fire from three AKs and a heavier PKM machine gun. A lot of spraying, but fire was only effective if it was close enough to make you keep your head down and not shoot back. This wasn't effective. The PKM was probably firing armor-piercing bullets at the Cherokee. The Cherokee!

Storey slid down to the bottom of the ditch and looked under the vehicle. A concrete tunnel ran right under the road. He scrambled back up to the top and slapped Troy on the leg. Troy looked down, and Storey indicated by hand signals what he wanted to do. Troy nodded.

Storey signaled him to go. Troy jumped to the bottom of the ditch and sprinted toward the Cherokee. Having lost the red-dot sight off his rifle in the crash, Storey popped up the backup iron sights and started shooting. The silver Mercedes had stopped broadside at the top of the rise, about forty yards away.

Judging that Troy had had enough time, Storey dug in one of his vest pouches and came up with one of the Austrian Arges mini hand grenades, just a little bigger than a golf ball. Small meant they could be thrown a lot farther. He thumbed the pin off the retaining clip in the plastic body, yanked it out, and heaved the grenade toward the far side of the Mercedes.

As soon as it left his hand he was back down in the ditch. The Cherokee was impaled directly across its width, so there was about a three-foot open space between the bottom of the vehicle and the bottom of the ditch. Storey crawled through that space, becoming aware that most of the incoming fire was being directed at the Cherokee. The grenade exploded when he was underneath—at first making him think that the gas tank had ignited.

Once he was through he could see why everyone was firing at the vehicle. The dummy was still sitting up straight in the backseat.

All the more reason to move faster. Troy was already through the tunnel on the other side of the road. Storey ran hunched over. While he was halfway through, the Cherokee exploded, the blast knocking him onto his stomach. That was what he'd been expecting. The AKs and the PKM were to take out the Cherokee's tires and run it off the road. Then an antitank rocket from an RPG-7 rocket-propelled grenade launcher to open it up like a tin can.

Troy was already back up on the road as Storey

emerged from the tunnel. Storey joined him, pouring sweat from the exertion. They didn't shoot, but covered each other while they alternated moving. Quite a few Pakistanis had gotten out of their cars to watch the action. They bolted when they saw Troy and Storey. The rest, more prudent, were huddled down on their floorboards.

Not wanting to expose themselves, the two Americans weaved between the cars, following the sound of gun-fire until they were even with the Mercedes. On his belly, Storey peeked underneath the car he'd been hiding behind. Two men were shooting from behind the Mercedes, one was loading another rocket into the tube of his RPG. A fourth was leaning against a wheel, hit either by a lucky shot or grenade fragments. They were laughing, still firing at the Cherokee. Too much target focus could be fatal.

He looked over at Troy. Troy nodded that he was ready. Storey mouthed silently, *one . . . two . . . three.* They both popped up over the car, firing. Storey centered his front sight post on one and slapped the trigger twice, watching his man fall. He was shooting with both eyes open, one to aim and the other watching. As he shifted to the next target he saw two more go down. Damn, but Troy was fast. Storey shot the fourth, but those little 5.56mm bullets didn't always guarantee a kill. Three rounds and the wounded man still managed to spin around the vehicle and get behind the trunk.

Storey saw Troy moving in his peripheral vision, so he kept firing to keep the man fixed in position.

Troy darted over to the cover of the next car in line, shifting left until he was looking straight at the front grill of the Mercedes. He dropped belly-down onto the road in a good prone firing position, but had to pause and wipe the blood from his eyes once again. Looking directly under the Mercedes, he had a clear view of two legs from the knees down.

Troy settled the floating Aimpoint red dot on one ankle and fired. The whole side of a body fell into view, and Troy emptied the rest of his magazine into it. He pulled another from his vest, slapping it into the well and letting the bolt ride home.

Now Storey was advancing on the Mercedes, firing into each body as he came up. Two in the chest, two in the head. He didn't stop but passed completely around the vehicle, making sure of the one Troy had just shot.

Troy met him on the other side of the Mercedes. "Cover," said Storey. While Troy kept an eye on the surrounding area, Storey gave each body a frisk, removing the Pakistani identity cards he knew were fake. He took a picture of each face with the camera in his Personal Digital Assistant. Then from a vest, a fingerprint card for each man, special paper that needed no ink, only pressure.

The Cherokee was still burning. "Let's clear the area," he said to Troy.

"We jackin'?" Troy asked.

Storey nodded.

They jogged up the line of stopped cars. Now that the firing had stopped, many were moving, popping U-turns in the road and speeding back to Karachi.

A quarter mile down the road was the reason for the traffic tie-up, a three-car and one-truck accident that had both lanes blocked and no way to go around. As usual, there was a great crowd of onlookers enjoying the diversion and offering advice. And everyone just stared in amazement as a white man and a black man carrying rifles ran right by them and disappeared down the road. As usual when someone or something was running, there was an urge to give chase. A few men gave in to that until Storey tossed a flash-bang over his shoulder and changed their minds.

Now that they were clear of the obstruction, Storey chose the first car that looked like it was in good running condition and didn't have an entire family inside. A compact Toyota with just one man in his early twenties behind the wheel.

And the young man's eyes tripled in size at the sight of Storey charging up with his rifle leveled.

"Get out!" Storey ordered.

The man just sat there, frozen.

Storey yanked open the door, grabbed him by the neck, and dragged him out, passing him to Troy, who threw him into the backseat. Troy got in beside him, making sure he himself was behind Storey in case the Pakistani spazzed out.

Storey shifted into drive, pulled out into the empty lane, and gave the car the gas.

The Pakistani was trembling uncontrollably. Troy didn't realize that part of the reason was several lacerations that had left his face covered with oozing blood.

"You speak English?" Troy demanded.

"Y . . . y . . . yes, sir," the man stuttered through the shakes. "Please do not kill me."

"Relax," said Troy. "We're not going to hurt you. What's your name?"

"Bilal, sir."

"Okay, Bilal. You're not going to come to any harm, and neither is your car. We just need a lift to our destination. Once we get there, we'll compensate you for your time and trouble, and you'll be free to go on your way."

"I hate to interrupt this," said Storey, "but is your radio working?"

Troy checked. "That's affirm."

"Then don't waste a lot of time with a situation report. Have them call the air base and make sure we're met. I don't want to be standing outside the front gate with our shit hanging in the breeze while the guard calls for instructions."

Troy did just that, brushing off a million questions from Al, who'd been monitoring Pakistani police radio reports of a major shoot-out on the road.

Bilal was now beginning to believe that he wasn't going to be shot and dumped into a ditch while his car continued on some journey without him. "Excuse me, gentlemen, but are you American?"

Storey let out a warning grunt for Troy's benefit.

"Let's just say we're foreigners who've had a little trouble on the road," said Troy, enjoying it. "And who really appreciate your assistance and hospitality."

Bilal took in a full view of the black man wearing sunglasses and shooting gloves, the strange rifle resting across his lap, the vest bulging with ordnance, and the thin radio microphone snaking from the earpiece to his mouth. "A little trouble? Yes, sir, I am sure you have had only a little trouble."

That tickled Troy's funny bone. He gave Bilal an appreciative smack across his very thin shoulders.

Storey took the turnoff to the air base. Troy was rummaging around in his vest and pockets. "Kick in," he said to Storey. "We got to hook our boy here up."

Storey passed a wad of bills over his shoulder. Troy added his own to it.

They pulled up to the air base gate. The guards eyed the car suspiciously, then raised their German G-3 rifles when Troy and Storey emerged.

Storey raised his hands to reassure them. And Bilal, trying to be helpful, stuck his head out the window and shouted in Sindi, another of the languages of southern Pakistan, that they were friendly.

It was help they really didn't need, so Troy slapped the bills into his hand, saying, "Thanks a lot, Bilal. Hope we didn't shake you up too bad." And then in his ear, "Better not tell too many people about this. There's some that would blame you for helping us, if you know what I mean."

Bilal nodded solemnly, then for the first time looked at the money in his hand. All green United States hundred-dollar bills, more and more as he kept unfolding them.

Five thousand dollars total, a princely sum to the average Pakistani, not even considering the black market exchange rate into rupees.

Bilal ran after Troy and Storey, insisting on embracing them even as the gate guards drew down on them all. "Thank you, gentlemen, thank you. God protect you both."

Then, the reality of the situation sinking in, he jumped back into his car. Before disappearing in a cloud of exhaust, he stuck his head out the window and shouted, "God bless America."

"Amen, brother," said Troy.

"Changing the world's minds," Storey said dryly. "Five grand at a time."

As they walked toward the gate with hands raised, two jeeps filled with military police sped up. A little shouting back and forth with the guards, then the MP lieutenant waving at Troy and Storey, saying, "Come, come."

They were driven right onto the airstrip, past French Mirage fighter jets and Chinese-manufactured MiG-21s wearing the white crescent and star on the green background. Right up to a gray Gulfstream in U.S. Air Force markings. Kasim al-Hariq was already inside.

The CIA man who'd driven him looked Troy and Storey over, and asked, "Nice drive?"

"Yeah, great," said Troy, removing his sunglasses to wipe the blood from his eyes again. "You?"

"Took the back roads. No problem."

Storey and Troy unloaded and cleared their weapons. When they stripped off their vests a dark, soaking wet outline remained on their shirts. They settled in as a crewman brought the air stairs up.

There was an air force doctor on the flight, standard on important prisoner transfers. He took a close look at Troy's head. "Let's go in the bathroom and wash this up, and I'll look for glass shards."

The jet was already airborne when they returned from

the bathroom. Troy had his head dressed, and was walking all hunched over. "His muscles are stiffening up from your car crash," the doctor told Storey as he dug in his bag for a muscle relaxant. "How are you feeling?"

"Not as bad as him," Storey replied. And then to Troy, "I've been meaning to ask you how you got out of the Cherokee so fast."

"Think I got thrown out," said Troy. "We crashed—I was in the ditch. Exactly *how* that happened, I don't know."

"We'll get you some X-rays as soon as we land," said the doctor, checking both their eyes for signs of concussion, and ears and noses for traces of blood.

Storey glanced out the window at the Indian Ocean, then back to the CIA man. "We're not going to Bagram?"

"Not for this guy. Diego Garcia."

A small island in the Chagos Archipelago south of India. A British possession, but a major U.S. logistics base, including port and air facility. Very isolated. There was a small interrogation center there for the most important terrorist catches, staffed by the best interrogators.

"Hot shit," said Troy, who hadn't been looking forward to a trip to Afghanistan. "You ever been to Diego?" he asked Storey.

"Just to refuel once. Never got off the plane."

"Best chow hall in the military," said Troy. "A dip in the pool, a few San Miguels at the club before we fly back home. This trip is looking up."

Now it was Storey's turn to shake his head.

9

The FBI agents were observing the interrogation room through the one-way mirror. Jabir al-Banri was handcuffed to a bar running along the table.

"You sure you want to go in solo?" Supervisory Special Agent Benjamin Timmins asked.

"Positive," said Beth Royale. "Otherwise, he'll just gravitate to the man."

"And you think a woman's touch is going to be the key here?" Timmins said, a little sarcastically.

"These guys grow up watching their fathers boss their mothers around," Beth replied. "Then they boss their wives and daughters around. They can't deal with women any other way."

"He won't talk to you," said Special Agent Ron Graham. "He won't even look at you."

"At first," said Beth. "Then he'll talk."

"For how much?" said Graham.

"Lunch of my choice?" said Beth.

"No way, that cost me fifty bucks last time, and all *I* ate was bread and water."

"You can't blame me because you never learn, Ronny. How about a new pair of shoes?"

"Christ, no. Ten bucks."

"Ten it is." Then to Timmins, "I want to run tape on this."

"You know how I feel about that."

"I know, Ben, but I still want to do it."

The usual refrain, "All right, all right."

Beth videotaped all her interrogations. The FBI never did that, feeling that an agent's word in court was paramount. But there had been enough scandals over the years that an agent's testimony from interrogation notes wasn't as unshakable as it had been. Beth liked to show a tape in court, or at least have it available so defense counsel wouldn't want to take her on.

She left. The rest stayed to watch.

Beth entered the interrogation room carrying a notebook computer, a legal pad, and some file folders under her arm. She didn't enter alone, though. She said to the agent who followed her in, "Uncuff him."

"You sure?" the agent said, just as she'd coached him.

"Go ahead," said Beth. "I didn't have any trouble getting them on him in the first place."

The agent unlocked the cuff from Jabir's wrist, and left.

Jabir sat glowering at her, rubbing his wrist. Beth totally ignored him, opening up her computer and arranging her papers.

When the door shut, Jabir spoke his first words. "Cover your head!"

Beth only laughed. "You're dreaming if you think you can tell *anyone* what to do around here, little man."

Furious, Jabir stood up, fists clenched.

Beth remained seated. "Go ahead. We'll show the video of me kicking your ass at our next Christmas party."

Jabir stayed standing for a few seconds to salvage his pride, then sat down as if he'd made his point. He turned his chair around so he faced the wall. "I will not speak to you. It is *haram*." Forbidden.

"Keep it up," said Beth. "Be stupid. Make my job easy. Make *sure* you spend the rest of your life in prison."

Jabir's head twitched ever so slightly.

"Oh yes," said Beth. "He's thinking to himself: I'm only under arrest for cigarette smuggling. And that's only three years on each count. Say we can file on at least twenty-three counts. Sixty-nine years, you do a third, that's twenty-three. And twenty-three isn't life. But you know you're not here for cigarette smuggling, don't you? That's just an easy twenty-three years to tack on the end of your life sentence."

Beth tapped at the keys of her notebook. "Turn around, see what I've got to show you. C'mon, it's your life sentence—you might as well look."

Jabir held out longer than Beth thought he could, but of course in the end he couldn't stand it. He glanced over his shoulder as if to just sneer at her. Then the computer screen caught his eye, and he swiveled around, apparently without even thinking about it. When he got a good look his face fell down to his chest.

"That's right," said Beth. "We got all your records. And now we've got the money laundering. Membership in the organization. Material support. All those reconnaissance photos and reports on the federal buildings, malls, the Silverdome, Tiger Stadium. Conspiracy. Conspiracy to commit murder. That's life right there." She shook her head sadly. "You're done, Jabir. There's over a hundred counts. We don't even have to win them all."

Having laid the groundwork she wanted, Beth was through emphasizing prison. After all, Bin Laden told his people that they would end up either as martyrs or in U.S. prisons, and either one was equally pleasing to God. Which was probably why Jabir hadn't screamed for a lawyer yet. She'd only done it to set up her next move.

"But you know the worst part?" she said. "You were very good. Very professional. You even chose your men right. Kalid, Feisal, Isam, Hamid."

Jabir's composure cracked a little more at the mention of the names.

"They were professional, too," said Beth. "None of them betrayed you. Until now, that is," she added, to give him something more to think about. "But that's understandable, isn't it? Given the weight of evidence?" She gestured toward the screen. "I'm sure you can understand. They're young, and now they're looking out for themselves."

"You lie!" Jabir shouted.

"You wouldn't be upset if you didn't know it was true," Beth pointed out reasonably. "But like I told you, it's not your fault. We never would have found you all if we hadn't found your controller first."

Jabir didn't realize it, but his face wouldn't have been twitching more if Beth had been giving him electric shocks.

"Did that bother you?" Beth wondered. "To have someone less competent put over you? I know that would bother me. But what am I saying, 'less competent'? Totally incompetent would be more like it. We couldn't have caught him any easier if he'd been wearing a T-shirt that said *Controller of Jabir's Cell.*"

Beth sensed that the play to Jabir's vanity was a winner. Everyone thought they were smarter than their boss. "And you know the worst part? Here you are, behaving like a soldier, keeping silence. And there he was, in this very room, in *your* chair. And he couldn't wait to tell us everything. He gave you up. He gave up all the other cells. He gave up the networks, the communications. He gave up *everything.*"

Jabir also didn't realize that his lips were moving in time with what he was thinking.

"How could we have caught you otherwise?" Beth asked. "Your tradecraft was immaculate. And you came in prepared to die before betraying him, while he had already betrayed you."

Beth sighed. "It will all fall apart now. Because we're going to have to charge your wife, Rubina, as an accessory. We've been told how you took her along on your reconnaissance jobs as cover. She took the video while you drove."

Jabir started again. Beth's interrogation of the wife had paid off.

"And when she goes to prison?" said Beth. "Well, the government will not allow us to send your son to the family of a terrorist. And your mosque will now be under suspicion. Your son will have to go into a foster home. All we can do is try to find a good Christian family to raise him."

"No!" Jabir shouted.

"My hands are tied," Beth said regretfully. "And since your controller is already cooperating, we have all the information we need. Why do you think your friends are talking to us?" She let silence do its work for a while, then slapped her hand on her legal pad, making Jabir jump. "Maybe if you confirm the information we already have, and you're truthful, *maybe* I can persuade my superiors not to charge your wife. That means she could go free and raise your son with your family. To be honest, my conscience would feel better if I could do that."

There was a make-or-break moment in every interrogation, and this was it. Beth knew not to press. She sat back in her chair and let Jabir make up his mind.

"The pig," Jabir muttered. "The dirty pig."

"Who?" Beth asked, as if she weren't really interested.

"Muhammad," Jabir said, almost under his breath.

But Beth didn't leap at the name. As if she were totally bored, she said, "I know who you're talking about." Though of course she had no idea. "But if you're going to cooperate, you'll have to state all names for the record. It's required."

"My wife and son will go free?"

"*If* you're completely truthful," said Beth. "I give you my word. But one lie, just one, about anything, and the deal is off. I leave the room and put your wife under arrest. No second chances, no appeals."

Jabir nodded glumly.

Though Beth kept her face blank, inside she was dancing. Jabir had now accepted her as his destiny, crossing over.

"His full name," Beth said sternly, tapping her pen on the legal pad like an impatient teacher. Any break in the mood could give Jabir a chance to wiggle off the hook.

"Muhammad al-Sharif."

"His address?"

"Fifty-one eighty-eight Michigan Avenue, Dearborn."

"His occupation?"

"He owns Absolute Performance Auto Repair, on Warren Avenue."

"Good," Beth said grudgingly. "Now let's go back. How and where did you first meet?"

"You know all this from him," Jabir grumbled.

Beth smacked the pad with her pen again. "How do you think I'll know if you're lying? Answer the question, and from now on lose the attitude."

Jabir all but said yes, ma'am. He named the primary Al Qaeda training camp outside Kandahar, Afghanistan. "We were introduced in 1998. October," he added quickly.

"By who?"

"Abdallah Karim Nimri."

Beth had never heard the name, but had no intention of betraying her ignorance. "Go on."

"It was Nimri's idea. He said that an American would have more freedom of action than we. He was looking into the future."

"And how did Nimri and al-Sharif meet?"

"In the camp," Jabir replied. "On entering, you were required to complete a form. They would search the forms for things that interested them."

"How did al-Sharif get to Afghanistan?"

"The imam of his mosque."

A talent spotter, Beth thought. Find a likely recruit, see if the jihad preaching took, keep an eye on him. If he worked out, a plane ticket to a madrasa, a religious school in Pakistan. More indoctrination, more eyes on him there, like scouting a baseball prospect. Then across the border to Afghanistan, to a real training camp. Religious, military, clandestine instruction. The minor leagues. If the prospect panned out, he was fully trained and sent out into the world. Wherever he ended up, he was expected to recruit and train others. All he needed from the organization was a little cash now and then, and his orders. "Was al-Sharif born a Muslim, or did he convert?"

"You are testing me," Jabir said, with a sly smile.

"Of course I am," Beth replied. "Answer the question."

"He found the true faith in prison. This is why I am here now. Not even a good criminal. Years in prison."

People in glass houses, Beth thought. "He told you what his name was before he converted." She phrased it as not quite a question, not quite a statement.

"I discovered it," said Jabir, indulging in a little boasting. "Samuel Foster."

"Did he grow up in Chicago?"

"As you know. I wish to see my wife."

And tell her to pass on the message that the network was compromised. It might be productive to see where she took it. Later. Beth shook her head. "First things first, Jabir." She decided to give him a little approval, so he'd keep trying for more. "You're doing well. You want something to drink?"

"Coke."

"You mean, you would like a Coke—*please*."

Chastised. "Yes, please. A Coke."

"I'll have someone get it." It wouldn't do for him to start thinking she was going to fetch him anything. Beth closed the cover of her laptop. "Don't touch the computer."

Out the door and into the observation room. And a hand out to receive Graham's ten dollars. "Did he touch the computer?"

"Are you kidding?" said Graham. "He's your bitch now."

"That was a damn fine piece of work," said Timmins. "We're running down Muhammad al-Sharif right now."

"Let's not go kicking in the door to his house or garage until we're sure he's there," said Beth. "Or he'll be long gone."

"He might have gotten the word already," said Graham.

"I'm just saying," said Beth, "we already lost our chance to pick one of these guys up quietly and try to turn and play him back into the network."

"We've already been over this," said Timmins, in his end-of-discussion tone.

Yes, we have, Beth thought. All the undercover work and use of informers that had taken down the Mafia was out the window for terrorists. There had to be arrests, and they had to be public, to show that the bureau was really doing something. "You know, when Jabir told me about his controller, I was thinking—"

"Yeah, I was thinking the same thing, too," said Timmins. "The Muslim convert that special ops took out in the Philippines."

Reminding Beth once again that, though an FBI politician, he was not at all stupid.

"I don't like it," Timmins went on. "I don't like that a non-Arab American citizen is controlling Al Qaeda sleeper cells. I especially don't like that I'm going to be on the phone all night with everyone in Washington once I tell Headquarters about this."

"To whom much is given . . ." said Beth.

"Yeah, right," said Timmins. "You want to partner up with someone on Jabir? Trade off so you can take a break?"

Beth shook her head. "We've got the relationship

now. It's me and Jabir until he's dry." She didn't mention that one wrong move might ruin everything, and she only trusted herself not to make it.

"Suit yourself," said Timmins. "We're going to get a treasure trove of nuts-and-bolts operational tradecraft. I want to know who's doing the talent spotting in the mosques, and I want him to remember everyone he ever met in the camps in Afghanistan. I'll enjoy trading that with the CIA."

"You'll get everything he has," said Beth.

"If I have anything to do with it," Timmins told her, "they'll be watching the video of that interrogation at the academy. It was beautiful, really beautiful. Big gamble—big reward."

Not immune to the flattery, no matter how much she pretended otherwise, Beth let her exterior crack open in the form of a pleased smile. "Thanks, Ben."

10

The music was loud, and the Thai girls were all parading around in their bikinis. Each wearing a discreet number, like the starting lineup of their country's team in the sexual Olympics.

People used to come to the Patpong area of Bangkok strictly for the sex. But its reputation from the Vietnam War onward made it a must-see on many tourist itineraries. So now along with the usual sexual adventurers one might see couples walking through the night market along Soi Patpong 1, checking out the bars and snapping photos of the hyperaggressive barkers out in front of their establishments trying to drum up business. The German sex tourists wearing socks with their sandals could be seen alongside twenty-something backpackers and the occasional Carrie Nation–style activist trying to save the native girls from a life of sin.

The hard-core perverts found this disillusioning and gravitated toward the Nana Plaza and Soi Cowboy areas. But Patpong still thrived in its notoriety.

Which was probably the reason the four Arabs had taken a table at the Kings Corner Club. If it was a deliberate choice, it was a good one for many reasons. The club was packed. And Kings Corner had the reputation for the prettiest bar girls, not to mention the snottiest.

They knew they were hot, and therefore it was a seller's market. All business, they wouldn't sit at a table unless a customer bought them a continuous stream of very expensive nonalcoholic drinks.

The Arabs weren't buying, and there were plenty of other *farangs* who were, so the girls left them alone. It was a multinational crowd, so they didn't stand out—not even by speaking Arabic. Arabs were regular customers of the red-light districts of Bangkok.

For the Arabs it was better than a hotel where they might be bugged by Thai security, or someone's apartment that might already be under surveillance.

Abdallah Karim Nimri had already passed the other three men a CD-ROM under the table. Talat al-Rashidi was the controller for all Southeast Asia. Majed Ismail, the controller for Thailand, operated a large scrap metal company in Bangkok that shipped and received all over the region. Nabil Zaydan was the controller for the Philippines.

"The four missiles have been shipped in a container of steel scrap from the port of Odessa in the Ukraine," said Nimri. "They should arrive by the end of the month. All the information is on the CD."

"All four missiles in one shipment?" said al-Rashidi, his disapproval quite obvious.

"If the missiles are discovered the operation is over," said Nimri. "Four shipments, four chances of discovery."

The others nodded in agreement.

"Shipped *here*, and not Subic Bay?" said Zaydan.

"That was the original plan," said Nimri. "The American disruption of our network there made the change necessary. The missiles will arrive here as scrap, and then be shipped air freight to Manila as electronic components. Is this a problem?"

"No," said Zaydan. "As long as they are paid, the customs search nothing. They are accustomed to me receiving shipments. And paying them. But what missiles?"

"Russian," said Nimri. "SA-16, the latest model. What the Russians call Igla. Needle."

Zaydan frowned. "I do not know this system. The American Stinger, yes. The Russian SA-7 also. But not this."

"Chechen brothers will operate the missiles," said Nimri. "They will fly in separately, before the security preparations begin. You will arrange their hiding, and provide a brother to each as an assistant. A Filipino brother, familiar with Manila. The locations must be chosen within the missile range envelope. The missiles and men must be positioned before the city is closed down by security."

"The locations have long been chosen, in anticipation of such an operation," said Zaydan.

Nimri expected nothing less. Al Qaeda was known for meticulous reconnaissance. "The locations must not be listed as either rented or owned by foreigners or Muslims."

"Of course," said Zaydan. "Even so, I must tell you that the security precautions make our chances very slim."

"There will be at least one decoy helicopter," said Nimri. "Four locations, all missiles fired simultaneously, so the aircraft cannot evade all. There must be mobile phone communications, and there must be backup."

"God willing, two missiles will launch," said Zaydan. "I cannot promise more."

"Prepare carefully and thoroughly," said Nimri. "Act bravely. The rest is in God's hands." He passed a slip of paper to Zaydan. He would receive the money for the operation by the *Hawala* system. This was used by Muslims to transfer money around the world.

In many countries, especially in the Middle East, the banking and money transfer systems were either unreliable, chaotic, or crooked. The reliable systems of Western countries were not trusted by immigrants who did not speak the language or understand the mores.

And terrorists preferred to avoid the international banking system, especially with the increased scrutiny after 9/11.

A *Hawaldar* moved money without the use of wire transfers, checks, or credit cards. Nimri had removed his operational funds, in cash, from a friendly bank in Dubai. The largest city-state in the relatively stable United Arab Emirates, a laissez-faire commercial and trading center, the banking system there attracted massive amounts of both clean and dirty money from all over the Middle East, Africa, and Asia. Like the Swiss a generation earlier, the Dubai did not want to upset this profitable arrangement by asking too many questions.

Nimri had then taken the cash to a Dubai *Hawaldar*. The *Hawaldar* would contact another of his acquaintances in the Philippines, giving him the amount and a code to confirm the recipient's identity. Zaydan would visit the Manila *Hawaldar*, give him the code, and pick up the cash. No receipts, no records. Untraceable.

The two *Hawaldars* would settle the debt in their own mysterious way, either by an offsetting transaction in the other direction, the payment of a debt, the purchase of equivalent goods or services, or a straight commercial banking transaction. This was done on trust, with no contracts, among the loose association of *Hawaldars*. Many of the same clan, tribe, or family.

Nimri had flown from Dubai to Bangkok, picking up part of the money, in cash, from a Bangkok *Hawaldar*. This he would give to Ismail to pay for the Thai part of the operation. The *Hawala* system freed all of them from having to pass through customs with large amounts of cash in their possession. Or to rely on traceable checks or wire transfers.

They talked awhile longer. Then Zaydan rose, embraced the others at the table, and left. Nimri then settled the details of the missile transfer with Ismail, passing him a thick envelope of high-denomination Thai baht notes.

Now it was just Nimri and al-Rashidi at the table.

"Many years, brother," said Nimri over the thumping of the music.

"Many years," al-Rashidi replied. "And still victory eludes us."

"Our survival is our victory," said Nimri. "God will reward us, in his own time."

"He must," said al-Rashidi. "To make up for our leaders' poor decisions."

A comment that would have sent Nimri into a rage coming from anyone else now only made him laugh. Al-Rashidi was another Egyptian, another former member of *Gama'at al Islamiyya*, Egyptian Islamic Jihad. Even more cosmopolitan than Nimri, which made exile from Cairo even harder. A short, squat man whose beard would never grow beyond a scattering of scraggly hairs. Cynical as only an Egyptian intellectual could be.

Both of them had been part of the team that made the failed rocket-propelled grenade attack on Egyptian President Hosni Mubarak's motorcade during a state visit to Addis Ababa, Ethiopia, in June 1995. Ruthlessly hunted by Egyptian security, Islamic Jihad had been on the verge of going under. Then both Nimri and al-Rashidi had followed, though others had not, when Islamic Jihad head Ayman al-Zawahiri folded the organization into Al Qaeda, becoming Osama Bin Laden's chief deputy in the process.

"There was no other choice," said Nimri. "Our money and morale were nearly exhausted."

"I thought so too, at the time," said al-Rashidi. "I also thought that the way to Cairo was through America."

"It may yet prove to be the case."

"This missile operation is another piece of desperation, my brother. If we must stay silent for three years to accomplish it, even a massive success could be worse for us than many smaller failures. You know I say this to you because you are my brother."

"I have thought the same thing myself," said Nimri. "And I hear you with an open heart. Because you are my brother, I will tell you about the part of the operation no one else knows of. I would not even tell you, my brother, but that I may require last-minute support. You are the only one I trust."

"Your own part?" said al-Rashidi.

Nimri nodded.

"I knew it," said al-Rashidi. "You are not like Khalid Shaykh Muhammad, our great operations genius, sending others out to execute his plan and then surrendering to the Americans, crying for his life. I knew you would be involved."

Nimri spoke, and al-Rashidi's eyebrows rose. "This makes me feel better about the operation. I had many doubts."

"But the losses, brother."

"Wars are not won without losses, brother. God will reward those in his service. But you are assuming much risk."

"Better so than losing again, God willing," said Nimri. "But now that you know my full plans, you must remove yourself to a secure location. Away from cities. But it must be a place where I can reach you, and you me."

Al-Rashidi thought it over. "By God, I know of such a place. And with satellites, communications are possible from anywhere. We will use the code we used in Sudan?"

"Excellent," said Nimri. "Now, brother, tell me truthfully. What do you think of my plan?"

"It may not succeed," al-Rashidi said bluntly. "But what else can we do? Act against places such as this?" He looked around the bar, scowling. "These will be the last, not the first. No matter how easy some of the brothers think they are. We must act according to our best, and allow God to pass judgment upon us. If we do not act, His verdict will be certain."

"These are my feelings also," said Nimri.

The two men embraced with great feeling, and Nimri walked out into the raucous Bangkok night.

almost too fast to be believed, followed by a tropical downpour that could unload as much as an inch of rain in fifteen minutes. Then the reappearance of the sun, making you feel as if you'd been thrown wet into a clothes dryer.

"It's lunchtime anyway," said Troy.

And at the dining facility they were joined by one of the interrogation team, an army lieutenant colonel, military intelligence officer.

"Mind if I sit with you guys?" he asked heartily. After getting a yes, he went up to the line to get himself some food.

"I sure hope he's a better interrogator than he is an operator," said Troy. "Like he just bumped into us, with the officers' mess over on the other wing of the building."

"Most people get pissed off when officers let you know they think you're stupid," said Storey. "I say, use it to your advantage. When he gets back he'll be all insecure, so he'll have to mention something about how much he loves us enlisted."

The colonel set his tray down. "Thanks, men. It's good to sit with the real people for a change."

He'd caught Troy in the act of drinking a Coke, and some of it started leaking out his nose.

"Don't mind him, sir," Storey said calmly. "Rotten table manners."

The colonel smiled uneasily as Troy dealt with the carbonated liquid sloshing painfully about his sinus cavity. He didn't give any hints that his visit wasn't social, talking instead of the Monday Night Football game, which was shown live via satellite on Tuesday morning.

It was only when they were through eating that the colonel suggested a little walk. Storey pondered the irony of the colonel worrying about being overheard when just on the other side of the island was a National Security Agency antenna farm that could pick up someone farting over the phone in Bangalore, India.

The baseball diamond was deserted. They talked, leaning over the chain-link fence.

"Your guy broke," the colonel said.

Troy wondered what they'd used on him. Sleep deprivation; he knew from SEAL Hell Week just how much that could mess you up. Food deprivation; a bland diet of unfamiliar foods, just enough calories to make you constantly hungry. Temperature; if you were used to the heat, they kept your cell cold, and vice versa. And the devastating psychological knowledge that they had you forever and life wasn't going to improve one little bit unless you gave up what they wanted. In a way, it was like SEAL Basic Underwater Demolition School. Everyone who volunteered knew what was going to happen and thought they could take it. And it was always a surprise to see how few really could. Rough stuff, but not nearly as rough as what the other side would do if they got their hands on you.

"He didn't strike me as all that tough, sir," said Storey. "Even so, that's pretty fast."

"Normally, we have to cover everything," said the colonel. "Then go back and focus on the areas where they resist interrogation. But the same informer who gave him up also gave us more than enough detailed background information to focus on. That made a big difference."

"Good news, sir," said Storey. His subsequent silence was his way of encouraging the colonel to get to the point of why it concerned them.

"Either of you ever hear of an Abdallah Karim Nimri?" the colonel asked.

Storey and Troy both paused for a moment to flip through the card files in their heads. Then both shook their heads no.

"Egyptian," said the colonel. "Up and comer. Dark horse candidate for Al Qaeda operations chief. He's working on an operation to kill the president during the upcoming Asia visit. Probably the Philippines. Your guy was the cutout between Nimri and the leadership."

"So this guy knows where Bin Laden and Zawahiri are?" Troy said excitedly, hoping that was why they were being briefed. Hell, the president could always skip his trip to the Philippines.

"We're working on that," said the colonel. "But there's not much hope there. As soon as the word got around that he got grabbed, all the people he knew about and all the money he knew about moved. That's their standard procedure."

Troy was about to say something else, but Storey nudged him. You didn't get briefed on information like this unless you had a need to know. And, given time, the colonel would eventually tell them why they needed to know.

"We haven't got much on the assassination plot against the president," the colonel told them. "He threw it at us; then once he realized what he'd done he clammed up. But we're getting it out of him bit by bit. Evidently this guy Nimri is using networks that are already in place. And evidently a while back you took out one of the Philippine players at Subic Bay."

Storey nodded. If you kept working them hard, the links would eventually appear.

"The rest of the Philippine network is fuzzy," said the colonel. "We don't know whether it's Abu Sayyaf, Jemaah, or strictly Al Qaeda. There's a firm connection in Thailand, though. Operative named Majed Ismail. Metal dealer. We get him, we could unbutton the whole operation."

Now attuned to the rhythm of the process, Storey and Troy waited him out.

"You're going to get orders to go to Bangkok," the colonel said.

Troy was about to open his mouth when Storey grabbed the bull by the horns. "All respect, sir, we could have gotten a message from Washington, so there's a reason you're speaking to us face-to-face. And I assume there's a reason we're talking beside a baseball diamond instead of in a SCIF." Which was a Special Compartmented Information Facility, a specially locked, screened, allegedly bug-proof space where conversations of the highest security classification were *supposed* to take place. "So might I suggest that the colonel tell us what that reason is?"

Enlisted men, even senior staff noncommissioned officers, didn't usually put lieutenant colonels back on their heels, and Troy admired how neatly Storey had done it. His bet was that the colonel was going to do himself a little yelling.

He couldn't have been more wrong. The colonel swallowed it meekly. "The CIA is already on this guy Ismail. They're working with the Thais. But the Pentagon wants to have a presence also."

"A presence, sir?" said Storey, without a single trace of emotion.

"That's right. The idea is for you two to fly to Bangkok, covertly, and become involved in the capture of the target."

Troy was just opening his mouth when he got the "shut up" look from Storey, who said to the colonel, "You realize, sir, that we're going to have to clear this with our command."

"Of course. Those are my orders. I can release any message traffic when you're ready to send."

"Thank you, sir," said Storey. "But we'll use our own links." He waited, but the colonel didn't seem to have anything to add. "Good afternoon, sir." Being in civilian clothes, he didn't salute, but he did come to attention.

"Good afternoon, men," the colonel replied, in that

hearty, low-register voice senior officers reserved for talking to the enlisted swine.

As soon as the colonel was out of earshot, Storey went through the gate and took a seat on the bleachers. Troy, of course, was forced to follow.

And he was spilling over with outrage. "Yes, sir? No, sir? What is this shit? This is fucking insane."

Storey was deep in thought. After a while he looked up and said, "Sorry, were you waiting for me to argue with you?"

"No, I was waiting for you to fucking argue with *him.*"

"It wasn't his idea. If a lieutenant colonel comes up with a harebrained scheme on his own, you can get rid of him pretty easy. Unless he's your boss. But he was just a messenger boy."

Troy was still talking fast. "If we go to Bangkok, we've got two options. We tell the CIA we're there to help, and they'll tell us to fuck off and go home. Or we *don't* tell them we're in town, go nosing around an operation they're running with Thai security, and bump into them by accident. Someone could accidentally get killed. Or thrown in jail. And I'm pretty sure it would be us."

"In case you're wondering," said Storey, "I'm still not prepared to argue with you."

"Well then, why didn't you fucking say anything to him? Only about a hundred questions popped right into *my* head."

"Oh, that's the one thing you don't want to do," said Storey, still unperturbed. "If this is coming from as high up as I think it is, we might actually have to do it. When you get ordered to do something stupid, and you can't get out of it, your first instinct is to ask a million questions and demand detailed orders. To demonstrate to them how stupid they're being. But that's a big old mistake. Because then you're saddled with all these *detailed* stupid orders that they expect you to carry out. Never ask any questions about a stupid order you *have* to carry out. Just salute, say 'yes, sir,' and get your ass out of the area. Then maybe, just maybe, you'll leave yourself some flexibility to inject a little common sense into the operation."

Troy just sat there with his jaw swinging open. The fuck if Storey wasn't playing chess while the rest of them were playing checkers. "You're right. This is so stupid it had to come from high up in the Pentagon. But what's the reason? Why do they want us bumble-fucking around Bangkok, tripping over an operation the CIA's already got up and running?"

Storey's expression was one of pity. "Because, you poor fool, this is a big score, an assassination plot against the president, and they don't want the CIA to get all the credit for foiling it. And that's exactly what the CIA wants, which is why they're moving so fast."

"Fuck," said Troy.

"Back in D.C. it's all about budgets, and all about politics. That's why it's more important we beat the CIA than Al Qaeda."

"Now I know why we've done so well so far."

"This goes back a long way," said Storey. "When the Iranians took over our embassy in seventy-nine, the CIA couldn't put any spies on the ground to support Delta's hostage rescue, so the army put together Intelligence Support Activity. And they actually put agents on the ground in Teheran. The CIA didn't want anyone but them running agents, so all of a sudden investigations of special operators padding their expenses gets leaked all over Washington. It was a bloodbath. ISA eventually gets back on its feet, and in Colombia they do a better job of pinpointing Pablo Escobar's cell phone calls than the CIA. Once Pablo's dead it's expense account fraud and sexual fraternization all over again. People in the Pentagon have long memories, and they carry grudges. A couple of the guys who got Pablo are in our support section."

"I guess we all *can't* get along. And we're the two dicks who have to run around Bangkok."

"I've been doing this for a while," said Storey. "And there's always a way around everything. Even if we have to go to Bangkok, we're the ones on the ground. Not them."

The reason Storey turned down the colonel's offer to release a message was that military communications, even highly classified communications, were read by an enormous number of people in addition to the sender and recipient. So he sat down again with his keyboard and PDA, composing his own inquiry.

The word back from Washington was what he expected. They were going to Bangkok.

Unlike the trip to Pakistan, which had been done under red diplomatic passports and cases of weapons with diplomatic seals, this would be totally covert. What was known in the trade as a low-visibility operation.

Blue civilian United States passports, though Canada and New Zealand were used occasionally. Impersonating any other nationality pushed the risk level too high. Legitimate passports, but names that were not Storey and Troy. However, the first names were variations on Ed and Lee. No doubt any good psychiatrist could explain why even highly trained operators always remembered a false last name, even under great stress, but frequently drew a total blank on the first name, even under the most mellow conditions.

There were no commercial flights to or from Diego Garcia. Storey and Troy caught the round-the-world C-141 that flew in from the Philippines. They both got off in Nairobi, Kenya, and went their separate ways. Businessmen traveling in pairs attracted attention.

The arrangements were easy. There was an international toll-free number back to the office, and staff that did nothing but book flights, hotels, and cars, under whatever business cover the operators were traveling under. Storey flew to Cairo, then to Abu Dhabi. From there it was a direct flight to Bangkok.

Troy flew from Nairobi to New Delhi. Then another direct to Bangkok a day later.

In his business suit. In business class. With a briefcase and a laptop, because every businessman has a briefcase and a laptop. Troy's contained nothing but reams of material on the injection-molded plastics trade.

A profession that he couldn't help but think Storey had picked out just for him, knowing he'd have to memorize everything about it to maintain his cover, and knowing it was just the most boring shit imaginable. But it was good cover for both the Middle East and Asia.

Troy hated flying commercial when he wasn't armed. And a Middle Eastern airline, yet. There were only a few passengers on the plane who *weren't* Arabs.

It was after dark when his plane touched down at Bangkok's Don Muang Airport. The traffic was always unbelievable. The cab from the airport took so long he could have caught a decent nap.

Troy was jet-lagged, and being jet-lagged always made him feel jacked-up, not tired. The hotel was a typical four-star businessman's choice, and the room was quite comfortable, but in his condition it felt like a cell. When the bellboy set down the bags, Troy could have sworn he heard an echo.

He was supposed to meet Storey in the morning, and he'd better be fresh to make sure he didn't bring any surveillance to the meet. Troy did sets of push-ups until he reached a thousand, then a thousand crunches. Exercise only made him feel more wired. It was almost midnight. Hell, it wouldn't hurt to go down to the bar for a while. Sleep was out of the question, and he had to get out of that room.

When most people walk into a bar they check out the action first, then look for a place to sit. When members of the special operations community enter a bar they scan for threats, first immediate, then potential. Then they make sure there are at least three viable ways out, rehearsing in their mind exactly how they'd accomplish a speedy exit. Then, and only then, do they position themselves in a place where no one can get near them without being seen. After all, the two most dangerous and proficient gunfighters of the old West, Wild Bill Hickok and John Wesley Hardin, were both shot in the back of the head by individuals they never even saw.

Americans who hated their current popular music might reevaluate that position after checking out what the rest of the world listened to. Troy normally hated pianos in bars. Now he longed for one.

There was a light ball over the dance floor, of course. Japanese businessmen dancing with Thai girls. Not wearing bikinis and numbers, but pros nonetheless. No matter how badly you danced, watching a Japanese businessman get down made you feel like Travolta in *Saturday Night Fever*.

Troy pushed his way to the end of the bar, where it blended into a wall. Before his vodka and tonic—the beer drinker's mixed drink—was delivered, the chairs on both sides of him magically opened up. One thing about Asians, they made no bones about their racism. Troy didn't give a shit—now that he had a place to sit down. He twirled his seat around so his back was to the bar and the wall, with good sight lines in all directions.

What Lee Troy did see was a Thai girl making her way down the bar. In a tight black strapless dress that was enough to bring tears to the eyes of any heterosexual male. Not cheap, though. And she sure knew how to move in it. Straight black hair that just touched the small of her back. A small sting of simple pearls around her neck that, for whatever reason, Troy found incredibly hot. No silicone tits, just lithe and beautiful.

She stopped at the open chair beside Troy, looking first down at it, then up at him. Troy made a welcoming gesture. She slid into the seat, tugging at her dress to prevent unsightly creases and delicately crossing her legs.

She took a cigarette from her purse. Troy didn't smoke, but he always carried a lighter—for just this sort of contingency, among others. He lit her up.

The girl smiled her thank you. "*Nous sommes Afriques?*"

Troy had run into this before, in other countries. African meant AIDS, and they were gone. "*Non*," he replied, matching her French. "*Je suis americain.*"

"Oh," she exclaimed, seemingly delighted and in good English, "that is so nice!"

"Really?" said Troy.

"Oh yes. I like Americans very much." As a gesture of reassurance, she rested her hand on his knee.

Which was a nice little zap of electricity that traveled right up Troy's leg. "I'm glad to hear that. I'm Leon. And what is your name?"

"Pai."

No doubt the short version of a multisyllable Thai name that, of course, was not her own. Troy gave her a big smile. "Your name is as beautiful as you are, Pai. May I buy you a drink?" He felt that at least half of American taxpayers wouldn't disapprove of him spending his per diem in such a fashion.

"Yes, thank you." Rapid chatter in Thai with the bartender, and something pink and fruity came sliding over. "First visit to Bangkok, Leon?"

"That's right," said Troy, deciding this was no time to be telling the truth about anything. "I just arrived tonight, but from what I've seen it's a beautiful country."

Pai dropped her eyes demurely. "You like to dance?"

"Baby, it's a myth that all the brothers can dance."

"Excuse me?"

Troy smiled and put a hand on the hand that was on his knee. "I'd rather talk to you."

The eyes dropped again.

When Troy finally glanced at his watch, it was closing in on 2:00 AM. "Pai, I have a business meeting tomorrow morning."

"Oh?"

"Perhaps you'd like to come back to my room?" He knew he really shouldn't, but that delicate little hand kept sliding up and down his thigh. After all, the place was full of pros—it didn't smell like a setup.

"Oh, Leon, you a wonderful man."

"Maybe we could work something out."

The hand slid *all* the way up his thigh. "Oh, I be so nice to you. You gift me what you want in morning."

Troy was reassured by that. Because if she'd pretended she was coming for free he would have told her to forget about it. He wasn't going for the settle-up-in-the-morning routine, though. That was an open door for two drastically different numbers and a potentially nasty dispute about someone's relative worth as a professional. They settled on four thousand baht, just under a hundred dollars, for an all-nighter. Evidently she had some kind of arrangement with the hotel because there was no fine to pay to the bar for taking her out, as was usual in Thai clubs.

On the way up in the elevator Troy gave her a thorough frisk, in the guise of feeling her up. Not that he didn't feel her up too, but it seemed wise to check for weapons.

Inside his room Pai excused herself and went to the bathroom. Troy took the opportunity to go through her purse. Regular ID; nothing out of the ordinary there. He raided the minibar to make them a drink. He wasn't about to let her do it.

Water was running in the bathroom. Pai came out and sashayed up to Troy, smiling. Then she twirled around, gathering up her hair to give him access to her zipper.

Troy drew it down very slowly. Then, with the back of the dress hanging open, he started at her neck, sliding his hands down her shoulders, then her back, sweeping around the front, and down. She was making nice little pleasurable noises the whole time. Troy's next objective was the waistband of her panty hose. Which he rolled down, methodically, inch by inch, until he reached her ankles.

She was naked, and he still fully clothed—which he found the hottest thing so far.

She took his clothes off, in nearly opposite fashion. Almost without touching him at all, just light whispers of touch, randomly here and there. Troy had to close his eyes and try to hang on.

Pai took his hand and led him into the bathroom, where the tub was almost full.

And she gave him a bath. Troy had been dick checked before, but never so elegantly. Troy washed every inch of her, and she washed every part of him except what he most wanted washed. Flicking her head back and forth, she playfully lashed him with her wet hair.

They toweled each other dry, she still taking her time while Troy was now in much more of a rush.

On the way to the bed Troy was diamond hard, as if he could cut glass. More teasing, more feathery touching. Trying to move things along a little faster, Troy moved the tip of his tongue over the erect tip of one nipple. His palm was pressed against her pubic bone, his fingers clasping and relaxing.

There was no way. She was in the driver's seat, and he was the one whose head was about to blow off. Troy wondered whether there was some kind of advanced degree program they sent these girls to.

Finally Pai pushed him back on the bed with two palms against his chest. She rolled on the condom the same way he'd rolled down her hose. Rising up on her knees, she lowered herself very slowly down on top of him. Troy groaned loudly. Finally.

But she didn't move. Troy started to move his hips, but she held him down.

Then Troy felt himself gripped. And squeezed. And . . . milked was the only word to describe it. And Pai still wasn't moving. Only her stomach muscles. She was smiling down at him.

"Jesus Christ," Troy said loudly. It came out not quite like a prayer.

Up and down. Side to side. He was pulled and squeezed and twisted, in a rhythm that kept increasing. Troy's face was all clenched up; he was making a series of panting, almost squeaking sounds that would have thoroughly embarrassed him if he'd only known he was doing it. And then a loud, groaning "aaaagh," muscles locked, almost levitating off the bed.

Both of them still, she still on top of him. Troy had to blink several times to clear up the spots in his vision field. His breathing was just steadying. "Holy shit, baby."

"You want me to go?" she asked, almost unbelievably coquettish considering her position.

"Hell no," Troy replied.

It was at the end of round two. Troy was on his stomach and Pai was rubbing his neck. And he was as relaxed as possibly he'd ever been in his life. And she handed him his drink. And Lee Troy took a big gulp.

"I wake up and I'm alone," he was saying to Ed Storey. "That's when I know I fucked up. I look around and my cash is still there. I'm four thousand baht light, but the rest of the cash is still there. That's when I know I *really* fucked up. No working girl is going to slip me a mickey and leave a nickel behind. So I figure, if I haven't been clipped, then all my shit's been searched and each piece of electronic gear has at least two new chips in it. I might even have a transponder up my ass."

Storey took the news with his usual calm. "So what did you do?" Not upset, just curious.

"Well, first thing, I leave all my shit exactly where it is. Outside the hotel I'm so fucking paranoid I think I've got GPS chips in my suit buttons. I even stop off, buy new clothes, and throw my old ones, shoes included, in a trash can.

"Now I'm in and out of cabs, in and out of buildings. I've got a different change of clothes in a shopping bag. I change again, go out a restaurant back door. I'm done fucking up—I am *not* bringing a tail here."

There were in an apartment just south of the Chinatown district, on the east bank of the Chao Phraya River. A safe house maintained by the Defense Intelligence Agency.

Storey had been waiting patiently until Troy was done. "You made a mistake but you didn't fuck up. The only way you could have fucked up is if you kept all this to yourself, trying to cover your ass. *That's* how people get themselves in trouble in this business. Besides, it doesn't seem like you did the right thing, but you really did."

"Now you're shitting me. I'm lucky I didn't get my throat cut. How did I even *remotely* do the right thing?"

"What's my second rule?"

"Always live your cover."

"Correct," said Storey. "You're a twenty-seven-year-old American businessman in Thailand for the first time. Do you stay in your hotel room your first night in Bangkok, watching TV? I think not. You at least go down to the bar for a drink—your hotel bar because you're the typical timid American in the exotic east. A beautiful Thai girl wants to come to your room—do you say no? I think not, at least if your cover is you're not gay. So you lived your cover. You got rolled. And now you just keep playing the game. If we want you to be followed, you take along your phone and your PDA. Otherwise you leave them in your room. And when we leave the country you wipe your PDA drive clean and leave everything behind. We'll buy you new gear. Okay?"

"Not anywhere near okay. I walked right into a honey trap, face-first."

"More like dick-first," Storey observed.

"Thanks for trying to make me feel better."

"Hey, it's a good lesson learned. In this business more guys get killed by their dicks than anything else."

Troy looked down at his crotch. "You hear that?" He shook his head. "*I* hear you, but I don't know about Big Lee. You can't talk any sense to him."

"Yeah, well, I don't want to get in the middle of any issues you and Big Lee might be having." Storey paused. "She really muscle-fucked you, huh?"

"She sure did."

Storey was wearing a faraway expression. "I was a young trooper. First time I got muscle-fucked, I almost married the girl right then and there. Trying to figure out how to ship her home in my duffel bag." He shook his head at the memory. "She had an act. Slipped a banana right into her pussy and it came out sliced. Sliced! I can't remember how many shows a night she did."

"I can't believe you didn't marry her," said Troy.

"I remember getting this mental image of her squatting over my cereal bowl every morning. Kind of ruined it for me."

Troy was grinning at him. "Thanks for sharing that."

"You're the one who got laid last night. Don't thank me."

"I won't," said Troy. "How do you think they got on to me?"

"CIA gave you up to Thai security. That's pretty definite."

"Then why didn't they just grab me and throw me out of the country?"

"That wouldn't be good counterintelligence. Once they've made you, they follow you around to try and acquire the rest of any network we might have. The Thais can get muscular if they need to, but they're also subtle."

"If they're subtle, then why did they tip their hand by leaving my cash?"

"They had no choice. Think about it. If they took all your cash, you'd be wondering why they left your phone and PDA, the answer being so they could bug your phone and PDA. Either way they take the chance of tipping their hand. They were probably hoping you'd think you just fell asleep, and couldn't remember if you paid her or not."

"Now I get it," said Troy. Old Storey didn't miss much.

"The girl was still the best way to get to you."

"Maybe I should send them a thank-you note," said Troy. "She was the best I ever had." Then something occurred to him. "Why didn't they tumble onto you?"

Storey shrugged. "Probably because there's a lot fewer twenty-seven-year-old black American businessmen arriving in Bangkok on any given day than thirty-four-year-old white American businessmen." He cracked a little smile. "Looks like racial profiling to me."

"Yeah, wouldn't be the first time that happened. First driving while black, now it's flying while black."

"Getting back to business," said Storey, "the surveillance team from support had a chance to look around. CIA and the Thais are on our metal dealer's business and house like a blanket. Team leader told me they were worried about getting made, and they never got closer than a quarter of a mile to the target."

"So that's it. We can scrub this bullshit op and quit playing these stupid games."

"The people we work for," said Storey, "these are the games they play. And they still want us here."

"So what do we do, sit around and jerk off?"

"Not you, that's for sure. I'll give you a choice. We can hang by the pool, and you can keep getting laid, or we can do something useful."

"Do what? Just because we're in town, if anything happens—the target makes the surveillance or gets away, you know the CIA's going to blame us. That's how those fuckers operate."

"I know. But they'll blame us even if we're sitting beside the pool. Hear me out, now. Since they couldn't get close, our surveillance team got up high and broke out their four-thousand-millimeter camera lens to watch everyone coming and going—"

"You ever carry one of those fuckers, and the foot-locker they come in, up a flight of stairs?" Troy interrupted.

"Yeah, a hundred-and-fifty-pound pack is easier to hump around. But you can pick out a zit on someone's nose from a mile away. Surveillance also picked up some cell phone calls. Just hit and miss, nothing like they'd get if they were closer. And something they noticed gave me an idea. Who knows everything that goes on inside a SEAL Team?"

"Command master chief," Troy said instantly.

"Okay, you've got everything the officers do, and everything the enlisted do. Who knows both? Who knows *everything*? Someone so insignificant no one ever thinks about them."

Now Troy gave it much more thought. "I got it. The admin clerk. Fuckers see every piece of paper, suck up to the officers, gossip all day."

"You're close," said Storey. "You're very close. As a

matter of fact, you're right. But there's one other guy I'm thinking about."

Troy kept thinking. Then he broke into a smile. "The commanding officer's driver. If he's not sitting there while the officers shoot the shit, he's hanging around the office. And if he's not doing that, he's back at the barracks with the troops."

"Correct. Always look for the weak link, the vulnerability. The man in charge isn't it. He's always worried about his security, about getting arrested. About getting snatched. He's got bodyguards. The guy who drives him around—he just lives in an apartment out in town."

"You think we should pay him a visit?"

"That's my idea. I've already taken the surveillance team off the big guy and put them on the driver. They're assembling a target folder on him right now. But after what happened in Pakistan, I'm not telling you. I'm asking you."

"Hell," said Troy. "I can get laid any time."

12

People joined the FBI to arrest criminals. But at least half an agent's career was spent sitting in cars and vans and apartments, watching something—usually nothing. And another quarter was spent writing reports about it.

So it was for Beth Royale and Paul Moody in a surveillance van belonging to the Organized Crime Unit of the Detroit field office. The van was painted to resemble an oil heater repair company, something that could sit on a residential Dearborn, Michigan, street all day without attracting attention.

Beth had binoculars to her eyes, looking through the tinted window. "And the car hasn't moved for two days?" she asked.

Neither of the Detroit special agents in the car answered her.

Beth lowered the binoculars, turned so she could face them, and repeated, "The car hasn't moved for two days?"

The older of the two, a crusty white male warhorse in his early fifties, continued to ignore her. But she locked eyes with the younger of the two, this one a new guy in his late twenties, until he said, "No, it hasn't moved."

"Thanks," Beth replied. "I guess you don't have to watch too many empty houses with the Mafia."

Muhammad al-Sharif owned only one car, and there it sat in front of his house. But there had been no signs of life in the house for the last two days except lights going on at dusk and off in the morning, evidence more of a timer than human occupancy. Al-Sharif had not opened his auto repair business either.

The older agent finally spoke. "It's easy to make cases when you get first crack at the national intelligence."

"We like to make cases, then make arrests," Beth fired back instantly. "Not make arrests hoping to make a case."

A stinging shot at the Detroit office's only antiterrorism case so far. Four Middle Eastern immigrants arrested as a "sleeper operational combat cell," or so the prosecutors had called it. Arrests had been made in the so-far-vain hope someone would confess and roll over, and it was looking like a major disaster if it ever went to court.

The van was parked near a corner, a blind spot so anyone entering or leaving from one side door could not be observed from the house they were watching. Beth slid over and opened the door. "I'll be right back."

"Bring back some coffee," said the older agent. It did not come out like a request.

Beth's eyes flicked over to Moody. He imperceptibly shook his head. "I don't drink coffee," she said, slamming the door.

"Bitch," the older agent said. "We ought to drive around the block. Let her come back and find us gone."

"I wouldn't," said Moody.

"There won't be a gap in the surveillance. Or are you worried about *her*?"

"No, I'm worried about you," said Moody.

"What, she's going to be on the phone crying to the bosses? So what?"

"You do what you want," said Moody. "I'll just tell you a story I heard. Her first assignment was New York, and they really gave her the business. Froze her out, messed with her desk, new centerfold pinned up every day."

"And she filed a complaint with O.P.R.," the older agent said assuredly. The Office of Professional Responsibility was the FBI's version of an internal affairs department, in charge of disciplining agents.

Moody shook his head. "One morning everyone came to work and opened up their e-mail. And all the guys who were giving her the business had something from Beth in the in-box. No message, just a photo. A guy on all fours, naked, and a dominatrix fucking him in the ass with a dildo. She'd taken every guy's picture and Photoshopped it onto the body of the guy getting corn-holed. Really convincing, or so I was told. The guys were pissed; then they noticed that she'd copied the photo to each of their home e-mail addresses."

"Jesus," the younger agent blurted out.

Moody nodded. "I heard that eight guys cleared the office at a dead run and headed home code three, lights and sirens, trying to delete the message before their wives opened it up."

"Jesus," the younger agent repeated.

"She never said a word about it," said Moody. "And no one ever messed with her again. I got told the story, not by her, after I started working with her. I didn't believe it at first, but I do now."

"Like I said, a real bitch," the older agent replied.

Moody nodded again. "But she can take care of herself. You go ahead, though. Do what you want."

The van didn't get moved.

Beth returned, without coffee, to a very quiet van, and went back to her binoculars.

The radio began crackling with back-and-forth conversation. The supervisors were getting tired of waiting.

All the units got a fifteen-minute warning to be ready to go in.

The occupants of the van began putting on their body armor, and over that the navy blue windbreakers with gold FBI lettering.

The agents of the Detroit office SWAT team, in their black assault jumpsuits, helmets, and MP-5 submachine guns, would be making the initial entry into the house.

All the different posts checked in that they were ready. The command went out over the radio, and the SWAT team flowed into the house. Then agents came running in from everywhere. Beth shook her head at all the drawn pistols and shotguns, hoping none of the boys had an accidental discharge.

As Beth and Moody came through the door, Supervisory Special Agent Benjamin Timmins was standing in the middle of the living room, trying to get the herd of agents under control.

Beth immediately noticed a bookcase standing empty in a corner of the room. Which was both immaculate and spartan. She kept noticing what wasn't there. No magazines on the coffee table, not even a *TV Guide.* Not so much as a crumpled gum wrapper, or half-full coffee cup.

She walked past Timmins and into the kitchen, stopping only to put on a pair of latex gloves before opening the refrigerator. It was completely empty, but cold. A faint smell of ammonia cleaner. Nothing but cans in the pantry. No perishables.

Timmins was still in the living room when Beth came out. "Let me guess," she said. "Not a piece of paper in the whole house."

Timmins was frowning.

Beth caught Moody's eye, and he followed her outside. The yellow crime scene tape was already up, and a neighbor was standing there, watching the show. There were others, but he stood out. It wasn't just that he was standing there in his T-shirt and boxer shorts, but that he seemed utterly unconcerned by the fact that he was standing out in public in his T-shirt and boxer shorts. Looking like he'd just got up, though it was late morning. White, male, late thirties. Beer gut. Unshaven, of course. Smoking a cigarillo.

"That's my boy," Beth said to Moody.

"Imagine my surprise," he replied.

"I'm Special Agent Royale," said Beth, flashing her credentials according to regulation, even though the windbreaker made it somewhat redundant. "This is Special Agent Moody. Are you a neighbor, sir?"

"Next door," he said, with a toss of his head.

Beth was smiling pleasantly. "Could I ask your name?"

A complete change of posture. From professionally surly to bright as a new penny. Even standing up a little straighter. Moody knew *he* would have just gotten the surly part. He kept eyeing the sagging waistband of those boxers, hoping there wouldn't be an accident.

"Tom," the new man said.

"Tom," said Beth, as if it was the best news she'd heard all day. "Tom . . ."

"Oh, sorry," he said, apologetic. "Tom Johansen. What do you want Muhammad for? Terrorism?"

"Mr. al-Sharif seems to be missing," said Beth, not quite answering the question. "What made you say terrorism?"

"What else? All his Arab friends in and out all the time. Arabs everywhere. I remember when it wasn't like that," he confided. "I guess they won't blow up their own neighborhoods."

Beth offered no comment on that. "Did you know him well?"

"Not really. He wasn't real friendly, but he wasn't unfriendly, if you get me. Hello; how are you; have a nice day; good-bye. That kind of thing. I'm not complaining, though. Compared to some of the people on this street."

Moody couldn't stand it. He'd be getting attitude and one-word answers, and here the guy was rambling on, trying to please her. He was a little curious about what old Tom thought was a bad neighbor, though. The stink of that cigarillo was making him nauseated.

"When did you see him last?" Beth asked.

"Must've been four days ago."

"That's really good," said Beth, giving up some approval to keep him sweet. "Most people couldn't pin down a date like that. How do you do it?"

"Oh, it was trash day," said Tom.

Moody hadn't thought it was his extraordinary mental powers.

"Trash day?" Beth said politely.

"Yeah, I was a little late getting the trash out, and the wife was giving me hell. I hate that goddamned recycling, pardon my French."

Beth only responded with a sunny smile to spur him on.

"Anyway, I'm dragging the can out from the garage, and there's Muhammad on the curb. With his bin, about three lawn bags, full, and two cardboard boxes. I want to know how he's going to pull this off, so I hang around. He doesn't seem too pleased about me hanging around, but I do it anyway. The truck pulls up, and the guys are giving him that look, like there's no way we're taking all that. But Muhammad slips each of them a few bucks, and helps them throw the stuff in the truck. About an hour later he leaves." Then he added, "I just happened to be going past the window then."

"Did you happen to see what was in his trash?" said Beth.

"All wrapped up."

"How did he leave? His car's still there."

"Couple guys picked him up. If he got kidnapped it wasn't them."

"Friends?" said Beth.

"They stayed in the car. Beeped the horn. That's how I came to the window."

"Did Muhammad bring anything to the car?" Beth asked.

Tom just looked puzzled.

"Boxes?" said Beth. "Bags . . . suitcase?"

"Oh, couple of duffel bags. Green, like army ones."

"Anything else?"

Tom shook his head.

"What kind of car?"

"What do you mean?"

"Sedan, pickup, SUV, minivan?"

"Compact, I guess. Toyota, Honda, something like that. It was red," he added helpfully.

"Did you happen to catch the license plate?" Beth asked.

"No way."

"A Michigan plate? Out of state?"

"Sorry."

"Is there anything else you can tell me about Mr. al-Sharif?"

Tom shook his head again.

"Well, thank you, Mr. Johansen. I really appreciate your help." Beth passed him her card. "If you think of anything else, please give me a call."

A wide smile at that. "I just might. I just might." He went to shake hands with her, then realized the card was still in his right hand. He went to put it in his hip pocket, then realized he didn't have any. And instead of switching hands, he jammed the card into the waist-band of his underwear.

Moody rolled his eyes. As they walked back into the house, he said, "He was your boy all right. You can sure pick 'em."

"It's a gift," said Beth. "Careful you don't look like that in ten years."

"Don't even joke."

Timmins was still in the living room. Still frowning.

"All the stuff that's gone," said Beth, "Al-Sharif

dumped it. Three lawn bags, two boxes in addition to his trash receptacle. Waited for the sanitation truck, paid the crew to take it. And no, Ben, I'm not going to the landfill."

Timmins smiled faintly, as if the idea intrigued him.

"He left half an hour later," said Beth. "Red compact, no make, no model, no plate. Two males in the car, no description. He was carrying at least two army duffel bags."

"That's just great news," Timmins said sarcastically. "The whole place has been Windexed. Good thing we've got his prints on file. I doubt we'll be getting anyone else's."

"He's off to do something," said Beth.

"I know," said Timmins.

13

While it was possible to walk down a Bangkok street, catch a faint smell of incense, and turn a corner to encounter a breathtaking gilded palace or *wat* in the classic architectural styles of every century from the ninth to the nineteenth, there were only so many palaces and temples. The other Bangkok was rows of drab shophouses, apartment buildings, high-rise office canyons, and dirty concrete towers. Seven million people jam-packed into an object lesson on the dangers of uncontrolled urban expansion, but also one of the world's most exiting cities—mainly due to the Thai love of a good time.

The outskirts were more spread out, though. On the far eastern edge of the city, Sukhumvit Road began in Bangkok and continued all the way to the Cambodian border. Few tourists made it out to Sukhumvit Road because it was far from all the attractions. But the road fed a growing business district that thrived on proximity to the airport. Popular with foreigners; good cover for Storey and Troy; good cover for their quarry—who lived in a ten-story apartment building that was home to a mix of nationalities.

"He's smart," said Troy. They were sitting in a car, watching the building after a thorough reconnaissance of the area. "If he lived in a Thai neighborhood he'd stick out like a sore thumb. He blends in here."

"Good choice for security, too," said Storey. "He's in the middle of the building, so he's hard to reach from the ground. He can look out, but not many can look in. And he stayed away from the top of the building—too expensive, attracts too much attention. What do you think?"

Troy consulted his notes. "He walks around the neighborhood, but not on any kind of routine or regular schedule. Which means we can't take him on foot outside, and that was my first choice. He parks his car in the underground garage—drives in, drives out. Security and cameras in the garage, so forget about that. The way I see it, we either take him in his car or in his apartment. Doing a vehicle snatch in Bangkok traffic? Yeah, makes the takedown easy, but the getting away is a bitch."

"I agree," said Storey. "We've got to search the apartment anyway, we might as well take him there."

This was for their own peace of mind, since the surveillance team had already done the full-court press on the target. Full-time photo and video observation. Tapped his phone and followed him around to intercept his cellular calls. Bounced a laser off his apartment windows to listen in on what was happening inside. The only thing they didn't do, for fear of compromise without enough payoff in return, was physically bug his apartment and car.

Storey and Troy already knew about the building security, through the simple means of sending in one of the surveillance team to ask about renting an apartment. Foreigners were concerned about security, and the management obliged. The previously mentioned cameras and attendants in the garage. Security cameras covering the outside of the building. A manned desk in the lobby. An alarm system in each apartment, with motion sensors and wired windows and doors. A private security company took care of the response. Actually, a lot better than most buildings in Washington.

Nothing they considered insurmountable. Hollywood loved the spectacle of rewiring security cameras and cracking alarm system PINs with portable computers as the seconds agonizingly clicked down. But reality was much more straightforward.

The most valuable information they'd received from the surveillance team member/apartment hunter was a list of the numbers and locations of the empty units, all of which he'd insisted on seeing.

Storey made the decision to go based on the information that came in every day from Washington. The CIA had intercepted the missile shipment before it cleared customs, inserting GPS transponders into the missile canisters so they could track them anywhere in the world. The missiles had been shipped out to the Philippines, and the CIA was preparing to move against Majed Ismail and his Thai network. With all that going on, the disappearance of Ismail's driver wouldn't get either side very worked up.

Storey and Troy were both in street clothes, but were also wearing wigs, moustaches, and eyeglasses. Both Delta and the SEAL DevGroup were trained in covert operations by the CIA, and the CIA loved disguises. A person's appearance could be changed very quickly with easily obtainable ingredients. Though there were also very expensive, custom-made full head and hand prosthetics would allow, say, a Caucasian to drive unnoticed in an African city. In fact, part of Troy's personal reputation stemmed from his demand, during his introductory Green Team training, for what he called a "white boy mask."

They waited until night, always the best time to make an approach. The apartment hunter had been very intrigued by the security camera monitors at the front desk, and picked out some dead space they didn't cover. Part of the wall at the rear of the apartment grounds was masked by the landscaping, and that's where they went over, accompanied by one of the surveillance team. They were still masked from the well-lighted part of the grounds, and the pair of security cameras on each corner of the building.

Their weapon against these would be a simple pen-sized laser pointer. Obligatory for any modern business presentation, obtainable in any office supply store. Attached to a miniature camera tripod, the kind that can be clamped to anything, like the branch of a tree. Which is what they did, aiming the red laser dots at the lenses of the two cameras. Anyone watching the scene from an inside monitor would see the screen brighten and bloom, and nothing else. Storey and Troy simply walked up to the building.

The first-floor apartment terraces were up high enough that no burglar could jump and climb into them. Except, that is, if you had a few feet of climbing rope with a titanium hook on the end to grab the steel railings. Once they were on the first floor, all Storey and Troy had to do was stand on the top of the railing, grab the bottom of the railing of the upstairs apartment, and climb on up.

As soon as they were up, the surveillance team member clicked off the laser pointers, stuck them in his pocket, and retreated back over the wall. If a guard had even noticed the problem, by the time he played with the brightness and sharpness controls, pounded on the unit a couple of times, and thought about calling someone, everything was back to normal.

The second-story apartment was one of the empty ones. The prospective tenant had also noticed that the alarm systems in the empty apartments were not turned on. And why should they be? There was nothing in them, and no one wanted a leasing agent to set it off during a showing.

As Storey came over the railing, Troy was picking the lock on the sliding glass door. Everything was going smoothly. Until a small dog began barking wildly in the apartment next door.

Storey kept one eye on the next-door terrace and one on Troy. Dogs were always the biggest problem. People were lazy and stupid, but dogs noticed everything. After a couple of minutes of steady barking, a light popped on in the apartment. And Troy didn't have the lock picked yet. Storey felt around in his back pocket and dug out a dog treat. He lobbed it onto the other terrace, then grabbed Troy and pulled him into the corner of their terrace, out of sight.

They sat wedged in tight together, listening. The dog still yapping, a glass door sliding open. A man's voice in Spanish saying to the dog, "*Qué es?*" As soon as the door opened the dog charged out to the edge of the terrace railing, still barking. Then it stopped abruptly, amid faint crunching sounds. Across the gap between the two terraces, a tired human sigh. The same voice to the dog, "*Vamos.*"

The door slid shut. Storey waited, listened. The surveillance team member watching that side of the building through a high-powered spotting scope came through his radio earpiece. "Light's off. No movement." Storey pressed his radio Send button twice to break squelch, indicating he'd received the message. A peek around the corner confirmed it. He pointed Troy in the direction of the door again.

Troy didn't like electric lock picks, didn't like the noise they made. So he had to get all the pins in the lock tumbler depressed manually. In the dark. By feel.

Storey heard a faint click as the tension wrench turned. Sliding doors were noisy; Troy was moving it an inch at a time. No bar in the door; agents didn't like to bend over and fool with it while doing a showing.

Inside the apartment they paused only long enough to ease the door back and lock it again.

Listening at the interior door for footsteps in the hall. Opening the door, one eye peeking out into the hall. No cameras in the halls. People didn't like that. There *were* cameras in the stairways and elevators. They took the stairway, leading with the laser pointer before turning a corner.

One might assume that the guard watching the monitors, if there was a guard watching the monitors instead of reading a magazine, eating a little snack, or catching a bit of night shift shut-eye, would notice the succession of camera flashes proceeding through the building and think something was amiss. But security guards didn't think that way. They thought they were dealing with a succession of equipment gremlins.

There was another empty apartment on the sixth floor, one floor up and two over from the target's apartment. Storey stood guard while Troy picked the lock. Ironically, the dead bolt opened easier than the terrace's sliding door.

Inside another empty apartment, Storey paused to check out the alarm controller box. An alarm system with room motion sensors meant the system had to be turned off while the occupant was at home. But higher-end systems had settings to deactivate the motion sensors and leave the doors and windows armed against intruders. This wasn't one of them—all the better.

Bangkok nights were not quiet, and they were not cool. Most people, and all foreigners, kept their windows and doors shut and the air-conditioning on. Storey and Troy were both sweating heavily and paused to slurp some water directly from the kitchen tap. They also put on spandoflage head nets. Spandoflage was stretchable camouflaged elastic mesh, much faster to get on and off than camouflage face paint, and much cooler than a balaclava hood. If anything went wrong now they'd have to leave the building at a dead run, with no time to dazzle the cameras.

This time, when out on the terrace, they climbed down. The tough part was next. Because the terraces on the same floor were separated by about fifteen feet of open space. Just a bit too far for a standing long jump, especially from five floors up.

Storey unzipped the small student's backpack Troy was wearing on his back. Fitting together the center sections of three identical four-piece travel fishing rods made one very long twenty-foot-long graphite fishing rod. Looped around the end of the rod was the titanium hook tied to forty feet of mountaineering rope. Holding the rod vertically, Storey let it down gently as if making a cast, until it rested atop the adjoining terrace railing. Pulling the rod back left the hook and rope attached to the railing. Troy pulled the rope taut and tied it to their railing with a figure-eight slipknot.

The shorter six-foot lengths of rope they'd used to climb before were tied around their waists and legs to form a climbing harness, what mountaineers called a "Swiss seat." Clipped onto the front of the seat was a carabiner, a very strong D-shaped aluminum ring with a spring-loaded locking gate.

This was a crucial moment. Any screwup would create a whole series of problems. While Troy broke down the fishing rod, Storey reached into his shirt and pulled out the tiny Glock pistol with the equally tiny sound suppressor attached. He waited, watching and listening for any signs of life from the apartment they were about to visit.

They hadn't brought the weapons into the country. All of the safe houses had a full weapons package cached away in the walls or under the floor. Even a bullet trap target box for test firing. The silenced weapons only, of course.

Only after an incredibly long two minutes of waiting did Storey give Troy the signal to go. The only question was whether the railings would support their weight. Troy hopped over, holding on with one hand while he snapped the carabiner onto the rope. Then he stepped off, dangling upside down, the oval aluminum carabiner the only thing connecting his seat harness to the rope.

Troy pulled himself hand over hand, the carabiner sliding along the rope like a pulley. The short trip only took four pulls. He grabbed the opposite railing and stepped over.

Now he pulled out his Glock. Covering the sliding glass door, he waved to Storey. Storey pulled himself over. He'd brought the free end of the rope over with him, tied to his belt. He gave that a hard tug; the knot fell apart and he pulled the whole rope over, leaving nothing behind. As he was stuffing the rope back into Troy's pack, Troy pointed to the railing, which had noticeably bowed outward under their weight. Storey shrugged; they'd made it across.

With all the climbing equipment stowed away, Storey attached two more pieces of gear to his belt. A Taser stun gun and an ASP baton. The Taser fired a pair of barbed dart electrodes that were connected to the gun by fifteen-foot wires. Pressing the trigger again sent fifty thousand volts through the wires and into whomever the darts were stuck into. That much voltage discouraged any further resistance.

The ASP was a blunter instrument, in case technology failed. A telescoping billy club that expanded from a concealable eight to a full twenty-four inches with a snap of the wrist.

With everything ready, Troy picked yet another door lock. All the practice he'd been getting made him much faster this time. While Storey covered him, he slid the door open a crack, feeling for any kind of homemade early warning like a bell. He kept moving the door a quarter inch at a time, until it was open just enough for them to slip through sideways.

Once in they spread out and followed opposite walls.

No one asleep on the couch—Storey had found them there before.

The sight of an insulated wire snaking across the carpet made Storey freeze. He held up a fist to signal Troy to do the same. The wire looked rust brown against the light-colored carpet. Storey followed it. The wire ended up at the front door, more specifically into a thick plastic rectangle sitting atop a pair of metal scissor legs that had been placed right in front of the door.

Storey unfolded his little multitool one-handed and quietly clipped the wire. A claymore antipersonnel mine: a sheet of ball bearings backed up by more than a pound of plastic explosive. Electrically fired, and the clacker was probably under their target's pillow. A stick with a drinking glass balanced atop it was propped up against the door to fall over if it was opened. Simple and effective. Coming in the back door was looking very much like the right move.

Storey very carefully and quietly moved everything out of the way in case they needed to leave quickly.

Troy was still frozen in place in the living room. Storey pointed toward the bedroom. Standing in the little hallway, he signaled another halt so he could think things over. Specifically, whether to enter the bedroom slow and quiet or fast and hard. Normally he'd lean toward slow and quiet, but that would be a mistake if there was another claymore and glass behind the door. He decided on hard and fast. Screw the noise and zap him with the Taser before he had a chance to do anything. He made his intentions clear to Troy with hand signals.

Storey holstered his pistol and readied the Taser. The unit had regular pistol sights, but also a visible red laser. Helpful for aiming in the dark.

Troy had his left hand on the bedroom doorknob, the pistol ready in his right. Storey had his left hand on Troy's shoulder. He squeezed.

Troy pushed the door forward and sprang into the bedroom, going left across the doorway. Storey went right. A pause to see where the bed was—against the far wall. A figure was already thrashing in the sheets and rooting under his pillow. Storey settled the laser dot and fired the Taser. A loud pop as the two nitrogen cartridges went off, propelling the darts. Storey pressed the trigger again to fire the electricity, but the target didn't fall back and start twitching from the current. Instead the hand under the pillow came up with a pistol.

Storey dropped the Taser and snapped out the baton, but he knew he'd never get across the room in time. Two hisses superimposed on the metallic snaps of a pistol slide cycling. Now the target fell back on the bed spasming, but from two 9mm slugs to the head.

Storey flicked on the light and went over to see what had happened. A young Arab staring up at the ceiling, two holes a thumb width apart in his forehead. Great shooting, especially in the dark. And two Taser electrodes stuck in his chest, right where they were supposed to be. Except that everything had turned out wrong.

Troy returned from checking the rest of the apartment, just to be sure. They were silent for a while, two perfectionists infuriated at having failed. Then Troy said, "What happened with the Taser?"

Storey was checking the unit. "I dunno. Who knows how long it sat in that cache? Maybe the battery connections corroded in this humidity?"

"You pissed at me?" Troy asked.

"For saving my life again? What else could you do, try and shoot the gun out of his hand?"

Not much in the mood for laughing, each of them gave only a couple of grim grunts. A fixture of the old westerns, and a physical impossibility in real life. Though Storey had heard of a SWAT sniper doing it to a guy who was sitting down and dangling his pistol between his legs.

"Motherfucker was quick," said Troy. "I hate prisoner

snatches. When they go bust it's like a ton of hard work for nothing."

"Maybe we'll turn up something here," said Storey. He hated failure—he felt it in the pit of his stomach.

"Hey, what could we do? Other than test-fire the Taser at one of the surveillance team to see if it worked."

"They'd probably balk at that," said Storey.

They spent all day on the search, and it was a small apartment. Sliced open all the furniture, pulled up the carpet. A closet held a folding-stock AK-47, loaded magazines, and a shoe box filled with an assortment of hand grenades. Nothing unexpected.

"Claymore in front of the door was a nice touch," said Troy, as they examined the ordnance.

"I knew an operator who spent a lot of time in Lebanon, used to do that all the time. Someone John Wayne's your door, you pop the claymore and go out the window." Storey had removed the blasting cap and was turning the mine over in his hands. "I thought it was one of ours but it's the Chinese copy, Type 66. You can probably pick one up in Cambodia for twenty bucks."

Storey expected the phone to ring some time during the day. It never did.

The only items of interest were found in a small desk in the bedroom. Road maps. Of eastern Thailand from Bangkok to Cambodia. And southern Thailand and northern Malaysia. Storey handled the maps very carefully. You could tell a lot about where someone had been by the way a map was marked and folded. In the same drawer as the maps was a manila envelope filled with what looked like gas station receipts. Storey and Troy both read Arabic, but the receipts were in Thai script and would have to be translated. They were in neat stacks held together with rubber bands.

Without removing the band, Troy flipped through one stack with a gloved finger. "Each stack a different trip?"

"Maybe he kept these to claim his expenses," said Storey. "Be nice to know where he was driving."

"Too bad these guys don't keep diaries," said Troy.

"The Marxist revolutionaries liked to keep one for when they wrote their memoirs after the final victory over imperialism. Too bad it's not Al Qaeda policy."

They bagged up the maps and receipts. The dead man had four different passports in four different names. Pakistan, South Africa, Yemen, and Belgium. All current, and at first glance genuine. And all with customs stamps the intelligence analysts would find interesting.

They took the dead man's photo and fingerprints, and a swab from the inside of his cheek for DNA comparison.

Working steadily into the night, they subsisted on tap water and Powerbars. They found nothing else. They took the papers and left the weapons, after recording the serial numbers. The Thai police could draw their own conclusions from them, and the shredded apartment, when the body was discovered.

After midnight they left through the front door, dazzling the stairway cameras on the way down. Then out a back service door, unobserved because the surveillance team had their lasers aimed at the cameras on that side of the building.

Back at the safe house the famished pair plowed through a pile of takeout while two of the surveillance team, fluent Thai speakers, looked over the papers. Happy they were near Chinatown, Troy stuck with *khao mu daeng*, Chinese-style red pork on fragrant rice. He watched Storey shovel down a bowl of *kaeng khiaw wan*, green curry and shook his head. "Figured you were one of those hot food freaks."

"It's good," Storey said with his mouth full, the sweat pouring down his face. "Try some."

"No way, man. I'm a Maine Yankee, remember? For me spicy food is brown mustard instead of yellow on my ham and cheese sandwich."

"On white bread," Storey said, grinning. "Before I joined the army, I never knew there was anything else. First time I ever saw wheat I thought it was burnt. Told everyone the bread had gone bad and they laughed their asses off." He said it jokingly, but couldn't keep out the hard edge that recalled the humiliation.

"Which trip do you want first?" the Thai-speaking army staff sergeant asked them. He'd originally been an electronic intelligence intercept operator, and also spoke Mandarin Chinese.

"Most recent," said Storey, still eating.

"Okay," said the staff sergeant. "This was only two weeks ago. He starts at Bangkok, heading west. Then down the peninsula. Overnight at a hotel in Surat Thani. Phatthalung; Pattani. The South African passport crossed into Malaysia, gasses up right at the border. Then nothing. Trip back, he crosses back into Thailand, gasses up at the same place. Almost a full tank. Now, I'm looking at meal receipts, and I'm thinking two people on the way down, but only one back."

"Drove someone to Malaysia, dropped him off, and came back," said Storey. "Interesting. When was the next to last trip?"

The staff sergeant picked up another stack. "Almost three months ago. To Cambodia."

"Too long," said Troy, going over the time line in his head. "We need to be looking at that Malaysia trip."

"What was he driving?" Storey asked the staff sergeant.

"Same Toyota Land Cruiser he dri . . . or should I say drove around Bangkok? Registered to the scrap metal business. Registration is on the customs declaration when he crosses into Malaysia."

"Northern Malaysia's jungle, villages, and a few small towns," said Storey. "If we know the mileage a Land Cruiser gets . . . and the size of the gas tank . . . and where he gassed up crossing the border . . . and how much he put in the tank . . . and where he filled up and with how much when he crossed back—"

"*And* we get ourselves some good topographic maps and a protractor," Troy broke in, "we should be able to figure out pretty near where he dropped his passenger off."

"You might be right," said Storey, putting down some more green curry. He loved the combination of the coconut milk and the green chilies. "If he didn't carry an extra can of gas to screw up our math."

"Good thing there aren't any officers here," said Troy. "Would have taken five times as long for someone to make up their mind."

Everyone laughed.

Storey was still eating and thinking. "We may just be able to pick up a trail."

14

Beth knew that when an investigation hit a dead end, only methodical, grinding police work could set it moving again. She also knew that she didn't know her way around Detroit, and that was just fine with the agents of the local field office. They wanted the counterterrorism superstars from Washington sitting in the backseat while *they* drove the investigation. As far as Beth was concerned, that kind of pissing contest was the bosses' business.

Looking for an end-around, she sought out the Detroit office's primary liaison to the Muslim community. She'd been really impressed by a brief he'd given them, though based on recent events she didn't expect much cooperation.

Beth couldn't have been more wrong. Special Agent Theodore Weaver was the kind of FBI agent whose credentials civilians always asked to look at twice because he just didn't look like the public image of an FBI agent. He looked like someone's favorite uncle, prematurely gray, a little fleshy, rumpled, and supremely laid-back. The absolute opposite of the typical territorial Doberman type.

Which he proved by cordially inviting Beth into his

cubicle and putting his feet up on the desk. Exposing, she noticed, a hole in one sock.

"I only met Muhammad a couple of times," he said. "I'd drop by his garage, and it was either charge me, show me a warrant, or get the hell out. A real hard-nose, with quite a reputation. If you were talking to someone on the street and he came walking by, one stare from him shut them up. Have you read his jacket?"

Beth nodded.

"Of course you have," he said, smiling.

This was the kind of agent she loved. Knew everyone on his beat, had three Rolodexes full of contacts. People liked him so much they just wouldn't stop talking.

"He grew up stealing cars," Weaver said. "Celebrated his eighteenth birthday with a tire iron assault with a deadly weapon on a guy who didn't want his car stolen. That ADW put him inside as an adult in ninety-one. Which was around the time the Nation of Islam really lost its monopoly among the prison population. The Saudis came in with their money. Pretty soon the only Islamic literature in prison was their hard-line Wahhabi brand. Hate the infidel—love holy war. The only chaplains who could afford to preach full-time were the ones the Saudis subsidized. It wasn't something prison staff had any interest in."

"And Muhammad converted," Beth said.

"He was eighteen, and he didn't want to end up as someone's punk. But he really took to it. Understand that the Muslims in prison have real stature. It seems more real than one of the gangs to a lot of kids. They look up to the older guys; they belong; they have something to believe in for the first time. You ever hear of the Lucasville riot?"

"No," said Beth.

"Southern Ohio Correctional. They were vaccinating against tuberculosis. Tuberculosis vaccine has an alcohol base, and alcohol is *haram*, forbidden to Muslims.

The authorities didn't pay much attention to that, so the brothers had themselves a real nice riot in 1992. Muhammad was right in the middle of that as one of the foot soldiers. Spent his time in solitary, which only boosted his credentials. Got out in 1994. Followed one of the prison chaplains up to Dearborn. Applied for a passport in ninety-five. No, we don't know where he went, but I wouldn't have any problem betting on it."

"Afghanistan," said Beth.

"Wherever he went, when he came back he opened up his garage. The prison chaplain, name of Najm, guaranteed the loan. Saudi diplomatic passport, but don't read too much, or too little, into that. Saudis handed them out like candy to their missionaries, or anyone who knew a sheik. Najm tried to take over a mosque in Dearborn. Usual Wahhabi model. Big donations, preach purity, get the young men all fired up. Then accuse the elders of not being Islamic enough, not enough segregation of women, cut off the money until changes are made. They tried to occupy the building, but in this case the congregation showed up with baseball bats and threw them out. Muhammad was one of the foot soldiers again, preaching jihad to the young men."

"I'd really like to talk to that preacher," said Beth.

"So would we all. As soon as planes started flying again after nine-eleven, he was on the first one back to Saudi Arabia."

"Anything else on Muhammad?"

"He was pretty quiet after that. Auto theft was looking at his garage as a chop shop, but they were a long way from making a case."

"This fills in a lot for me," said Beth. "I really appreciate it."

"That was a nice interrogation you did the other day."

"I took a gamble and got lucky," said Beth. So that's what got her invited to sit down.

"I understand you know Harry Lime," Weaver said out of the blue.

"At the academy," Beth said, surprised.

"What did you think of him?"

"Harry's my mentor," Beth said simply. "Taught me everything I know."

"We worked together in Miami. I was just talking to him the other day."

"Oh?" said Beth.

"Yeah. He was telling me you decided right from your first day not to take any crap off anyone. And that was why he liked you. I told him the word around the office was you still had that philosophy."

Beth didn't reply to that, hoping to start a rumor that she could actually keep her mouth shut.

"Harry and I don't look like your basic FBI poster boys," Weaver said, smiling at his own wit. "But we've done all right for ourselves. We never wanted to be one of the drivers back at headquarters anyway."

Beth decided to continue her policy of keeping her mouth shut.

"Don't worry about it," said Weaver. "There's a difference between not taking any crap and running around looking to give it out. I'm going to meet one of my C.I.'s this afternoon. Want to come along?"

"I'd love to," said Beth, a little stunned at having the old boy network work in her favor for once.

Weaver picked the location for the meeting in Rochester Hills, north of Detroit. At 1:00, while they were driving there, he said to Beth, "This guy is very devout. You know the deal, I'm sure. Don't try to shake his hand."

Without a word, Beth opened her purse, took out a silk scarf, and tied it over her head, covering her hair.

"Didn't know if you'd balk at that," Weaver said approvingly.

"To make a case, I'd wear a burka," said Beth. "I just wouldn't wear it to the office."

"My kind of attitude," said Weaver.

Beth quickly appreciated Weaver's deceptive attention to detail. He wasn't laid-back about meeting his informant. His choice of location left less chance of accidentally bumping into someone who might recognize either party. A diner was a nice mix between public and private, a place where no one noticed unfamiliar faces.

They arrived early, circling the area, looking for anything out of the ordinary. Weaver even sent Beth inside the diner to check it out. But he made sure she came back to the car. You never wanted to be sitting at an agreed-upon meeting place for an informant to show up.

"Agents get comfortable around their C.I.'s after a while," said Weaver, like the best ones, always teaching. "Too comfortable. A C.I.'s not your buddy; a C.I.'s at least half a crook, or he wouldn't be a C.I. in the first place. Maybe he woke up this morning feeling bad about himself and not wanting to be a snitch anymore. And because he's a stupid mutt the only way he can think of how to do that is to shoot you. Maybe he was running his mouth, and instead of him a few people show up who want to kill themselves some FBI agents. Doesn't pay to be careless. We'll wait for him to sit down, make sure he's alone; *then* we'll go in."

From a parking lot farther down the street, they watched a young Arab man in his mid-twenties enter the diner.

"Bassam's from Yemen," Weaver said, seemingly in no hurry to go in. "Illegal, of course. Cabdriver—the usual entry-level immigrant jobs. Fell in with the group who tried to take over the mosque, but those baseball bats scared the hell out of him. After that he kept his distance from that group, but he didn't lose touch with them. Got picked up for credit card fraud. Wife and baby, so he rolled over. Okay, I'll go in first. Give me five minutes, then come in. I'll do the talking, right?"

"He's your guy," said Beth.

After five minutes by her watch, Beth took the walk. The lunch rush was over, and Weaver and Bassam were sitting in a booth off by themselves. Beth sat down next to Weaver.

"This is my colleague," Weaver said.

Bassam had a scraggly beard that was as thin and wiry as he was. He snuck a quick look at Beth, then, being in close quarters with an unmarried woman, kept his eyes down on the table. "I want to see her identification."

Beth was just about to reach for it when Weaver went from fatherly warm to fatherly cross. "If I tell you she's all right, she's all right."

Establishing control, Beth thought. And doing it well.

Now Bassam really kept his eyes down on the table.

The waitress came over, shutting everything off. "What can I get you, hon?" she asked Beth.

"Just coffee please," said Beth. "Black."

They all waited until she came back with it. Then Weaver was much softer, following the formula of bringing the carrot back after the stick. "You know why we're here."

"Muhammad al-Sharif," Bassam said.

"That's right," said Weaver.

"He told the men at his garage he was closing," said Bassam. "They were shocked. They questioned him, he said business was bad even though they knew it was not. He gave them their pay and sent them away, letting them take whatever tools they wished. They talked much of this. Two went to his home, to ask him to reconsider. And if not, to let them take over the lease. He was gone. No one knows where he is."

"Then why are we here?" Weaver demanded.

Bassam took another quick look up, and decided that

he was losing his audience. "Two others have disappeared with him."

Weaver was skeptical. "Two others are gone some-where, or two others are gone with *him*?"

"These two, they would be with him."

"Who?" said Weaver.

"Omar and Dawood."

Now Weaver was interested. "Both of them?"

"Both of them. If one is gone, they are together."

Okay, keep the poker face, Beth ordered herself in the face of rising excitement. The more coconspirators, the more chance that careful interviews of their family and friends might bear some fruit.

But if Weaver was showing Bassam some love, it was tough love. "We know they hang together. Tell us some-thing we don't know."

"Dawood borrowed his brother-in-law's boat," said Bassam. "He said he wanted to go fishing."

"What kind of boat?" Weaver asked, keeping his cool.

Bassam shrugged. "A fishing boat."

Beth knew she would have raised her voice, but Weaver still asked the questions as if he were barely in-terested. "A canoe? A rowboat? A sailboat?"

Because informers were informers, it was very im-portant that this be a one-way transaction, that they not give Bassam any information that he could sell to anyone else.

"With a motor on the back," said Bassam. "Maybe four, five meters. I do not know boats," he said apologetically. Then, trying to be helpful, "They drive it on a trailer, towed behind a car."

"Did Dawood say where he was going fishing?" Weaver asked.

"He said the Upper Peninsula. Something white."

"Whitefish Bay?" said Weaver. "Whitefish Point? White Pine?"

"This is all I heard," said Bassam. "In this situation I

must be silent. If I ask more questions everyone wishes to know why I am asking more questions."

"Did Dawood say how long he was going to be gone?" said Weaver.

"A week perhaps. His brother-in-law did not want to give him the boat, but he did."

"Omar and Dawood," said Weaver, "did they make the same kind of exit Muhammad did—just up and leave everything?"

"Yes," said Bassam. "Except Dawood. But he lived with his sister and brother-in-law."

"Did you hear anything else?" Weaver asked. "Anything small, anything you didn't think was important at the time."

"Nothing more," said Bassam.

"It's not much," Weaver said grudgingly. "If you hear anything else, if anyone gets a call from one of them, you give me a call right away." He passed an envelope under the table.

Bassam turned toward the window and stuffed it into his belt. "I will," he said. Then he looked up at Weaver— a different look, full of knowledge. "Muhammad has said that he will never go back to prison, Mr. Ted. Please be careful." As he got up he nodded his head at Beth, almost a little bow.

"Are two Arabs and an African-American going to stick out up North?" Beth asked after Bassam had left the diner.

"They are if they're traveling together. And if they really are traveling up North. I don't see why Dawood would tell his brother-in-law the truth." A pause. "You can do a lot of things with a boat. Lot of big ships travel Superior and Huron."

"You mean like the *Cole* bombing?" Beth asked.

"Or using a little boat to hijack a big ship. Or anything."

"At least now we've got relatives to talk to."

"My guys better go out and do that, though," said

Weaver. "It's not a turf thing. We go out and do interviews in the community all the time, keeping tabs on people. If different agents start doing it, agents no one's ever seen before, there'll be talk."

Beth saw the wisdom in that.

"The only link they left to anyone they knew was the boat," said Weaver. "And that was because they obviously had to have it."

"Do you have to register a recreational boat in the state of Michigan?" Beth asked.

"Yes, you do. A physical description and registration hull number will help, even though there's thousands of boats in this state. But that's not what I meant."

"What did you mean?"

"I meant that all three of them left their lives behind. They aren't planning on coming back. Just like the nine-eleven hijackers."

"I know," said Beth.

15

"We could have rented a plane, and jumped, and been there by now," Lee Troy complained, the bouncing of the SUV making the words rattle on their way out of his voice box. "You can find a clearing in any jungle."

"It hasn't come up until now because it's way down on my list of rules," said Storey, behind the wheel. "It's a two-parter. Don't parachute unless you have to. And even if you have to, figure out something else. Too many things can go wrong."

"Yeah, I'd much rather drive until I need a kidney transplant," said Troy, sitting back in his seat, arms folded across his chest, the classic body language of pouting. "If we're going to drive, why not drive straight through?"

Storey glanced over at him and smiled. "If I'm a Malaysian border guard, and I'm looking at two guys pretending to be tourists who just drove twenty hours straight from Bangkok and didn't stop off anywhere, I'm going to take their car apart down to the last bolt and strip search 'em, because they sure as shit ain't tourists. We'll take at least a couple of days and build ourselves some cover."

Storey actually would have preferred to save time by

flying to the resort town of Phuket and renting a car there. But they were transporting a few items it wasn't advisable to try and carry onto a plane.

They'd rented a Honda CRV out of Bangkok, using one of their alternate identities. And gone to four different agencies, Storey passing up various four-wheel-drive vehicles because they were all in light or bright colors, until he found the black pearl CRV.

They left Bangkok heading west and then down the southern peninsula, skirting the border with Burma. The road shifted between single and double lanes, with the second lane under varying degrees of construction in most places.

There were police roadblocks on the highway at regular intervals. Some manned, some not. Some manned by alert cops who flagged them down, and some who just wanted to stay in the shade. The roadblocks were there to check for illegal immigrants, so after a quick check of their passports they were always waved right along. None of the police spoke any English.

Outside Bangkok the Thais weren't crazy drivers. Most of the traffic in the country was pickup trucks, cargo trucks, and motorcycles. The bikes were everything from little 100cc Hondas to big road cruisers, and they took a little getting used to since their drivers were in the habit of motoring along the shoulders of both sides of the road, and in the wrong direction. The rest of Thailand drove on the left. The truck drivers were cool, though. If you were stuck behind them they'd flash their turn signals when it was safe to pass.

The terrain varied from jungle to cultivation. Rice paddies, of course. But also plantations of coffee, pineapples, and oil palms. And slender rubber trees with pale, almost white trunks that from a distance reminded Troy of New England birches.

The humidity was as high as the heat, and the air-conditioned vehicle was a sanctuary. Every stop meant leaving its cocoon, and they always returned dripping sweat.

The highways went right through most villages, and Troy and Storey often had to slow down. It was the Third World quandary. You could build a modern highway, but you couldn't keep the barefoot kids and chickens off it.

There were other hazards. Troy was driving and Storey sleeping, and a road empty of traffic practically demanded more speed. Coming around a curve at a good clip, Troy found himself zooming up on a large black object. He cut the wheel and stomped on the brake.

Storey awoke to the sound of screaming tires. He found himself in midair, restrained by his seat belt, then slammed back against the seat. The CRV was skidding across the highway. Even though he didn't have one, Storey automatically put his foot down on the brake.

Troy was still fighting with the wheel. To keep from going into the trees on the other side of the highway he finally used the emergency brake. They halted in a cloud of brown clay dust.

"What the hell just happened?" Storey asked slowly, carefully enunciating each word.

Troy was still a little breathless, but he managed to get out, "Water buffalo."

"*Water buffalo?*" Storey said, just as slowly as before.

"Who the fuck grazes their livestock in a highway median?" Troy demanded, having recovered sufficiently to be pissed off. "What kind of mental fucking defective would even think of something like that? And then think it was a good idea?"

"Just off the top of my head, I'm guessing that median grass doesn't get chawed on very often," Storey observed calmly.

"And there's a good fucking reason for that!" Troy shouted. "I came around the corner and one of the fuckers was right in the middle of the road."

"Good thing you didn't hit it," Storey said, still mildly.

"No shit," said Troy, still loudly. "Be as bad as hitting a moose. We'd be looking for a new ride, if we lived."

"I'm not going out that way," Storey informed him. "You know what kind of shit I'd have to take in Valhalla if I got killed by a water buffalo?"

Troy had calmed down enough to grin at that.

"So try not to let it happen, okay?"

"No shit," said Troy.

Storey opened his door. "I'll take over driving. I'm awake now. Oh, and while you're going around, crawl underneath and see if we dislodged anything."

After frequent stops at tourist attractions whose tickets they bought but whose sights they never visited, they overnighted at the beach resort of Phuket. Adding to the collection of restaurant receipts and tourist brochures they were painstakingly assembling though haphazardly scattering throughout the vehicle.

"You check out the red-light district?" Storey asked Troy in the morning over breakfast.

"No, I didn't make the scene."

"You ordered in then?"

"What are you talking about?"

"Don't tell me you didn't let Big Lee out to play last night. And you on such a roll?"

"No way, man. I'm one with the monks for the rest of this trip. Not pushing my luck anymore."

As they drove farther south the culture changed gradually. The *wats* became mosques, and the wailing calls to prayer could be heard in the villages they passed through. Women's clothing became baggier—long sleeves and skirts down to the ground. Most were wearing white head coverings like cowls that draped over the shoulders and down to the chest, with only a small oval for the face to emerge from. The sight of them gave Troy a tingling feeling of alertness, a realization that they weren't as safe as they'd been.

The terrain was hillier, and the mountains that had been in the distance drew closer. It was mostly tropical rain forest now. At the commercial town of Hat Yai the highway turned into an expressway that shot right down to the border. Very soon they were at the Sadao crossing.

Storey had timed the drive to make sure they arrived during daylight. Darkness always made customs agents more suspicious.

The road was lined with trees and neatly bordered by beds of flowers. The Thai crossing was a large open-air metal roof on pillars, the top painted in strips of red, white, and blue that the rains had faded. Under the roof the road spread out into a number of lanes, and along each lane were small booths that housed Thai officialdom.

Storey was driving. As they entered through the gate Troy jumped out to pick up the forms they needed at the little kiosk. He filled out the arrival/departure cards as Storey followed two trucks to the immigration check-point. Troy jumped out again to join the line at the immigration booth.

The passports were checked and the forms stamped. A constant of border crossing is that little attention is paid to people leaving a country. Customs waved them through.

They left Thailand and after a drive of a couple hundred yards through no-man's land were welcomed to Malaysia and pulled under another metal roof. They felt no call to stop at the duty-free shopping complex. Storey pulled over and sent Troy to the first booth for more forms. A Malaysian arrival/departure card and currency declaration form. Again filled out while waiting in line.

Troy presented the documents at the immigration booth.

"What is the purpose of your visit?" the agent asked

him in the British-accented English befitting a member of the Commonwealth.

"Tourism," Troy replied. "We were driving through southern Thailand and thought we'd spend a few days in your country."

"And how will you leave the country?"

"We'll drive back to Thailand, probably through here."

The agent finished checking his computer and handed back the stamped passports and arrival cards. "Enjoy your stay, sir. You do not require a visa for stays of thirty days or less."

"Thank you," said Troy.

The next stop was the customs booth. Now it got dicey. Storey drove slowly, hoping for a pass, but the agent pulled them over.

This one also spoke English, but less well. After he had the passports and eyed the occupants of the vehicle, there came the inevitable, "Anything to declare?"

"No, sir," said Storey, operating under his standard procedure for dealing with any kind of government official: neat dress and good manners equaled fewer hassles.

"Step out," came the command.

"Yes, sir," said Storey. He popped the rear hatch before complying.

The agent took one look at the luggage in back before signaling one of his colleagues. "Luggage into building, please."

Storey turned to Troy. "You're younger than I am."

"I knew it," said Troy, for effect.

Storey smiled at the agent, who let a slight grin crack through his professional demeanor.

Troy humped the bags into the booth and, as directed, dumped them onto an X-ray carousel.

The agent watched the screen intently. When the bags came through the other end he went right to one and opened it up. He fished around and came up with a toilet kit. A careful examination of everything, then a slight look of disappointment that the pill bottles only contained antimalaria medication. He zipped everything back up and motioned for Troy to take it away.

As he dragged the bags across the sweltering asphalt, Troy saw the other agent's legs sticking out the back of the CRV. There hadn't been anything in the bags except clothes. But stashed throughout the body of the vehicle was enough weapons, ordnance, and assorted military equipment to guarantee both an unpleasant interrogation and a very, very long stretch in a Malaysian prison. Something the U.S. government would do absolutely nothing about.

Storey was up near the front of the vehicle, slouching against the body. A good customs agent was like a good poker player. They didn't play the cards, they played the people. Specifically, their body language.

And Storey was the perfect picture of boredom and driving fatigue. But he must have seen something else as Troy set the bags down beside the Honda. Maybe he didn't care for Troy's body language. So he roused himself, reached in the open door, and plucked a map from the visor. He ostentatiously snapped it open and spread it out on the hood. "Hey, Leonard, come on over here."

Troy obeyed, giving him a little look for the "Leonard," even though it was the name on his passport. Knowing that the identity he'd used to enter the country was compromised to Thai security, they'd switched to different passports. "What?"

"I've been thinking," said Storey, bending over the map. The agent was still in the back, and had pulled up the upholstery. They could stand a detailed search, but if he started yanking plastic off, it was all over. "We've only got a few days here. It might not be worth driving over to Perlis State. Let's stay here in Kedah. We can drive around and check out the sights, go to Pedu resort and play some golf." Even without looking, he knew the agent was listening to them.

As did Troy. "Yeah, but I wanted to check out the royal palace at Arau. And maybe the caves at Gua Kelam." There was a tapping of metal from the back. Troy was a bit relieved that his pistol was hidden in the frame—he might have been tempted to shoot someone.

"You sure you wouldn't rather play some golf?" Storey asked. "I would."

"That's because you're an old fart," said Troy. "You get more exercise eating a sandwich than you do playing a round of golf."

"Look, I'm tired of driving," Storey said reasonably. "Let's hit the resort, maybe play a round or two, then see what we feel like."

"All right, all right," said Troy. "You've got to humor the aged." He knew Storey was doing this little theatrical piece for him, and it pissed him off to see the bastard so cool. At least he didn't have to worry about sweating. *Everyone* was.

The agent was now in the spare tire well.

Troy wondered how it would go down. Probably nothing as dramatic as spotlights, sirens, and dogs. The Malaysians would just walk up, pull their pistols, and put them under arrest.

The customs agent climbed out of the back of the CRV and walked over to the booth.

Going to get some backup, Troy thought. Storey was still studying the map.

The agent emerged from the booth and headed toward them. Troy hated feeling this helpless. He'd already checked out the area—running wouldn't do any good. Fight? With what?

Car horns in the background, the smell of exhaust. Voices chattering in several different languages. The tapping of leather soles approaching across the asphalt.

The agent handed a sheaf of papers to Troy. "Enjoy your time in Malaysia."

"Thank you, sir," Storey replied.

Troy was still standing there holding the papers. Storey plucked them from his hand. "*I'm* leaving," he said. "You do what you like."

He'd already started the engine when Troy decided that was a good idea.

The final stop was the police checkpoint, a stand-alone booth with an aqua-blue pagoda roof. Storey, being Storey, had a letter from the rental agency giving them permission to take the car across the border. And he'd already purchased a Malaysian car insurance policy.

As they pulled out Storey glanced at his watch. "Hour and a half. That wasn't bad at all."

"You know, they only searched us because I'm black," said Troy.

"I suspected as much," Storey replied.

They were now in the northern Malaysian state of Kedah, though their destination was the neighboring Perlis state to the northwest. Which they could have reached directly through a different border crossing, but Storey insisted on an indirect route.

They drove south on the North-South Expressway until they reached the town of Changlun, then west on the Changlun-Kuala Perlis Highway into Perlis. Near the town of Arau they turned north on single-lane roads. Their objective was a large sugar plantation near the Thai border. That was where their study of the captured maps and the computation of gasoline consumption from the fuel receipts had led them.

Storey stopped for a leisurely dinner, timing the drive so they reached the outskirts of the plantation around dusk. He had his spot all picked out from the satellite photos they'd studied in Bangkok. A dirt trail off the road they were traveling on, which weaved through some jungle forest.

A stop, and a check on foot to make sure the jungle wasn't so swampy that the Honda would get stuck. Then a shift to four-wheel drive, off-road and backing right into

the jungle. There was a machete in the tool kit. A few
minutes working to push the flattened vegetation back
up, cutting new vegetation to camouflage the tire tracks
and the gap they'd made in the foliage, and the Honda
disappeared into the forest. The black pearl color that
Storey had so carefully chosen blended well into the
green.

Now they pried open the interior panels and removed their cargo from the frame. First what looked like
padding, but were actually two sets of the black cotton
pajamas Southeast Asian peasants still wore to work
their fields. The pajamas had been spray-painted with
streaks of brown to make an improvised camouflage pattern. Two pairs of running shoes, also spray-painted
brown. Storey and Troy were still using their spandoflage mesh head coverings. It wouldn't do to complete the mission, get stopped by a cop on the road, and
have him notice camouflage paint in your ears that
you'd missed washing off.

Two load-bearing vests from the safe house cache in
Bangkok, filled with the usual mix of ammo magazines
and grenades. And two small day packs, purchased in
Bangkok and camouflaged with spray paint.

At first glance the two rifles looked like the usual
M-4 carbines. But they were actually the Knight's Ar-
mament Company SR-47, which had been developed se-
cretly for the Tier-1 special operations units. An M-16
carbine chambered for the Russian 7.62X39mm short
round of the AK-47. With a special cut-down magazine
well that accepted the standard thirty-round AK-47 magazine.

The cave complexes of Afghanistan were such an isolated and target-rich environment that the special operators fighting in them found that they literally couldn't
carry enough M-16 magazines to do the job. So they
asked for a weapon capable of using magazines they
could pick up on the battlefield—which meant the

AK-47 magazines of the opponents they'd already dealt with.

Why not just use AK-47s? The most important thing in weapons handling was the muscle memory—the operation of the weapon, the location of the safety, the grip, the sights. Plus, the AK series, while unbelievably rugged and reliable, was also notoriously inaccurate. And the sights were just terrible.

So a contract went out and Knight's virtually hand-made six SR-47s. A few more were ordered later, but there weren't very many in the inventory.

Ironically, the SR-47 solved the number-one problem with the M-16 series of weapons, the lack of lethality of the U.S. 5.56mm bullet. The Russian 7.62mm short round was a man-stopper. An added benefit for covert operations was that there would be empty Russian casings and magazines left lying around after everything was over, not American ones.

Both rifles had PEQ-2 infrared laser aiming devices mounted on them. These projected a laser dot that could be seen through night-vision equipment.

Troy had an Aimpoint red-dot sight mounted on his weapon, and he was wearing a single-tube PVS-14 night-vision goggle over his right eye.

Storey thought he moved better at night without night-vision goggles. So he mounted a PVS-17 mini starlight scope on his rifle, which could be used for both shooting and observation.

Storey programmed waypoints into his civilian GPS unit and set the correct azimuth on his wrist compass.

Troy said, "How's my hair look?"

"Perfect," Storey replied.

As darkness fell they headed off into the brush.

There were villages on the outskirts of the plantation, but repeated calculations of the mileage and gas consumption seemed to indicate that their objective was inside it. That led to further study of satellite photos.

Plantations used every spare bit of ground for cultivation. There were garages, of course, and workshops, but few dwellings—mostly for staff. Storey doubted that anything would come of it, but they had to be checked out. Satellites were powerful tools, but when you were hunting individuals only eyes on the ground could tell you what you really needed to know.

The land had been scraped bare to plant the sugarcane. All except for the limestone hills that jutted up between the fields, occasional thin tree lines between the sections, and scattered ponds. It made movement easy but risky. The full-grown fields were almost impassible, but with any other level of cultivation there was plenty of space between the rows. Except the loose earth left footprints—Storey did not like that at all. It was enough to make him wish for rain.

At least the night sounds gave them plenty of cover. A million insects buzzing and chirping, frogs croaking, and night birds screaming.

It was past 10:00 when they reached the first dwelling, backs aching from moving hunched over through the immature cane. Storey brought his rifle to his shoulder and checked out the area through the 4.5-power lens of his starlight scope. No lights on. No vehicles of any kind in the area.

Wanting to be sure before they went any closer, he tapped Troy and Troy removed the SOPHIE from Storey's pack. SOPHIE was a 5.3-pound long-range thermal imager that looked like a large pair of binoculars. Storey turned it on and waited for the detector to cool to operating temperature.

SOPHIE detected heat. The image it produced was the heat differential between every object in its field of view. When he looked through his rifle night sight, which magnified any ambient light from the stars and moon, Storey could see cane fields. Through the SOPHIE he could see the bright body heat of rats walking through the fields and birds perched in the trees for the night. A metal water tank in the distance glowed bright against the ground that had cooled off faster in the evening air. Nothing with any body heat was in the house.

Now they crossed through the trees. Storey covered while Troy peeked through a window. Some kind of staff housing, but it was empty. No signs of any recent occupancy.

The second house was over a mile away. It turned out to be equipment storage. This was why you couldn't rely on satellites.

Storey was concerned. They might have to spend a week reconning each village in the area, and still not be able to pick out someone who didn't belong there. He could accept a fool's errand, but not one so risky. It was looking like a wasted trip.

But they still had to check out the third house. This one was nearly four miles away. Storey cupped both hands around one of Troy's ears. "We'll be a long way from the car by daylight. Do we go on now or move the car closer and come back tomorrow night?"

Troy just pointed. *Go on.*

Storey had saved the third for last because it was the hardest to approach. A cane field on one side, and another across a dirt road. A few surrounding trees for shade, but otherwise wide open all around. Only a thin tree line to make an approach, which was why Storey didn't want to approach through it. But there was no other choice.

He was on point, and moved even slower than before. A very careful step. Vision sweep. Listen. And only then another careful step. It was why he didn't wear night-vision goggles. They made him feel less alert. It was like looking through a toilet paper tube—you could only see what you were looking directly at. They unbalanced your head, and made you concentrate on your feet. And he felt they killed the rest of his senses.

After stepping forward and putting his weight down, Storey felt the pressure just below his knee. He eased back, sliding his hand down his leg until it was next to his knee. It felt like fishing line. Keeping a light finger pressure on the line, he took a step back and crouched down. His fingernail followed the line to the right until it touched metal. As lightly as a blind man reading Braille, he traced the outline of a tin can wired to a tree trunk. Simple and effective. The pin removed from a hand grenade, wedged into the can to keep the spoon under pressure. The fishing line tied to the grenade. Any pressure on the line pulls the grenade from the can, releasing the spoon. Tracing the line to the left found another can and another grenade. By the time you figured out that it wasn't a vine wrapped around your legs you were dead and the noise had alerted everyone in the vicinity.

The booby trap made Storey very happy. It meant they were on to something. He signaled Troy to turn around and take the point, and they backed away.

Far enough away that they could converse in whispers. Storey told him what had happened. "You want to come back tomorrow night?"

"No," Troy whispered back. "We're going to have to make a daylight recon eventually. Can't do a positive ID any other way."

"You're the sniper," said Storey. "Take over."

For their observation post Troy picked the field directly across the dirt road from the house. The cane plants were slightly less than two feet high and the leaves spread out just enough to conceal the rows.

Storey approved. The new plants were so low to the ground that it would be dismissed as a hiding place. The least likely spot was always preferable. Unless someone picked that day to spray the field with pesticides, or come through and weed.

They crawled into the field and down the rows, Troy

leading and Storey brushing away any sign their passage
had left in the dirt.

The rows, as Murphy's Law always arranged things, ran
perpendicular to the house. So Troy used a pair of garden
shears, the sniper's best friend, to carve out an area for
them to lie down side by side. He was careful not to cut
away any of the leaves that would drape over them.

For daylight observation Troy set up a Kowa spotting scope. A 20–60-power zoom telescope, 3.25 pounds
and seventeen inches long. He attached a Canon digital camera body to the scope mounting.

They knew what it was going to be like. Before the sun
came up they made sure their trouser legs were tucked
into their socks, and sleeves into their light cotton gloves.
They donned beekeepers' hats purchased in Bangkok and also spray-painted for camouflage.

The dawn revealed a light mist over the fields that
quickly burned off. The heat rose. The leaves draping
over them provided shade but also shut off any air flow,
sending the humidity up near 100 percent. There were
thick clouds of small bugs the size of gnats. The fertilizer smell was strong. Probably cancer in about twenty
years, Storey thought.

They switched off every hour to stay sharp. The heat
was too brutal for napping, but at least they could roll
over, an inch at a time to keep from disturbing the foliage, to allow some blood back into the muscles they'd
been lying on. They drank water from the Camelbak
water bags in their packs, and munched energy bars. Uri-
nating into plastic bags so more insects, and anything
else, wouldn't be attracted to the smell.

Troy was in his element, and Storey was impressed. He
just needed a rifle in his hand. Totally focused, utterly
patient. The classic sniper.

Storey knew they were well concealed when the
wildlife began moving around them. Rats scampered
down the rows, only skidding to a halt and fleeing after

almost bumping into them. And before the ground got too warm a black-and-white-banded krait glided by, on the way home after a night hunting rodents. A southern upbringing gave you the instinct to kill every snake you laid eyes on, but Storey had learned that most species, even poisonous ones like the krait, didn't bother you unless you bothered them.

The house was modest and single story. With enough magnification, it was amazing how much you could see through windows. At 10:18 in the morning, duly logged into Troy's notebook, a short chubby man wearing only underwear stepped in front of one. An Arab man. Troy zoomed in the spotting scope and took four photos before the Arab disappeared. He nudged Storey, who looked at the images in the camera display.

Storey attached the serial cable to the camera and downloaded the photos to his Personal Digital Assistant. Then the cable to the satellite phone. He wrote a brief message requesting identification if possible, and sent the photos off to Washington. Though not with high expectations.

The hours passed. They convinced themselves that the Arab was in the house alone.

At 4:42 the satellite phone vibrated with an incoming message. The decoded text came up on Storey's PDA. The Arab was believed to be one Talat al-Rashidi, or so said the facial recognition software. The command center didn't ask them whether they could put their hands on the guy, they wanted to know whether they could get him across the border into Thailand.

Storey knew the deal. Unlike with Thailand, no one was going to ask the government of Malaysia for help they weren't going to give anyway. And it seemed that the Pentagon was still going to play games with the CIA, not ask it for help.

If he'd known the border better, Storey would have considered it. He'd grab the guy, but someone else was going to have to run bodies across the border. He worded his reply much more tactfully, but that was the essence of it.

Washington came right back with orders to maintain observation, making Storey regret sending them the photos in the first place.

At 6:07 PM a red Toyota pickup truck with Malaysian registration came down the dirt road and pulled in beside the house. Two young men in their twenties, who looked to be Malaysians, got out and went inside the house. Storey was on the spotting scope at that time and took their pictures. They didn't bring anything into the house, like groceries.

This created a whole set of problems. Their water was almost gone, and they wouldn't last another day in that field without more. So one of them would have to leave the hide and refill the bags. And if they let the target leave with his visitors they might never see him again.

It was the subject of a whispered conversation. The consensus was that they couldn't risk it—they'd have to go in.

By now they had a very detailed sketch map of the area, and they used it to make their plan.

The last thing they wanted was to be crawling into position only to have everyone pile into the pickup and drive off. To keep that from happening, as soon as it was completely dark they split up and began crawling through the cane, aiming for the road on either side of the house. They didn't have far to go, but had to do it very slowly so their movement didn't make a weaving pattern across the surface of the cane.

When he reached the edge of the field facing the road, Troy reached into his pack and brought out a 2.2-pound green metal box, square on three sides with an oval on the top that looked like a stereo speaker diaphragm. An M2 SLAM, or Selectable Lightweight Attack Munition, a smart mine. He wired the box to a cane stalk so it faced the road, setting the selector switch to ten hours, removing the cover from the passive infrared sensor, and pulling the pin. When a vehicle passed in front of the passive infrared port the change in background temperature would fire the mine. The part that looked like a speaker diaphragm was an explosively formed projectile, a high-velocity metal slug that could penetrate 1.75 inches of steel armor. It did much better on auto bodies. After ten hours the mine would self-neutralize, and it would just be a harmless green metal box with no identifying markings.

A three-quarter moon came up over the limestone hills. Troy and Storey still waited in the field. The house-lights went off at 1:00 AM. They didn't move until 3:10.

For a special operator the only thing more important than terrain was microterrain. Even what looked like perfectly flat and open ground would still have dips and hollows and rain channels that would completely conceal a crawling man. The trick was not to blunder across but carefully study the terrain before making a move. And Storey and Troy had had nineteen hours to carefully study the terrain in front of them.

The road was slightly lower than both the cane field and the house. Troy slid down the bank on his belly, made a final check in both directions, and quickly high-crawled across the road on hands and knees. The spot he'd chosen put a tree trunk between him and the house.

Once across the road Troy slowed way down. He had to operate under two worst-case assumptions: that there was someone alertly standing guard in the house, and that they had night-vision equipment.

Holding his rifle near the barrel so the weapon draped over his forearm and out of the dirt, Troy pushed himself forward using just his forearms and toes. It was called a sniper crawl, and he moved only four inches at a time, including a long pause in between to look and listen. The side of his head pressed against the dirt, the night-vision goggle trained at the house. Any sign of life and he'd have to make the call whether to lie there out in the open, hoping not to be seen, or get up and assault.

His joints were soon aching, though his chest was thankfully numb. He was sick of the smell of dirt. But rather than use it all as an excuse to hurry, Troy embraced the pain and discomfort as a mark of personal discipline. Mind over matter, they were always saying to the trainees at BUDS. If you don't mind, then it don't matter.

Inside the microterrain, Troy knew where the house was, but if he couldn't see it, then they couldn't see him. All the more reason to plan his route around all the obstacles in the area, no matter how small. The pickup truck was his friend. When there was no cover he crawled along the shadows cast by the trees. All the more important because sometimes black clothing showed up almost white in moonlight. The human eye senses movement before anything else, and his movement was slow enough to be imperceptible. It took him an hour and a half to move less than forty yards.

With the back door of the house now in sight, Troy still waited. Then, very faintly, the hoot of an owl. That was Storey in position on the other side of the house.

This was what you trained for. Not just to operate at the highest level, but to operate at the highest level at the time you were the most tired and uncomfortable. Troy tossed a very small pebble into the bed of the pickup truck. It made a lovely sound hitting the metal and then rattling around. A sound not connected to anything natural. Not the kind of noise that sets off sirens, the kind that brings a dozing man's head up off his chest and makes him say to himself: what the hell was that? Then Troy tossed another pebble against a metal wheel. That was the sound that puts a man on his feet and sends him off to investigate.

It took some time, but a silhouette eventually appeared at the back door. Looking around, listening. But there was nothing to see, and nothing more to hear. Now Troy imagined him trying to decide whether he really heard anything.

So there was someone on watch. Not alert enough to discover their movement, but too alert for them to enter the house undetected.

Troy had another pebble ready if he didn't come out, but he did.

The screen door squeaked—something that was good to know. It was one of the Malaysians, in a tank top, jeans, and bare feet. Pistol in his right hand.

Lying prone with his rifle at his shoulder, Troy had him dead to rights. His SR-47 had a Knight's sound suppressor attached to the barrel. It brought the rifle's report down to the level of a .22. That was quiet, but not quiet enough in the dead of night with two men still in the house.

The Malaysian moved to check out the pickup. Until Troy tossed his pebble against a tree trunk. The pistol came up, and now Troy knew exactly what they were dealing with. Because instead of dashing to the nearest available cover and *then* trying to determine what was going on, he advanced slowly across open ground, both hands on the pistol out in front of his body.

Off to his right Troy saw a dark upright figure gliding through the trees. He tossed another pebble. Into the dirt this time—a much more subtle sound. He was steadily drawing the Malaysian's attention toward him and away from what was coming up behind. But a lot of things could go wrong, just as they had done in the Bangkok apartment building.

Most human beings have a continuous inner dialogue going on, one part debating with the other about the best course of action. While this is happening the information from their senses is not being processed. The predator has no inner dialogue. The predator is fo-

cused on the prey, waiting for *it* to give the signal to
strike. Troy was careful not to look directly at Storey;
sometimes you could feel those eyes.

Storey was moving crouched over. On his toes but
lightly, not pounding. First weaving through the trees.
Then as the Malaysian turned toward the fall of the third
pebble, he committed himself. Springing forward, still
on his toes, adrenaline pumping and heart pounding,
holding his breath so the sound wouldn't give him
away. He came up from behind, as would the tiger.

The Malaysian finally sensed something and whirled
around, but Storey was less than ten feet away. *Pfft, pfft,
pfft, pfft,* so close together they were almost one sound.
Four rounds to the head from the little Glock pistol.
Storey's momentum carried him forward and he had his
left arm around the man's chest before he dropped. The
pistol still pressed against the head, just in case, Storey
carried the body to the cover of the nearest tree and quietly lowered it to the ground.

Troy had only watched the first part. Once it was resolved he kept his rifle trained on the back door, ready
to fire and then assault if anyone appeared.

Storey holstered the pistol, going back to the rifle
slung across his chest. A hand signal to Troy and he went
for the back door, sprinting across the open ground.

Storey paused only to ease the door open, letting
Troy slip in first. Rifles at their shoulders, they tiptoed
down a short entry alcove, pausing only to confirm
that the kitchen was empty.

Nothing was certain now. Either they still had surprise
or people were going to be jumping out shooting.
Storey listened hard for any indication of that. The
house smelled like chicken that had been burnt in
cooking.

An opening into what looked like a living room. Troy
crouched down and peeked around a corner as Storey
covered him. He pulled his head back and signaled: *on*

the right; one man; asleep; I'll take him, you cover. When
Troy had his own Glock out, Storey put his hand on his
partner's shoulder. *Ready.* He squeezed. *Go.*

Troy leaned around the corner and double-tapped two
rounds into the head of the Malaysian sleeping on the
couch. Almost the only sound was the two ejected shell
casings falling to the floor.

Storey moved up to cover the room exit. Troy made
sure of his victim and fell in behind.

A hallway with three doors. Wonderful, Storey
thought. Pick the right door and win a prize. Make any
noise picking the wrong one and ruin everything.

On closer examination one door was ajar. They tiptoed toward it. Yes, that was the bathroom. Empty.

Storey went to the next door, signaling Troy: *quiet.* Troy
nodded. Storey turned the knob a millimeter at a time
until the latch was completely retracted. Then he opened
the door, very slowly because everything wood squeaked
in a humid climate. Just enough for Troy to look in. Troy
shook his head. Storey would have left the door open,
but he was afraid of it moving and making noise.

On to the next door, which hopefully held the prize.
With another hand signal, Troy asked if Storey wanted to
go first. Storey shook his head. Troy had done the last one
just fine, and he still felt unlucky from Bangkok. He did
signal Troy not to look around this time—just go in fast.

The same routine with the doorknob. Storey flung the
door open. This time the bed was against the near wall.
Troy raised his rifle and brought the butt-plate down
onto the exposed stomach.

Talat al-Rashidi folded at the middle as the air went
out of his lungs in a loud grunting gasp. Troy threw him
off the bed, and Storey put a foot on his neck to hold
him still while Troy looped the plastic flexcuff band
around his wrists.

He hesitated over the gag. "Might suffocate the way
he's breathing," he rasped hoarsely. Speaking in a

normal tone for the first time in over twenty-four hours
will do that.

"Gag him," Storey ordered.

They each grabbed an upper arm and dragged al-
Rashidi out to the living room. "Watch him," said Storey.
"I'll clear the house." You always had to check, even if
you were 99 percent sure. It was the 1 percent that
killed you.

The house was empty. Storey returned to the living
room. "You better go get our packs, just in case."

Troy's return trip to the field took him less than a
minute. When he came back Storey was writing a message into his PDA. Al-Rashidi was tied to a hardwood
chair, his legs tied to two chair legs. They left him there
for the moment, chest still heaving and eyes locked on
the dead man on the couch.

"How come you hit him in the stomach?" Storey
asked while he worked the stylus across the screen.

"Didn't want to crack his skull by accident," said Troy.
And then, "I can't believe the fucker didn't wake up."

"When you're home alone you pay attention to
noises," Storey said. "You don't when you have company."

Troy was almost looking forward to the day when
Storey didn't think of everything.

Storey hooked up his phone and sent the message off.
"You been working hard," he said with a thin smile.
"Keep an eye on them and I'll look around."

"My pleasure." Troy was about to take the scratchy
spandoflage hood off, but didn't because al-Rashidi
couldn't take his eyes off it—which made it good medicine. He didn't bother watching the road; the SLAMs
would alert them to any traffic.

Storey came up with a laptop computer and two
nylon cases filled with CDs. A satellite phone had been
charging on the dresser. Four regular cell phones. Pre-
scription bottle with Xanax—someone had trouble
sleeping. Two suitcases were packed and zippered up for

a quick exit, which made him doubt that anything was hidden away in the house. Nothing but clothes and toiletries inside the suitcases, but when he slashed the lining open with his knife there were four different passports. In four different names, but all with al-Rashidi's photo. Bunch of credit cards. And about twenty grand in cash, U.S. hundred-dollar bills. The international currency of choice.

Storey checked his watch. It would be dawn soon. Washington needed to pull their thumb out of their ass—he wasn't going to hang around in daylight. He packed all the contraband into plastic bags, stacking them next to the door.

Twenty minutes later his phone began to vibrate.

He watched the message scrolling across the PDA screen. He'd just known something like this was going to happen. *Motherfuckers!*

"What?" said Troy.

Storey realized he'd muttered it out loud. He was tired, which meant he'd have to bear down and focus. He showed Troy the screen.

The message read: *Impossible to send you assistance to exfiltrate target. You are not permitted to transport target to Kuala Lumpur or U.S. Embassy or Consulate. If unable to exfiltrate target across Thai border resolve situation as you determine best. Out.*

Storey knew the deal. No one at the embassy in Kuala Lumpur wanted to get off their ass and take a drive north. And the U.S. hadn't asked the Muslim government of Malaysia for permission to run an operation on its soil, so they certainly weren't going to ask them for any assistance. This guy al-Rashidi was probably under the protection of some heavy hitter just to be on this plantation. Someone was a sympathizer; someone got paid off; someone got their life threatened. Everyone used the Mafia model: governments, criminals, *and* terrorists. And his own government had just been very careful to give him orders without anyone going on the record ordering him to do anything specific. Which put him out on the end of a very long limb.

Troy finished reading. "Well, that's that." Then, as if it was a second thought, "We're not taking him across the border, are we?"

"How?" said Storey. "In a suitcase? Wired to the undercarriage of the CRV? Folded around the engine?"

"Hey, I was just hoping you weren't going to tell me how." Another pause. "It'll be dawn soon."

"Yeah, and we're going to be gone by then. But that guy Nimri is still out there somewhere trying to kill the president, and I worked too damn hard to leave empty-handed."

"Get some," said Troy. "How does the master's in psychology play it?"

"The guy with the master's in psychology might not know much, but he knows the difference between claiming you're ready to die and being ready to die. You can wait outside if you want."

"I'm in."

"Think about it," Storey warned. "This could blow back on us—in a big way."

"I told you I was in."

Storey ripped off al-Rashidi's gag.

The Arab promptly howled, "*Help me!*"

Actually, only half that, because Storey's light open-handed strike across the windpipe cut him off.

"I did not tell you that you could yell," Storey told him calmly. Besides his native tongue, he spoke two languages fluently: Spanish and Arabic. "In the future do not do anything unless I give you permission."

By this time the other side of the conversation had gotten his voice back.

"We know who you are, Talat al-Rashidi," Storey said. "We have a few questions for you."

"Go to hell, you shit-eating son of a pig—"

Storey's raised right hand had shut off the invective. It sounded almost elegant in the Arabic.

Storey removed his Glock pistol from the holster under his pajama shirt.

"You are afraid to die, American. I am not."

Storey actually smiled at that. A smile that even creeped out Troy, who was watching the whole scene. Then Storey shot the Arab in the kneecap. An ear-splitting howl rocked the house. Storey tied a tourniquet around the thigh, not being careful about moving the leg. Al-Rashidi screamed at every jolt.

Storey grabbed his hair and shook it to get his attention, holding the satellite phone up to his face. "I need names to go with the numbers on this phone. Or I will shoot you in your other kneecap next."

A quick gasp of "Wait. I will tell you."

Storey picked up the phone, scrolling down the numbers in the address book and reading them off. Al-Rashidi put a name to each one. Troy laid his rifle across his knees and wrote them down in his pocket notebook.

Storey plucked his pistol back out of the holster and shot al-Rashidi in the other kneecap. Another piercing scream. Al-Rashidi bent over as far as his bonds would allow, crying, snot pouring from his nose.

"We are fools, is that it?" said Storey, tying on another tourniquet. "You can tell us any lies, and we will believe them?"

"I spoke the truth," al-Rashidi sobbed.

Storey grabbed him by the hair again. "We have all the names, do you understand? You think we do not know that you lie as easily as you breathe? I have plenty of time, and plenty of ammunition. I will say the numbers again, and I want to hear the name of Abdallah Karim Nimri."

Al-Rashidi looked up at him.

"That is correct," said Storey. "I know everything.

Match the names with the numbers. God will forgive you. After all, the final victory will be his, will it not?"

The pain got worse. Storey went through the numbers again, and al-Rashidi gave a completely different set of names. Including Nimri's.

"Again," Storey commanded. He read the numbers in a different order. Then once more, in another order, and faster. He looked over at Troy, who was still writing the answers down. Troy nodded. Storey looked out the window. Faint light was beginning to show at the horizon. No more time for questions.

Storey shot al-Rashidi in the head.

Troy was outwardly unmoved. But he was remembering something the master chief had told him. You didn't want to be on the side Ed Storey was fighting.

Storey flicked out his folding knife and cut off al-Rashidi's cuffs. "Let's go drag the guy outside in here. We'll light the house on our way out. Any luck, there's no CSI around here, and the locals won't figure it out."

After that was accomplished, Troy took fingerprints and DNA swabs. Storey slashed open the furniture to reveal the padding. Troy walked around the house setting fire to the curtains in every room and any paper he could find.

Loading up the pickup, he said to Storey, "You know, they're going to find the SLAMs."

"Can't be helped."

"Why don't I go get them? They're neutralized by now."

"They're *supposed* to be neutralized," Storey said. "If someone had a bad day at the factory the antitamper feature'll set them things off in high order right in your face."

Troy tried not to smile, because he was beginning to recognize those rare moments when the West Virginia cracker peeked out from Storey's usually perfectly enunciated English. "I'll risk it."

"It ain't worth it," Storey insisted.

"Yes, it is."

"It's your funeral," said Storey.

Troy rushed off. Storey started up the pickup, waiting for something to go boom. He could see flames flickering through the windows of the house.

But Troy returned with a huge grin on his face and the two SLAMs, which he stuffed under his passenger seat.

"SEALs," said Storey.

Racing the dawn, they sped down dirt roads toward the camouflaged Honda CRV. After quickly changing back into their vacation clothes, Troy led in the CRV, Storcy following in the pickup.

Choosing a lonely stretch of forest a mile away from where they'd hidden the CRV, Troy dug a hole while Storey smashed or otherwise disabled all their equipment. Doing that to perfectly good and very expensive gear went against every one of his Staff NCO instincts, but there was no percentage in having it with them in case they got stopped. Everything went into the hole: weapons, equipment, pajamas, and boots. They filled it up and replaced the foliage, scattering the excess dirt and brushing away their footprints as they retreated back to the road. The jungle would take of everything soon enough.

The pickup was abandoned in the next village they passed through, the keys in the ignition. That would take care of the last of the evidence.

They'd been without sleep for over forty-eight hours, but this was not a condition unknown to either SEALs or Delta operators. And Storey had no intention of stopping for a nap. He also did not intend to cross a border again. They drove straight south, heading for the Malaysian capital of Kuala Lumpur.

"You did good," he told Troy as they were driving along.

"Thanks," said Troy. "You really didn't think I was up for it?"

"Thought you'd be," said Storey. "Didn't know. You never know until it comes up."

"It was a lot more pleasant than it would have been if they'd caught *us* out there in that cane field. You must have seen some kneecapping when you did your tour with the Brits."

"Saw the end result a couple of times. The IRA does it for terror. As a way to get someone to talk, it's useless. They'll tell you whatever they think you want to hear. It only works when you've got a specific question that you absolutely know that *they* know the answer to." Storey paused for a moment and said, "This is a test of wills."

"You mean like some kind of Nietzsche thing?"

Storey was impressed that Troy had even heard of the German philosopher. "No. What I mean is, Al Qaeda's hoping we'll become their partners in atrocity. If the only way to beat them is to become like them, they're betting we'd rather go home. They're testing our will. But the difference, the way we win, is that they do it indiscriminately and we do it to *them*. Only. They do it with pleasure, and we do it with disgust. They do it at every opportunity, and we only do it when we have to."

"I don't worry about the deep thinking," Troy said emphatically. "I just fight the motherfuckers."

"That's what a master's in psychology will do for you," said Storey, sounding more like a master sergeant now. "Consider yourself warned."

Troy wasn't sure if Storey had been trying to explain himself or convince himself. "What were we supposed to do? Give him a candy bar and send him on his way because the rules don't let you kill someone after you take them prisoner?"

"Geneva Conventions don't apply to terrorists," said Storey.

"You know what I mean."

"I surely do. Today we're the heroes of the war on terrorism—forget about all the hard things we had to do. Five years from now it's Vietnam, and we're on trial for first-degree murder. Which is why neither of us is going to put anything that happened after we entered that house down on paper or in any communications. He died of wounds incurred in capture."

"Fine with me."

"Take it seriously. Because Washington was real careful how they worded those last orders so no one took any responsibility but us. Someday some general or politician—"

"Same thing," Troy interjected.

"Some general or politician is going to get theyselves into trouble and need someone to throw to the wolves. Like us. Or some Dudley Do-Right staff officer who spent his career behind a desk might stumble across our report one day and decide it's his duty to report a war crime."

"Hey, you don't have to convince me. Didn't bother me, and I didn't see it bother you."

"That's why my wives both said they left me. Among other things, they said I was emotionally unavailable."

"Yeah?" said Troy, amused by that. "Well, don't worry about it, man. It's easy to be emotionally available if you're a fucking hairdresser. Be an emotionally available warrior and they'll be feeding you Thorazine in your padded cell."

"Words of wisdom," said Storey.

It was over three hundred miles to Kuala Lumpur. Once in the city they parked the Honda and left the keys in it. Too bad for the Thai rental agency, but they weren't about to complete a paper trail by turning it in. The identities they'd used to rent the car and cross the border would be discarded, and they'd leave Malaysia on new passports.

Once clear of the car they flagged down a cab to the U.S. Embassy. It was okay for the big boys to play games, but Storey knew their asses were on the line if they delayed turning over their intelligence. So the first stop was the CIA duty officer, who took them right in to the chief of station, who went by the name of Gordon and listened very carefully to Storey's briefing.

"It's a shame al-Rashidi didn't make it," he said coldly. "If you'd bothered to get in touch with me I could have gotten you some help."

Storey didn't bat an eye. "You'd have to take that up with our chain of command, sir. Not us."

"Oh, I will. Depend on it. That's all we need, the Pentagon fighting their own private wars on *my* turf."

Storey didn't feel a need to comment on that.

"And you say you've got names to go with the numbers on this satellite phone," said the chief of station. "How?"

Storey reminded himself to be careful. This guy was no dummy. "They were on a list, sir."

"Then where is the list?"

"The list didn't make it out, sir. It was badly damaged and not transportable. We copied the names and numbers."

"You copied them. You've got all the passports and ID, the phones, the laptop and CD-ROMs, but you *copied* the list?"

"Yes, sir." Storey didn't particularly care whether he was believed or not. "If you'll permit me, sir, we need to move on those numbers before they perish on us."

"Do we? Thank you, *Sergeant*. Thank you very much for that insight."

"You're very welcome, sir," said Storey, acting as if the sarcasm had gone right over his head. "I'll be noting that I have turned them over to you, on this date and time. And hopefully a quick exploitation just may wrap up the plot on the president's life."

Troy enjoyed that one, and not just for the look it put on that snotty-assed chief of station's face. *Go ahead, you Ivy League prick, fuck around and get the president killed. See what happens to you then.*

Evidently it did start things moving. Because Storey and Troy were both woken from a sound sleep two hours later and brought up to the chief of station's office again, who started off by saying, "I'm told you're both Arabic speakers. Who's the most fluent?"

"I am, sir," said Storey.

"You're the only ones in the embassy," said the chief of station. "And we need you right now."

It spoke volumes about the lack of language proficiency within the government in general and the CIA in particular. Arabic wasn't one of the primary languages of Malaysia, but with the level of Islamic fundamentalist activity you'd think they'd have someone around who could speak it. But there weren't all that many people in the entire CIA who spoke Arabic. Damn near all of them had French, though, for that posting to Paris.

The chief of station explained what was going to happen. The National Security Agency, the arm of the intelligence community that intercepted communications, had shifted them priority on all assets. They would call all the numbers on al-Rashidi's cellular phone, and the NSA would try to locate the parties on the other end.

Storey knew a bit about it. The NSA had listening stations all over the world, not to mention satellites in orbit. That movie *Enemy of the State* was pure fantasy, but the NSA could intercept an ungodly amount of communications traffic. Though less now that the world had turned to digital cellular and fiber-optic landlines. And much more than they were ever able to listen to, translate, and analyze. Which was why, unless they were listening for something or to someone in particular, most of the information they gathered was after the fact. After something like 9/11 they'd go back over the tapes and find out everything the U.S. should have known in the first place. Luckily satellite phone transmissions, which went straight up to the satellite, over, and then back down, were easier to trace than run-of-the-mill cellular calls.

Storey wasn't just going to call up a bunch of Al Qaeda on the phone and chat about the weather. He borrowed a tape recorder and went outside, getting down traffic, horns, and street sounds at close range.

Then he took up al-Rashidi's Iridium phone. The CIA guys were on their own secure phone links to NSA headquarters at Fort Meade, Maryland. The NSA knew both numbers. They knew the location of the Kuala Lumpur embassy, and therefore which of the Iridium satellites the outgoing call was going to hit. The odds were pretty good.

When the connection was made Storey turned on the tape recorder at high volume, placing it close to the phone. But he spoke into it at arm's length. And a little scratching on the plastic to make a sound like static. Under all that noise saying, "Hello? Hello? Is this . . . ?" and then the name of the party. "I cannot hear you, brother. Can you hear me?" And then repeating it over and over and over again until the other party was either screaming with frustration or finally hanging up— hopefully not too soon.

It was working. The word came back from Fort Meade. Pakistan. Mindanao. Java. One right there in Kuala Lumpur. Vietnam. China. Laos. Cambodia.

And finally the one he'd saved for last. His act didn't give Storey much chance to listen closely to the other party's voice. But he did pay particular attention to Abdallah Karim Nimri's.

Storey couldn't help extrapolating. Nimri had hung up quicker than all the others. He was sharp.

They waited for Fort Meade to do their magic. "Is he in the Philippines yet?" Storey asked. It was taking too long. They hadn't been able to make the trace.

The CIA agent on the line with Maryland frowned, and said into the phone, "Say again?" He listened some more, put his hand over the mouthpiece, and announced to the room, puzzled, "Parry Sound, Ontario. He's in Canada."

"Oh, Jesus Christ," said Storey. "Jesus Christ, the Philippines is just a diversion. They're going to do something in the States."

16

As usual on Lake Superior when late summer blended into fall, the shoreline was shrouded in fog before the sun came up. The wind was light at five to ten knots, and the waves were only one to two feet. Perfect conditions. *God is great*, thought Abdallah Karim Nimri.

He could only hear the boat. It was showing no lights. With the global positioning devices a set of longitudes and latitudes could be passed over the telephone, then located with perfect certainty.

The waves lapped against the rocky point. Closer to its edge there was a fishy, seaweed smell. Not altogether unpleasant.

The sound didn't grow much louder, because as it came in the boat engine was throttled down. Then a thump as the hull contacted the rocks.

Nimri had forbidden flashlight signals. The American Coast Guard Web site asked people seeing boat-to-shore signals to immediately report them. The GPS was enough. He would hear the boat, and he would find it himself.

Nimri threw off the heavy wool blanket he'd been huddled under. Holding the plastic bag containing his clothes, he gingerly stepped down the rocks to the water. Fool. He should have kept his shoes on.

The first step into the water, and his heart almost stopped. By God, the water was cold. He had never felt water that cold. He tried to hurry, but the rocks under his feet felt as if they were covered in slime. Two more quicker steps and he slipped and fell face-first with a splash. The water was only deep enough to make noise; Nimri felt the pain shooting through his knee, and knew the skin had been scraped off his palm. He felt like shouting, but his anger always boiled over at the times when he could not make a sound.

Afraid that if he got up he would only fall again, he crawled across those cursed rocks until the water was deep enough to swim in. At least the cold was dulling the pain in his knee, but then his legs were turning numb.

The fall had disoriented him. He could not see the boat in the fog, and it was no longer making any noise. He might even swim right by it, then turn in circles, not being able to find the shore again before his limbs froze. *God is great,* Nimri repeated to himself.

A few more strokes, and off to his left he thought he saw a darker shape inside the fog. He swam toward it. The plastic bag his arms were wrapped around was really keeping him afloat.

It was the boat, God be praised. But it was the bow of the boat. Once again Nimri wanted to shout out his frustrations, but he knew God in His Infinite wisdom was testing him. He could no longer feel his feet. His breath was coming in gasps.

There was a shining metal ladder at the back of the boat. Nimri grabbed it with his left hand and threw the clothes bag into the boat. He was moving, even though he could not feel his feet on the ladder. As soon as he was out of the water to his waist, hands grabbed his arms and pulled him up.

Then, soaked and shivering uncontrollably, he was locked into a tight embrace.

"Brother Abdallah," the black man exclaimed into his ear. "You are with us at last. God be praised."

Nimri's teeth were chattering so hard he could barely get the words out. "A blanket."

"A blanket," the black man grandly commanded the shorter, stocky Arab who was the only other person on the boat.

The Arab didn't move.

"A blanket," the black man repeated. "Quickly, the brother is freezing."

"There is no blanket," the Arab replied finally.

"You forgot the blankets?" the black man said in disgust.

"Open the bag. My clothes." Nimri did not think he would ever be able to get the words out.

They tore open the plastic bag and helped Nimri into his clothes. Which was necessary, since his fingers felt like pencils. The black man made the Arab put his jacket around Nimri, and they both rubbed his limbs.

Nimri still felt like ice even inside his clothes. His teeth were still chattering, but he could finally get more words out. "Quickly, brother Muhammad, we must be away."

Muhammad al-Sharif snapped to the Arab, "You heard him. Start the engine." While he pulled up the anchor.

The engine came up but the boat didn't move. Nimri sat glumly in the fishing seat at the rear while the cold wind beat his face. *Of course* the boat would not move.

The Arab kept goosing the engine, and eventually the boat moved with another grinding of rocks against hull. Then the wheel was turned hard, the boat whipped around in a half circle, and they sped out into the lake.

They soon broke free from the fog. A carpet of stars blended down into the brighter nuggets of light along the far shoreline. Nimri knew that was the United States.

His shivering had subsided, but he still felt frozen to the bone. Though the parka hood was wrapped tightly around his head, Nimri could see another set of lights in the distance. Except these were moving. "Bother Muhammad," he called out, pointing. "What is that?"

Al-Sharif was quickly beside him. "A cargo ship. Have no fear. The lake is huge. There are only two large Coast Guard cutters, and few smaller craft. If they come near, we will see them on the radar detector first."

"Very good," said Nimri. Then he remembered something. He felt through the plastic bag until he found his satellite phone. Then he threw it into the water.

"Why did you do that?" al-Sharif asked.

"A suspicious call," said Nimri. Al-Sharif was still giving him an inquisitive look. "No matter. Now I am safe with you, I no longer need it."

"I am sorry about the blankets. Dawood is young. He becomes excited, and he forgets."

"No matter, brother. But we must remember everything from now on."

"It will never happen again. I swear it to you."

"I believe you," said Nimri. "We must all speak English from now on, also. No Arabic."

"Okay," said al-Sharif, in English for the first time.

Even though their trip from Canada was across a narrow part of the lake, the crossing still took time. The small sport fishing boat slapped into every wave, and Nimri was feeling nauseated in addition to frozen. The GPS brought them back to a line of concrete boat ramps that were deserted during weekdays.

A minivan with a boat trailer attached was backed down onto the ramp. The trailer was in the water. Another Arab was waiting. He caught the thrown line and winched the boat onto the trailer.

Nimri had been swallowing down his vomit for the past half hour, and was grateful to be on dry land. Al-Sharif now formally introduced him to the two Arabs. Dawood, who had driven the boat. The one at the van was Omar. Taller and more muscular than Dawood. And older. In his late twenties, while Nimri was certain Dawood was barely twenty-one.

He would ask their ages only when there was a need to put them in their place. They were both in awe of him, and to make it easier he would have to keep it that way. No familiarity.

As they went to get into the van he heard Omar say to Dawood in Arabic, "You forgot the blankets and towels, fool. God's mercy that the commander is still alive."

"Speak English," al-Sharif hissed to Omar, with one eye on Nimri. "Only English from now on."

"As you wish," Omar said. Nimri noted that he was less deferential to al-Sharif than was Dawood.

They took the boat up the ramp, Omar driving and al-Sharif guiding. In the parking area above the ramp, al-Sharif unhooked the trailer from the hitch.

"Will this be noticed?" Nimri asked him.

Al-Sharif shook his head. "Tourists leave their boats here all the time while they go off to get food or bait. No one notices a boat parked near a boat ramp."

"Very good," said Nimri.

Dawood overheard them. "We are leaving the boat?"

"What do you think?" asked al-Sharif, continuing what he was doing.

"But this is my brother-in-law's boat," said Dawood, appealing to Nimri.

Nimri could scarcely believe it. What did he expect them to do, drop the boat off at the brother-in-law's house on their way? Drag the boat with them on the mission? He didn't say anything, though, beyond giving Dawood a stare that was as cold as his body felt. This was for al-Sharif to handle. But Nimri did not like the fact that the boat had been borrowed from a family member, not purchased or stolen. Al-Sharif had been given money to buy a boat. It bore watching.

"Use your head," al-Sharif snapped.

Dawood looked resentful. He seemed about to say

something, then glanced over at Nimri and decided to keep his peace.

Nimri did not like starting off with reservations about his companions. At least Omar had the wit to turn the van heater all the way up. Soon the others were pulling their jackets off, though he could still feel the chill.

It was also in the van that he got his first good look at al-Sharif. Only six years since their first meeting in Kandahar, though al-Sharif looked older. It made Nimri wonder how much older *he* looked. Nimri remembered the fire-breathing convert, brimming over with his new faith, who had been carefully watched at the madrasa, the religious school in Quetta, Pakistan. Then passed along until he reached the Afghan camp. Only halting Arabic, and how pleased he had been to hear the English Nimri had honed at the University of North Carolina after leaving Egypt for the first time.

Each night at the camp they screened the forms that each new arrival had filled in. Looking for special talents. A non–Arab American was like a gift from God. But also could be a trap of Satan. How carefully they had watched al-Sharif, allowing him only the basic weapons training, looking to see if he was familiar with heavy military weapons and grenades the way an American special services operative would be. Every word that issued from his mouth was heard by men alert to falsehood. Finally al-Sharif had been brought to a room where Nimri told him, "We have work for you."

Then the advanced clandestine training in earnest. Nimri had tested him repeatedly. Al-Sharif had never failed. A thief brought before him, told it was an American spy. And no hesitation, emptying his Kalashnikov into the man almost before the guards could get out of the way.

The same man now? A few pounds heavier, but that was to be expected. Nimri remembered that the food in the camp had given al-Sharif diarrhea until he could barely walk. No fat though, still lean on the six-foot frame. The once bushy Afro now cut close, though with streaks of white visible. The lighter black skin of the Africans whose blood had mixed with that of their slave masters. And the same aquiline nose that Nimri had always flattered him for, to al-Sharif's delight, saying it marked Arab blood.

But the same man? Nimri knew he would have to watch carefully. But what he said was, "It pleases my eyes to see you, brother. I have missed you since Kandahar. You look well and strong."

Al-Sharif was pleased. "I am. And I've missed you. Did you have any trouble in Canada?"

"No. The Canadians are very polite. I traveled on one of their passports."

"It's the best border to cross. Here." He passed Nimri a pistol in a leather holster. And a leather pouch with two magazines.

Nimri examined the pistol and checked the chamber. It was loaded. "Heckler and Koch. Excellent."

"Snap the loops onto your belt, and wear the holster inside the waistband of your pants," said al-Sharif. "The magazine pouch the same, on the other side."

It took a moment for Nimri to figure out, but when he did, the pistol and magazines were perfectly concealed.

"There's work to do," said al-Sharif.

"There is," said Nimri. "Important work."

"What work, brother?" Dawood broke in.

Nimri's expression turned to ice again. "Work that you will know when it is time for you to know."

Behind the wheel, Omar shook his head.

They stopped at a Burger King for food. Nimri ordered three cups of tea to warm his still-frozen belly. The hot liquid was a blessing, even though it tasted like hot urine. He'd almost forgotten the American tea, which came in cloth bags. God willing, he would not be there long enough to have to get used to it again.

17

"So it was Whitefish Bay," said Special Agent Ted Weaver.

Beth Royale was looking out over the water. "Canada's what? Twenty miles away?"

"Twenty, thirty. Depending on where they landed."

"And they don't need their boat anymore?"

"They don't need their boat anymore. Ranger drove by it all morning, not thinking anything of it, before he checked it out and ran the number."

Paul Moody walked over after conferring with the crime scene technicians on the boat. "It's definitely been in the water. Gas tank's just about empty."

"Thanks, Paul," said Beth, giving him more than the usual maintenance. He'd been temperamental since she'd gone to meet the informant with Weaver and didn't bring him along. "At least they didn't blow anything up with the boat. That gives us time. I was afraid they were already moving into an attack and we didn't have any."

"Even money al-Sharif's prints are all over the boat," said Weaver. "When he stole cars he never wore gloves— always went in bare a . . ."

Beth rolled her eyes. "I'm familiar with the word *ass*, Ted."

"Sorry."

"Well, get over it."

Supervisory Special Agent Benjamin Timmins had been off in a far corner of the parking area talking on his cell phone. "Anything new on the boat?" he asked.

"Other than it's definitely been in the water, nothing," said Beth. "No tire tracks, so we have no idea what vehicle towed it."

"People in remote places notice things," said Timmins. "We've got agents and state police canvassing every home and business in the area."

The Bureau playbook, thought Beth. Just dump a load of people on a problem. "Ben, when they were done with it they just left the boat here. To me that means they were planning on moving so fast they didn't care about us finding it."

"Or they're just stupid," said Timmins. "Here comes Karen the Spook. Let's see what she has to say."

In the aftermath of 9/11, CIA intelligence analysts were permanently attached to the FBI in an attempt to smooth the flow of intelligence material. Which had been totally chaotic before. According to the CIA, that was because their FBI liaisons were country-clubbing mediocrities, and the FBI computers and dissemination procedures slower and less reliable than the Pony Express, and because the FBI would then leak to the media blaming the Agency for their own deficiencies. According to the FBI, it was because the CIA withheld everything of value to feather their own nest, then leaked to the media blaming the Bureau for every disaster. Neither viewpoint was necessarily incorrect.

Spook is a sometimes complimentary, sometimes not, term for a CIA agent. Karen the Spook, as she was called by the agents, was an experienced analyst who, Beth thought, was worth her weight in gold. She had real-time access to the CIA databases and, more importantly, knew how to interpret intelligence reports. Which were never black and white, and usually contradictory.

Karen was short, with blue-green eyes and shoulder-length brown hair. Very assertive, with an evil laugh. She'd originally been in the operations or spying side of the Company, but an accident she always claimed was a car crash had left her with a replacement hip and rebuilt leg. Aside from having to become an analyst, her only complaint about the accident was that she could no longer wear her favorite spike-heel boots. She'd occasionally look down at her sensible shoes and sigh.

Beth suspected that Karen had been sent to the FBI because she was a woman. They'd become fast friends. Karen loved sports and loved to bet on them. Not money—just something humiliating to the loser.

She'd been in the van playing with her secure communications equipment.

"What's up?" Timmins demanded as soon as she joined the group.

Karen consulted her notes. "Day before yesterday the Al Qaeda coordinator for Southeast Asia was taken out in Malaysia. His satellite phone and names to go with the numbers in the phone directory were recovered. The numbers were called, and the NSA ran traces. One of them was Abdallah Karim Nimri. And they traced the call to Parry Sound, Ontario."

"Well, we know who al-Sharif and his boys picked up," said Beth.

"And every intelligence asset we have is focused on Asia for the president's trip," said Timmins.

Everyone else was digesting the fact that a top Al Qaeda operative was in the United States with a non-Arab supporting him.

"Royal Canadian Mounted Police is still trying to run down how he got into Canada and what ID he's traveling on," said Karen. "The only thing they know is that he didn't do the usual: get off a plane, apply for political asylum, and then get released into town. He probably flew in on a non–Middle Eastern passport."

"Who got the guy in Malaysia?" Weaver asked. No one could resist a war story.

Karen gave it some thought before answering. "Two Missionaries. They hid in a cane field all day in hundred-degree heat, reconning the house the target was hiding in. It looked like he might fly, so they went in that night and took him out along with two bodyguards."

"Two on three," said Weaver, impressed. "And they got away clean?"

Karen nodded.

Beth couldn't hold it in any longer. "We *are* going to raise the terror threat level and put al-Sharif's picture in the media, aren't we?" she said to Timmins.

"I just got off the phone with Washington about that," said Timmins. "The answer is no."

"You're kidding," said Beth. "Why the hell not?"

"Justice is afraid it'll end up just like the D.C. sniper case. A total media circus, public going ape-shit, a million worthless tips to run down, local cops leaking everything to the press."

"So we only raise the threat level when the administration's in political trouble," said Beth. "Not when there actually is a team of terrorists driving somewhere in the United States to attack something."

"Beth, that's the biggest banana skin you've ever seen in your life," said Timmins. "And I advise you not to step on it."

Since Beth had already articulated what everyone else was thinking, and gotten in trouble for it, no one else said a word.

Beth said, "Fine, Ben. Then what are we going to do?"

"Do we have a photo of any kind on Nimri?" Timmins asked Karen.

"Nothing," said Karen. "Neither does any friendly agency. That they're willing to share with us, at least."

"Okay," said Timmins. "Nationwide law enforcement APB on al-Sharif and his two Arab accomplices. Keep working leads here and in Dearborn. Hope we get something from the Canadians."

"And you think that nationwide all-points bulletin isn't going to leak to the media?" said Beth.

"If it does, it's not my responsibility," Timmins replied.

Beth just nodded slightly, as if that was the answer she'd expected.

Weaver and Moody found something else to do just then.

Karen took Beth's arm. "Let me ask you a question."

When they were out of earshot, Beth said, "What?"

"Oh, nothing," said Karen, flashing her killer smile. "I just thought I'd better get you out of there."

Beth shook her head, still royally steamed.

"Shouldn't tell you this," said Karen. "The two Missionaries were Ed Storey and Lee Troy."

"Ed's a very good man," said Beth. "Next time I get pissed off about my job, I need to think about him and Lee out there in a cane field all day long. Thanks for telling me."

"There is something else," said Karen. "Patriots at Redskins on Sunday."

"You poor deluded homer," said Beth. "The Pats are going to cream them."

"Oh?" Karen said demurely. "Name your poison."

They did this all the time, and Beth knew Karen's style. "You have to wear a Dallas jersey to the next available home game. In plain sight. And a cowboy hat. *And* I get your husband's ticket, so I can watch."

"Bitch," said Karen. "Okay, the Skins win and you have to go to a country bar and ride the mechanical bull."

Beth opened her mouth to say something.

"*While* wearing a red cowboy hat and red cowboy boots," Karen added.

"Bitch," said Beth. "There will be no recording of this. None of your frigging spy cameras. And no one from the office will be there."

"Agreed," Karen said reluctantly. "Do we have a bet?"

"We have a bet," said Beth. "But I think it's going to be a while before either of us gets a chance to collect."

18

They had been driving for almost twelve hours. Nimri let them stop only for gasoline and drive-through food. They made more of those stops than usual, because he only let one man leave the van at each location. Three Arabs traveling together was going to attract attention.

Soon he thought the whining to go to the bathroom was going to drive him mad. They drank American soft drinks in cups the size of buckets and wondered why they had to urinate every fifteen minutes. And then the bickering over which fast food restaurant to stop at. As if they tasted any different.

It would begin as soon as the bags came in the window. Al-Sharif always taking it upon himself to distribute the food, and always serving Nimri first.

Omar ordering 7-Up in restaurants that only had Sprite, and Sprite in restaurants that only offered 7-Up. And complaining bitterly when he did not get what he ordered.

"This isn't my chicken sandwich," said Dawood. "This is a hamburger."

Al-Sharif rooting around in the bag. "There's no chicken sandwich." Then to Omar, behind the wheel, "Didn't you order a chicken sandwich for him?"

"I ordered a chicken sandwich," Omar replied. "I order a chicken sandwich every time."

"Eat the hamburger," al-Sharif told Dawood.

"I don't like hamburgers."

"Then eat nothing," Nimri finally snapped.

Momentary silence. "I will eat *his* french fries and apple pie," Dawood announced, pointing to Omar.

"Fine," said Omar. "Eat my french fries and apple pie in good health. Next time I'll kill you a chicken myself."

Nimri finally noticed the cardboard cup rack. "Did I not tell you to order the smaller size drinks?"

"Sorry, brother," Omar replied.

"Drink them slowly, at least," Nimri ordered. "For a change." *I have traveled alone too long,* he thought.

The miles passed. But all of America looked the same beside a highway, Nimri felt.

He was asleep and heard sirens. He woke up and thought he'd been dreaming. Except he still heard them. Disoriented, he looked back and saw the blue and red flashing lights. "What has happened?"

"Dawood was speeding," Omar announced.

"I told you to drive under the speed limit," said al-Sharif.

"I was passing and the signs changed," Dawood protested. "It's not my fault."

"Shut up," Nimri commanded. To Dawood he said, "Pull over immediately. Admit you were speeding. Accept the ticket. Do not argue. No one is to do *anything.* Keep your hands in your laps. Do not make this policeman nervous. Do you all understand?"

Dawood followed the instructions and pulled the van over onto the shoulder. The white Ohio Highway Patrol cruiser settled in behind them.

Al-Sharif, in the passenger seat, found the registration

in the glove compartment. "Have your license ready," he hissed at Dawood. "Put your window down, stupid."

The van windows were tinted. Nimri watched the trooper come up. He was wearing the strange hat American highway police wore, with the brim that went all the way around. Black pants, gray shirt, black tie. His hand was on his pistol. Nimri prayed that none of the others would do anything stupid.

The trooper looked closely through the tint to get an idea of who was in the van. Then he was just behind the driver's window. "License and registration, please."

Dawood handed them over.

The trooper's head loomed in the window as he took a better look at them. He glanced at the documents. "This isn't your vehicle, sir?"

"It's mine, sir," said Omar, sitting behind al-Sharif. He leaned forward to pass Dawood his driver's license. Then had to say, "Give it to the officer," before Dawood woke up and took it.

The trooper took the documents back to his cruiser.

Nimri looked back. He could see the trooper's mouth moving. He was talking on the radio.

"What's happening?" Dawood asked nervously.

"Shut up and keep cool," al-Sharif told him.

Five minutes passed.

The trooper walked back up to the van. But Nimri noticed that he did not have his ticket book out. And he did not tell them why they had been stopped. The first thing he said, to Dawood, was, "Where are you headed?"

And the fool froze. "Ah . . . ah . . . ah . . ."

Nimri cringed as the stuttering continued.

Then Dawood blurted out, "Washington."

Nimri could hardly believe his ears.

The trooper said, "Step out of the van."

Nimri twisted in his seat, toward Omar, to unsnap the seat belt.

The trooper saw it and said, "Just the driver."

When Nimri turned back the pistol was in his hand. He fired through his window, just behind Dawood's head. The glass exploded.

The trooper stumbled back and pulled his pistol just as al-Sharif joined in. Omar bailed out the side door.

Nimri's pistol stopped working. He noticed the slide was back and thumbed the button to drop the empty magazine, fumbling at his belt for a new one. Al-Sharif was still firing, leaning over Dawood.

The trooper fell back on the ground, managed to get up, and lurched back toward his cruiser.

Just as Omar came around the back of the van, firing.

The trooper fell back on the ground. Omar, remembering bulletproof vests, closed the distance and kept firing into the head.

Cars were swerving all over the highway.

"Get the licenses and registration," Nimri shouted to Omar, though without sticking his head out the window. He knew the American police cars had video cameras. His ears were ringing from the gunfire. "Is anyone shot?" he shouted.

"No," al-Sharif shouted back.

"You drive," Nimri ordered.

Omar found the papers propped up on the computer screen inside the cruiser. He sprinted back to the van.

"Quickly," Nimri said to al-Sharif. "More police will be here soon."

As al-Sharif stepped on the gas, Nimri kicked the remaining glass from his window, so it would look as if it was open. "Take the next exit."

The sign said ZANESVILLE. Nimri watched through the rear window. A red car followed them onto the exit. "Slow down," he said to al-Sharif.

Al-Sharif tapped the brake, and the car behind responded in an even more exaggerated way. A man was driving, a woman beside him on her mobile phone.

"Take the next side street," Nimri ordered. "Good citizens are following us, talking to the police on their phone." To Omar he said, "Be ready. We go out the door when I signal. We will stop this conversation. Is your pistol reloaded?"

"Yes."

Another side street, with trees on the corner. "Turn again here," Nimri said, pointing. "Stop when I tell you. Omar and I will get out. Then you continue slowly. When you hear firing, come back for us quickly."

"Got it," al-Sharif replied.

As soon as al-Sharif made the turn, and they were out of sight of the street they'd just been on, Nimri said, "Stop."

He and Omar went out the door, and the van continued on. They ducked behind the trees, though the two spies would be concentrating on the road. "As soon as they turn, while they are still slow," he said to Omar.

The car took the turn and they ran out of the trees, firing through the windshield at the driver. He might have saved them by stepping on the gas instead of the brake, but did not. Nimri was fascinated by how the bullet holes appeared in the glass as he shot. The driver's head fell back against his seat. The woman threw her phone out the window and screamed, "Don't kill me! Please don't kill me!" Nimri moved to shoot her through the open window.

The van, backing up fast, came to a stop with tires squealing.

"Go!" Nimri shouted to Omar.

"Should we make sure of them?" Omar shouted back.

"Into the van!" Nimri yelled. It did not matter whether the Americans were alive or dead, only that they were no longer following.

"Quickly," he said to al-Sharif, as he slammed the side door shut.

"We need a new car, fast," said al-Sharif.

"That I leave to you," Nimri replied.

It took them three wrong turns and racing down residential lanes and past a park until they found their way back onto a main street. There was a parking lot behind a business building. Al-Sharif pulled in.

Sirens could be heard in the distance. Following al-Sharif's directions, Nimri tore through the green duffel bags in the back of the van. He couldn't find it in the first. Then in the second there was the small, flat plastic toolbox.

Al-Sharif found what he wanted, a white Buick with Ohio plates. He parked right behind it, and Nimri passed him the toolbox. "Look now for whatever you do not want to leave behind," he told the others.

Al-Sharif bent casually over the door of the Buick as he slipped the Slim Jim into the window frame. He yanked up and the car alarm went off. But there is one sound that absolutely no one pays any attention to, and that is a car alarm in a parking lot. Al-Sharif disappeared inside the car, and a few seconds later the alarm cut off with an abbreviated yelp. A few seconds more and the trunk sprang open.

"Quickly, quickly," said Nimri. They threw the green canvas duffel bags inside. He now noticed the bullet holes in the side of the van. That and no passenger window would attract attention.

Dawood was picking up empty shell casings from the floor of the van. "Leave them," Nimri said impatiently. The police already had the description of the van. The cases were meaningless. There would be no trial.

"You drive," al-Sharif said to Omar. "Follow me in the van."

The Buick seats were comfortable, but the smell of cigarettes made Nimri want one badly. He noticed the short screwdriver sticking out from the steering column in place of a key. Then he studied the road atlas while Omar followed al-Sharif down the road.

Al-Sharif was clever. He found a parking space against the side of a building, against which he parked the side of the van with the bullet holes and missing window. A sign warned that there was no public parking, and all vehicles would be towed. Nimri prayed that would happen.

Al-Sharif replaced Omar behind the wheel. Nimri had found where they were. "The police will be waiting for us back on Highway 70. We will take this Route 60 south, until it joins with Highway 77. The police will expect us to go east. But we will go south, into West Virginia and then Virginia. And only then turn north. It will be a long journey, but safer. Are we agreed?"

Al-Sharif and Omar in the front seat nodded. Nimri paid no attention to Dawood beside him. He gave directions and they pulled out, driving the speed limit. A police car passed them, lights flashing. It did not turn around.

"Brother Muhammad," he said, "each new state we pass into, we will need a new car. With license plates of that state."

"Maybe more often than that," al-Sharif said grimly. "We *have* to keep changing cars."

"I leave it in your hands," said Nimri.

A helicopter fluttered back and forth overhead. Its sound faded as they turned south, and they saw no more police.

"God is great, brothers," Nimri said. "Truly God is with us."

"All praise to God," the others murmured.

Nimri leaned forward to put his hands on al-Sharif's and Omar's shoulders. "You conducted yourselves well, brothers. You kept your heads in battle. And you," he said to Omar, "blocking the infidel from his car and consigning him to the fires of hell. We are in your debt. And, brother Muhammad, who moved and drove so coolly. Well done."

He now turned to Dawood, who was waiting for it. Nimri merely asked a question. "Washington?"

Dawood seemed to shrink in size.

"You could think of nothing else?" said Nimri. "Nothing except to tell the policeman that four of the Faithful were traveling to Washington? To visit the Smithsonian, perhaps? The Lincoln Memorial? Mount Vernon?"

Dawood's stammer was even worse. "I . . . I . . . I'm sorry, brothers. I couldn't think of anything. Not one city. Not one town."

"When have you ever thought?" said Omar.

"Be quiet," said Nimri, cutting them all off. "You have blundered," he said to Dawood. "But you are also God's instrument, as He ever tests us. Your blunder allowed us to prove ourselves to Him, and feel His deliverance. But you must not blunder again. You must prove yourself worthy. Will you do this?"

Dawood was near tears. "I swear before God, brother Abdallah. I swear before God."

19

The Michigan Air National Guard Blackhawk helicopter settled down, without a lot of clearance for the rotors, in a parking lot near the Zanesville, Ohio, police station.

Out stepped Supervisory Special Agent Benjamin Timmins, his deputy, two assistants, Beth Royale and Paul Moody, and Karen the Spook.

Beth had been at many of these scenes, and they were all the same. Cruisers from every nearby jurisdiction, all parked with lights flashing. Why? It was policy. It was dramatic. Dramatic for the other half of the equation, outside the line of cruisers. A line of television station mobile vans. One to feed off the other. TV lights going on and off, cutting the darkness as the reporters did their stand-up.

Closer to the station, a million cops drinking coffee and gossiping with each other until someone gave them something to do.

Inside the station, the FBI windbreakers getting that look from everyone. Timmins did the grip-and-grin with the local chief of police, who was looking like a deer in the headlights from all the attention. The special agent in charge of the Cincinnati field office was also there. Zanesville was his jurisdiction, even though he'd had to fly across the state to get there. And a major from the Ohio Highway Patrol.

With the sheer number of people, just the noise of everyone talking in a normal tone of voice was like a dull roar. All the brass and the FBI pushed past everyone else and made their way to the station conference room. A TV and video player were already set up. Karen the Spook immediately appropriated a corner of the room and got her laptop fired up.

"Chief Gast," Timmins said to the Zanesville man, "why don't you take us through the sequence of events?"

Beth had to give him credit: Timmins was smooth. Treat the locals to a quick hand job; ensure their cooperation; get everything from them—give them nothing.

Chief Gast was just about to start when the Highway Patrol major shouldered his way in. "At 2047 hours on Interstate 70, Trooper Andrew McLaughlin executed a speeding stop on a blue 2000 Toyota Sienna minivan, Michigan license GVT-8007. He ran the license and registration, which were clean. The occupants, three Arab males and one African-American male, aroused his suspicions. He was informed of the FBI terrorism alert, and backup was dispatched to his location." He slid a tape into the machine and pressed Play.

It was the tape from the cruiser video system. Everyone kept their game face on as they watched the trooper die. From Special Agent Weaver's mug book of Dearborn Islamic militants, Beth recognized Omar delivering the coup de grace behind the van. She'd been counting. The entire gunfight lasted just over twenty seconds. That was typical. After the van drove off the major stopped the tape.

Now Chief Gast jumped back in. "At 9:06 PM our 911 system received a call from two witnesses to the shooting." He produced a mini tape recorder and played a copy of the 911 audio tape.

"Nine-one-one. What is your emergency?"

A woman's voice, very excited. "We just saw a police officer shot."

"Ma'am, what is your location?"

"Interstate 70. They shot him on the highway. We're following them now."

"Who are you following, ma'am?"

"The people who shot him." An unintelligible male voice in the background. Then the woman again. "They're in a blue van, Michigan GVT-8007. They're taking the 22 exit."

"Ma'am, what is your name?"

"Betty Adams." She gave each street they turned on, the operator cautioning her not to get too close.

Then, "They just turned. I can't see the street sign yet. I can't see them. Oh, they're down at the end of the street."

The popping sound of gunshots, and a piercing scream. A noise that sounded to Beth like the phone hitting the ground. The male voice shouting, the woman screaming, "God, don't kill me! Please don't kill me!" More gunfire. A car door slamming. The sound of tires.

"Dennis and Betty Adams," said Chief Gast. "From South Zanesville. Both pronounced dead on the scene. They were ambushed as they turned the corner. Same nine-millimeter shell casings as the interstate shooting." He paused. "All my cruisers were responding to the interstate. This went down ten blocks away."

"The van?" said Timmins.

"Recovered in a parking lot off Main Street. We also had a 2002 white Buick Park Avenue, Ohio BV-2786, stolen off Main Street at approximately the same time."

"How far from here is that?" the Cincinnati special agent in charge asked.

The chief turned red. "Three blocks. All my cars were on the interstate."

"We'll need every other stolen vehicle," said Timmins. "Just in case."

"That's every one," said Chief Gast. "We don't get many grand theft autos. Don't get many murders, either."

"It's on the air," said the Cincinnati special agent in charge.

The Highway Patrol major added, "It's possible they got back onto 70, but roadblocks were up at Cambridge and Wheeling, West Virginia, within fifteen minutes."

"Thank you, Major," said Timmins. "Thanks, Chief."

At that all the FBI agents moved over to Karen's corner of the room. The chief and the major both looked at each other. It was quite obvious they weren't invited.

Karen had already called a national highway map up on her computer. Everyone bent over it.

"Washington or New York," said Beth.

"Or Baltimore, or Philadelphia, or Norfolk Navy Base," said Timmins.

Beth shook her head. "New York or Washington, Ben." She didn't say anything more about threat levels.

And neither did Timmins. "They're going to be stealing more cars. We're going to have to tie in every report that comes in within twenty miles of every interstate east of West Virginia."

"It'll be a day or more from now before all of today's even come in," said Moody.

Beth inwardly cringed, and waited for it.

Timmins let him have it. "We're not going to catch them from stolen vehicle reports. We're going to use the stolen vehicle reports to determine their destination."

"Are you taking this?" the Cincinnati special agent in charge asked, knowing Counterterrorism took priority now.

"No, this is yours," said Timmins. "We're going back to Washington and work it from there."

20

A doorbell rang in Manassas, Virginia. Yasmin Oan came from the kitchen, wiping her hands on a cloth. She opened the front door. And froze. He husband always told her to look before answering the door. Today she wished she had.

"Good day to you, sister."

The man spoke Arabic in the Egyptian dialect.

"You can't come in," Yasmin said quickly.

"Spoken like a good Muslim wife," said Abdallah Karim Nimri. Yasmin tried to shut the door; his left hand held it. When Nimri turned sideways his jacket opened and revealed the right hand holding the pistol. "Please do me two favors, sister Yasmin. Do not be afraid, and do not make any noise."

Yasmin took a step back. Her legs were shaking so hard she almost fell over. Nimri entered the house. Behind him Omar paused in the doorway and nodded at the car parked across the street.

"What do you want?" said Yasmin, her voice shaking like her legs. She felt stupid as soon as it left her lips. She knew what they wanted—only the particulars were a mystery. But it was as if her mouth was giving voice to all her terrors.

"To speak to your husband," Nimri replied pleasantly.

"To stay with you for a day or two. Then we will leave you in peace."

Yasmin wore her skepticism across her face.

"You have my promise," said Nimri.

Yasmin's face also made plain what she thought of that. From the top of the stairs, "Mom?"

"Ah, Steven," Nimri said in English. "Come down and join us."

No response. Nimri turned to Yasmin with a look that chilled her. "Steven!" she shouted. "Come down right now!"

A dark-haired boy came down the stairs slowly.

"It's good to meet you, Steven," said Nimri. "Your uncle was my friend."

"Then why do you have a gun?"

The boy was so calm and self-possessed he made Nimri uneasy. Perhaps he was retarded. "How old are you, boy?"

"Twelve."

Nimri moved closer to him. "Steven, this is serious. You cannot leave this house without my permission. You cannot contact anyone outside this house without my permission. If you do any of these things, your mother will die. Do you understand?"

Nimri expected the boy to cry. Or beg. The boy did none of these things. Steven merely stared up at him and said, "It is written that he who kills a believer by design shall burn in hell forever."

Nimri had not expected to have the Holy Koran thrown in his face by a child. He felt like hitting the boy with his pistol, but held himself in. "Such are God's words to the Prophet, peace be upon him. It is also written that if a believer commits aggression, it is permissible to fight against the aggressors until they submit to God's judgment. To refuse to support jihad is to commit aggression upon the faithful."

"So you say what is written," Steven shot back. "It is also written: fear Me, and do not sell My revelations for a paltry end."

"I will not debate the word of God with you, boy. God the Merciful and Compassionate will judge us all. Listen to me and know that what I say I will do, I will do. Now, do you own a mobile phone? Do not lie to me."

"I don't own a cell phone," said Steven.

"Then go upstairs with this man. Unplug all the phones and bring them down. Any computers also." Nimri nodded to Omar. Then to Steven, "Remember your mother."

When they went up the stairs Nimri turned to Yasmin. "Sister, if you do what I say you and your family will come to no harm." He repeated his warning to Steven, but this time made him the object. "Do you understand?"

She at least did not argue with him.

Al-Sharif and Dawood came in the front door. "Bring in the bags?" asked al-Sharif.

"Wait until dark," said Nimri.

Steven and Omar came down the stairs, Steven carrying telephones and Omar a computer tower.

"Sister Yasmin," said Nimri, "now that Steven has returned to us, perhaps you should make some tea. After you give me your mobile phone."

Yasmin handed it to him and went into the kitchen.

Commuting in northern Virginia had been known to literally drive people crazy. Joseph Oan never minded it. He spent all day in traffic anyway, and he knew all the back roads between his work in Springfield and his home in Manassas. He was singing along with the car radio, and his hair was wet. He always showered before leaving work—his wife hated the smell of gasoline.

After parking in the driveway, Oan walked back out to the street to roll the empty trash container back to the garage. Steven should have done that, but getting a boy to remember anything to do with work was an impossibility.

Closing the garage door, Oan went through the gate in the wooden fence that bounded his backyard. Steven was usually kicking his football against the garage when he came home. He must have had extra homework.

Oan couldn't resist touring his garden. He was going to have to prune his roses back before it got any colder. Maybe this weekend. The grass needed to be mown again, but in a week or two he wouldn't have to worry about that until spring.

The back door was open. Trying to get his wife to lock doors was like trying to get his son to do his chores.

"I'm home," he called out. No answer. Oan's stomach tightened slightly, registering his alarm. His family was always home when he returned from work. His wife's car was in the driveway. Could something have happened that they had to call an ambulance? "Is anyone home?" he called out again.

Oan moved faster through the kitchen and into the living room. At the sight of his wife and son on the couch he stopped, relief flooding through him. Then he followed his wife's eyes and his gaze found the two Arabs sitting off to the side. His stomach contracted again. A noise behind him made him turn about. Two more appeared, cutting off his retreat.

"Greetings, Youssif al-Oan," said Abdallah Karim Nimri.

Oan's chest felt numb. He could not move his legs. It was as if, wide awake, he had walked into the exact same nightmare he had in his sleep once a month. "Who are you?" he said, and just like his wife felt like an idiot for saying it.

"Friends of your brother, Rashid," said Nimri.

Oan did not ask them what they wanted. He knew exactly what they wanted. He looked over helplessly at his wife.

Even though he didn't ask, Nimri told him anyway. "We require your hospitality," he said.

21

"Sweet," said Lee Troy. "Welcome home. Great job. Thanks for uncovering the plot. Thanks for saving the fucking day. Take a slap on the ass out of petty cash—now go out and play with the FBI."

"You're sounding a little bitter," said Ed Storey. "Were you expecting a cash bonus and tickets to Maui? You'll get over it, eventually."

They were down in the basement of their office building headquarters, in the equipment lockers. Each operator had a gear locker the size of a single-car garage. Parachutes, diving gear, mountaineering equipment. Two of every kind of weapon, from the mini Glock pistol to the brand-new 7.62mm MK 48 machine gun. One to train with and shoot to pieces, the other—pristine—to take on operations.

Storey was stripped to the waist, removing his shoulder holster. He rummaged along a shelf until he found a padded leather holster with two short bands. He wrapped it around his left ankle, cinching the two Velcro-covered bands tight.

"Okay," said Troy. "So the Glock'll be backup." He slipped his SEAL standard SIG-Sauer P-226 9mm into the waistband holster just behind his right hip.

Storey did the same with his Delta Force Model 1911A1 .45 automatic.

"Don't you get tired of those seven-round magazines in that dinosaur pistol?" said Troy.

"You need your twenty-round mag," Storey replied. "Once you start peppering the bad guys with those little nine millimeters, they might get mad at you."

"Okay," said Troy, enjoying the eternal pistol caliber controversy. "What about long guns?"

"I'm worried about vehicles."

"I suppose the FBI would get a little twitchy about me packing an MK 48 in D.C."

"I think you can count on it," said Storey, removing the SOPMOD M-14 from his rifle rack. A new version of the 1960s-era M-14, commissioned by the SEALs, who in Afghanistan had become discouraged by how many times you needed to shoot someone with an M-4 carbine before they went down. The Special Operations Peculiar Modification was an M-14 with a sliding metal stock, a pistol grip, rail mountings for sights and lights, and the barrel cut back to the forward hand guards. A special muzzle brake handled the recoil. Troy mounted a four-power Trijicon Advanced Combat Optical Gunsight telescopic sight on his. Storey stuck with the Aimpoint red dot.

"Better load up some hollow-point along with the armor-piercing," said Troy, rooting around in his magazine boxes for some M-14 twenty-rounders. "We don't want to get in close quarters and have rounds going through three different walls."

"Just don't mix them up," Storey advised. "You know, you'd better bring a McMillan, too. We might need to take a long shot."

"Which one?" said Troy. "The .300 Winchester Magnum or the .50 caliber?"

"I was thinking the .50 cal.," said Storey. "What do you think?"

"The fifty," Troy replied. "It can stop a car or a man." The bolt-action sniper rifle was already in its case. "I'll go to the ammo locker." Troy volunteered because he knew Storey would send him anyway.

"Don't forget a breaching kit," said Storey. Then something popped into his head. "Oh, and stop by the tech locker and grab that prototype jammer."

"The Warlock?" said Troy.

"Yeah."

"Support's going to be pissed," said Troy. "They're still giving that thing the once-over."

"They're not here—let 'em bitch. You know, I'd like to take a couple of LAAWs, too," Storey said, referring to the 66mm one-shot antitank rocket launcher, "but the FBI really *would* shit."

"Running ops in the U.S. makes me nervous," said Troy. "If FBI agents end up in court, you just know our asses are going to get blamed for anything that happens. I don't want to go up in front of any grand jury."

The Posse Comitatus Act of 1878 made it unlawful for military personnel to act in a law enforcement capacity in the United States. But the president could suspend the act in the interest of national public safety. In that case the attorney general had to issue a finding determining if the specific circumstance warranted an exemption.

On May 3, 1994, President Bill Clinton signed Presidential Decision Directive 25, whose classified contents have never been released. A particular favorite of conspiracy theorists, who believed it outlined a plan for world government under the United Nations. Actually, PDD-25 was in response to the U.S. intervention in Kosovo, in the former Yugoslavia. It specified the lines of command and control for U.S forces participating in multinational peacekeeping operations. But another part of PDD-25 exempted Joint Special Operations Command—Delta Force/Combat Applications Group, SEAL Team Six/Naval Special Warfare Development Group, and the 160th Special Operations Aviation Regiment—from the Posse Comitatus Act. So, by the direction of the president, they could be used to enforce U.S. law without the attorney general issuing a specific exemption. The nice thing about making such a directive classified, from the government's point of view, was that then no one had to worry about any legal challenges.

"Probably," said Storey, conceding Troy's point. "So, as always, the best course of action is not to screw up. Oh, when you're in the ammo locker, just flash-bangs, okay?"

Troy had to chuckle. "If we tossed a frag in the U.S., they really would lock us up and throw away the key."

The FBI National Academy is located on the Marine Corps base at Quantico, Virginia. Twenty years ago marine second lieutenants from the nearby Basic School used to jog through the grounds. But in the age of terrorism the FBI Academy and the adjacent Drug Enforcement Administration Academy were walled in, tightly guarded, high-security areas. The only way for the average citizen to see it was to rent the movie *The Silence of the Lambs*, which was filmed on location. In addition to training new agents, the academy grounds also housed various technical units, a high-speed command center, the Hostage Rescue Team and its aviation component, and the Counterterrorism Division.

"Let me have your attention, please," Benjamin Timmins said to the roomful of agents.

That only cut down on the noise. It didn't stop it.

"Listen up," Timmins said, much louder. The room quieted. "Settle down." He tapped on the laptop mounted on the podium, and a PowerPoint presentation came up on the screen behind him.

They could live without food and water, but not PowerPoint, Beth Royale thought. As far as she was concerned, PowerPoint was the explanation for everything.

Because no idea too complex to be turned into a bullet that could fit on a slide could be permitted.

"According to the best analysis of the stolen vehicle reports," said Timmins, "we believe there's a ninety percent probability that the terrorist cell's destination is Washington. However, they've used deceptive measures before, so we have to concede the possibility of an attack elsewhere. Or that one or more additional cells is out there, preparing a coordinated attack or a series of attacks."

Well, that about covered every possible contingency, Beth thought. No one could ever accuse Timmins of not hedging his bets.

"The FAA's been notified," said Timmins. "There was no trace of nuclear material on the boat that went to Canada, but the Nuclear Emergency Search Teams have still been alerted. We have APBs out for the murder of the Ohio trooper. We're sure this Abdallah Karim Nimri was in the van, but we didn't get his face on the trooper's video. We do have makes on the other three, though. Even though we're treating it like nothing more than a traffic stop cop-killing, the media is starting to sniff around the terrorism aspect and I'd better not hear anything along those lines coming out of this office."

No, of course not, thought Beth. Timmins was the little Dutch boy, sticking his finger in the dike by threatening *them*, while the FBI bosses had lunch with their favorite national correspondents every week.

"The Hostage Rescue Team is on alert," said Timmins. He nodded to the HRT special agent in charge, standing off to the side. "Unfortunately, most of the military units are fully committed overseas. But what isn't is on alert." He paused, looking down from the podium to the front row of chairs. "Now, as Beth was about to ask, what are *we* going to do?"

Laughter. For a moment Beth wondered if her face had given her away. Then she gave Timmins the evil eye.

"Okay, Beth," Timmins said. "To answer the question, we're going to do the only thing we can do. Check out every hotel, motel, rest area, and camping park in northern Virginia, Maryland, and D.C. Follow up on all our previous leads. Visit and reinterview everyone on our watch and surveillance lists. We've broken them down for you and will assign them geographically. The New York field office will be taking these exact same steps.

"Now, we've got four suspects that we know of. So I'm not sending pairs of agents out on their own. We're getting everyone available from every federal enforcement agency. Secret Service is fully committed to the protection mission, but we have DEA, marshals, and . . . other agencies also. Let me welcome all of you here at this time, and thank you for your assistance. Every pair of FBI agents will be assigned two other officers."

Typical, Beth thought. The Bureau always had to be in control. Couldn't send four DEA agents off on their own to work the case—someone else might get the credit.

"I want to stress one thing," said Timmins. "No four-agent team is going to try and take down these suspects on their own. You get any indication of them at all, even a hunch, you secure the area and call it in. We'll get you backup and the Hostage Rescue Team. They used pistols on the Ohio trooper, but we don't know what else they might have. They could be planning a suicide attack, wearing explosives on their bodies, and if so they certainly wouldn't mind taking you with them."

"Doesn't that take care of the threat, then?" came a voice from the back, to more laughter from the crowd.

Beth knew Timmins hated being jocked around with while he was briefing. The agent who said it was going to end up checking the Washington sewer system.

"It takes care of the threat," Timmins said tightly. "If you can guarantee that no civilians get hurt or property gets damaged, feel free to encourage the suspects to blow you up."

His tone didn't allow for much laughter, and there wasn't any.

"Any questions so far?" said Timmins. There were none. "All right, you'll be given your team assignments and list of interviews. Stand by and we'll have those for you momentarily."

Storey and Troy were in the back of the room. In jeans, running shoes, and long-sleeve shirts, they stood out, since everyone else was in a suit. Storey wasn't going to try and move fast in a suit, no matter how professional it looked. Their jackets were off, revealing Storey's .45 and Troy's P-226, along with more extra magazines than *any* cop carried.

Neither weapon was standard in the federal law enforcement community. It was inevitable that as soon as Timmins was done they'd attract some curious soul.

"Who you guys with?"

Storey ignored him.

Troy said, "No one. We're just hanging out."

"No, really. Who you with?"

"Boy Scouts of America," said Troy, hoping he'd get the hint.

"Spooks, huh? Let me ask you something."

Troy sighed.

The other guy didn't even notice. "These people are all fanatic Muslims, right?" It must not have been a rhetorical question, because he didn't give Troy a chance to answer. "They're all willing to die, so death doesn't scare them. But their religion says they can't have anything to do with pork. So wouldn't wrapping them in a pig skin or something make them talk, make 'em think they're not going to heaven?"

Troy could hardly believe his ears. He was tempted to just walk away, but the guy carried a badge and couldn't be allowed to walk around thinking the way he did. "You mean pigs are to Muslims like garlic is to vampires?"

The irony flew right over the head. "Well . . ."

"The Koran says pork is unclean and forbidden," said Troy. "But it also says that whoever is compelled through necessity, intending neither to sin nor transgress, will find that Allah is forgiving and merciful."

A snort in response to that.

"You should read it some time," said Troy. "The nine-eleven hijackers drank alcohol and got lap dances. And since they were doing Allah's work they figured he'd forgive them."

Another contemptuous snort. Storey had already moved off.

"Excuse me," said Troy, and hurried to catch up.

"You through?" said Storey.

"Thanks for helping me out."

"Don't look at me. You were the one who let him start humping your leg."

"Man, if that's the way we know our enemy, it's a wonder anything's still standing around here."

"Don't speak too soon," said Storey. "In a few days it may not be."

"If he's the one who's going to be interviewing Muslims."

They came up behind her. Storey said, "Hello, Beth."

Beth whirled around, and her face opened up into a brilliant smile. "Ed! Lee! It's so great to see you two. You're going to be with us."

"Pull some strings?" said Storey.

Troy just loved to watch Storey around her. He became as bashful as a three-year-old.

"As long as it's nothing important, they give me what I want to shut me up," said Beth. "Guys, this is my partner, Paul Moody. Paul, Ed Storey and Lee Troy."

They all shook hands. Troy wondered how she'd drawn such a weenie. Then he reminded himself to be cool on the first impressions and snap judgments.

Beth said, "Ed, what's the real chance of any military support?"

"Slim," Storey replied. "Everybody's out of town except the Bowstring Squadron."

"You just lost me," said Moody.

"Delta has three combat squadrons," Storey explained. "A, B, and C. One squadron is always ready to move out in two hours. That's Bowstring. SEAL DevGroup has three assault teams: Red, Gold, and Blue. They call their alert the Standby Team. Only the Bowstring Squadron is home right now. Other two are deployed overseas. Same with DevGroup, and their Standby Team is in the Far East getting ready to shadow the president's trip. Except for us, our unit is all overseas too. So we're really thin on the ground right now."

"Why do I think that's an intentional part of their plan?" said Beth.

"Because you're smart," said Troy.

Storey thought he ought to start off by clearing the air. "Beth, our orientation is overseas. So as far as we're concerned, you're in charge of this one."

"You don't have any problem with that?" said Beth.

"Hell, you outrank us anyway," said Troy, smiling.

"I'll try not to pull it on you," said Beth, smiling back at them. "Of course we're going to have to play it by ear. But if we do interviews, we don't want to have four people pounding into someone's house. No one will talk to us if we do that. Maybe you guys could back us up from outside, be ready and cover the exits."

"Fine with me," said Storey.

"Interviewing's really not our thing anyway," said Troy. He didn't think the FBI would be down with shooting anyone's kneecaps off. "We speak Arabic if you need it."

"Both of you?" said Beth.

They nodded.

"I did not know that," said Beth, grinning slightly as she saw them in a new light. "I'm assuming you guys are armed to the teeth, as usual."

Storey wasn't quite sure how to reply to that. "We've got a few things in the car. But we're not planning on laying waste to any neighborhoods, if that's what you mean."

"That's not what I mean at all," said Beth. "It's why I wanted you two with me instead of a couple of postal inspectors. If anything happens, I've got a feeling we're going to need all your stuff. And we'll need it fast, so keep it handy."

Storey and Troy both looked at each other. A little surprised, but pleased to hear it.

"Okay," said Beth. "We've got radios for you both, so you'll be on our system. Let's pick up our assignments and go to work."

22

Nimri handed Joseph Oan the cordless telephone. "Call your work. Tell them you are sick today. But you will definitely be at work tomorrow. Do you understand? Promise them you will return tomorrow."

Oan dialed the number while Nimri watched to make sure it was not 911. "Mike? This is Joe. I can't come in this morning. Terrible diarrhea. I guess it was something I ate last night. No, no way I can drive—I'm in the bathroom all the time. No, I'll be fine by tomorrow. Positive. I'll be in first thing. Thanks, Mike. I'll see you tomorrow. Bye." He handed the phone back to Nimri.

Nimri put down the one he'd been listening in on. "Very good." Then he was shaking his head.

"What?" Oan asked.

"Joe," said Nimri. "Joe. At least that is not your true name, but you have given your son a *Christian* name. You deny your blood, Youssif. You deny your people. What would your father say?"

Oan never would have thought that anything this gunman could say would embarrass him, but it did. Perhaps because he himself often thought about what his father would have said.

"You will all go upstairs now," said Nimri.

Oan was alarmed. "Why?"

"Because I must talk with my people," said Nimri. "I have given you my promise that if you do what I ask, you and your family will not be harmed. If you hear our plans, I will not be able to keep my promise."

For the first time Joseph Oan held out some hope that they wouldn't be killed. Then he told himself that was his American nature. His Lebanese nature told him that was exactly what the gunman wanted him to think.

The three Oans were tied to chairs in the parents' bedroom. The windows had been nailed shut the previous night. Dawood shifted the chairs and turned on the television.

"What are you doing?" said Omar.

"The TV'll help them pass the time," said Dawood. "I'll turn on *The Today Show.*"

Omar shook his head, though he didn't make Dawood turn off the TV.

When they came back downstairs Nimri had the dining room table spread with maps and diagrams. "Sit, brothers. Make yourselves comfortable."

They obeyed him with an air of excitement and anticipation.

"I thank you, brothers," Nimri began. "I thank you for your patience. And I thank you for your discipline in not questioning me about our mission. You have risked your lives without knowing. You are true mujahideen."

He watched them swell up at being given the title of Holy Warriors. It was as important to motivate men as it was to command them.

"Now I will tell you why I have activated you," said Nimri. "This is our mission. We will kill the arch-criminal Donald Rumsfeld. The American secretary of defense. The man who has killed thousands, nay, tens of thousands of our brothers."

"God be praised!" exclaimed al-Sharif. Omar and Dawood beamed at each other.

"This will be our first strike in America since the Blessed

Tuesday," said Nimri. "The eyes of all the Faithful will be upon us."

"I only wish to God it was Bush," Omar muttered.

"Bush is too well guarded," said Nimri. "God willing, his time will come. But he does us service. While he travels in Asia, all eyes are turned away from us here."

"I'm starting to see," said al-Sharif.

"As I knew you would," said Nimri. "Now, Rumsfeld. The Pentagon is too well guarded. He cannot be touched there. His home is less well guarded, but enough to make any attack require too many men for a low probability of success. And vehicles cannot approach either place. Aircraft? The Americans expect aircraft after the Blessed Tuesday. When Rumsfeld travels between these places, he travels inside a limousine with armor. And the limousine travels in convoy with security vehicles, filled with bodyguards, traveling in front and behind. The guards are from the American Army Criminal Investigative Division. Military police. Not the best, perhaps, but well armed enough to hold off an attack until police reinforcements arrive."

Without needing to see it, Nimri knew their eyes were all on him. "And so you ask yourselves, what can four men do, brother Abdallah? The answer, my brothers, is that four men can do nothing if they attack this Rumsfeld the way he expects to be attacked. But we will not attack him in any of these ways. Brother Muhammad knows the things I have asked him to assemble. Brother Muhammad, what did these things tell you?"

"A bomb," said al-Sharif. "A bomb to open that nice black limo up like a tin can."

"Exactly," said Nimri.

"But no explosive," said al-Sharif. "We'll be making it? It'll take time."

"No," said Nimri.

"Another group will be joining us?" said al-Sharif.

"No again," said Nimri. "The explosive we need will be provided by our host al-Oan, upstairs."

"Him?" said Omar. "Then why is he tied up?"

"He is not willing," said Nimri. "But he *will* help us. He drives a truck. A *gasoline* truck."

"Aaaah," the others said in unison.

"To be specific," said Nimri, "a Heil low-center-of-gravity, double-taper petroleum tanker. Aluminum. Four compartments. That holds a maximum of ninety-two hundred gallons of gasoline."

"Beautiful," said al-Sharif. "It would take us a month, a warehouse, and truckloads of fertilizer and chemicals to build a bomb like that. What's the explosive force? And no metric system please, brother."

"One gallon of gasoline is the equivalent of twenty sticks of dynamite," said Nimri. "Under ideal conditions."

"Almost a two-hundred-thousand-pound bomb," breathed al-Sharif. "The only military bomb that big is nuclear."

"Let us say nearer to ten thousand pounds," said Nimri. "The aluminum tank will add to the blast. The fireball will be . . ." He did the conversion calculation in his head. "Fifteen thousand degrees Fahrenheit."

Al-Sharif whistled.

"We could never keep the construction of such a bomb hidden," said Nimri. "But this one will be delivered to us, the keys to it handed over. This Heil trailer is towed by a Peterbuilt truck. And our brother Dawood has been to a school to learn to drive a Peterbuilt truck, has he not?"

"First in my class," Dawood said proudly.

"This truck will be in the breakdown lane of the highway when Rumsfeld's convoy passes," said Nimri. "As he is a servant of Satan, it is only right and proper that he should be speeded to hell by fire."

"The brothers have done a lot of surveillance and research," said al-Sharif.

"They have," said Nimri. "Many of them. They have observed Rumsfeld. They have learned everything there is to know about al-Oan upstairs. Much painstaking work. We will not fail them."

"When will we do this?" said al-Sharif.

"Tomorrow," Nimri replied.

"Tomorrow?" they all echoed.

"Tomorrow," said Nimri. "It is the only possible date. Rumsfeld has been traveling to Colorado and California. He left Washington on the sixth and returned on the thirteenth. On Saturday he flies to North Carolina. Tomorrow, the sixteenth, the Americans' Afghan puppet Vice President Hedyat Amin Arsala visits the Pentagon at three-fifteen. There will be ceremonies and meetings. Then they will both go to Rumsfeld's home in Bethesda, Maryland, for a dinner party. Rumsfeld's security detail takes many different routes to and from his home. But they always leave the Pentagon the same way. They will pass by our truck here." Nimri pressed his finger on a road map of Washington. "Not too close to the Pentagon that the security will notice it. Not too far that they take a different turn and we miss him. With ninety-two hundred gallons of gasoline, we do not have to be close."

"The lethal area of the blast?" said al-Sharif.

Nimri took a pen and drew a circle on the map. It encompassed over ten square blocks of tightly packed streets in Arlington, Virginia. "At the chosen spot the height of the trailer will be above the concrete highway barrier, so the blast will be unimpeded. And the highway is level with the surrounding area, neither above nor below. The highway will be crowded with vehicles, also."

"We could exceed the number of the Blessed Tuesday," said Omar.

"That is in God's hands," said Nimri. "What is important is that we destroy Rumsfeld. The Afghan puppet is an extra bird with the same stone. They will have nothing to bury but ashes."

"Beautiful," said al-Sharif. "A beautiful plan."

Nimri wanted to tell them it was all his, but did not.

The Faithful loved to boast, but it tempted God. There would be time enough for boasting if God granted them success. "At first it was thought to take him when he drove to the Pentagon in the morning. But the logistics were wrong. The truck would have to be exposed for a day and a night. This way, it leaves the depot in the morning, full of gasoline, and everything is done that same day."

"This Rumsfeld is a Jew, is he not?" said Dawood.

"Many of them pretend not to be, but they are," Omar confided knowingly.

"Even those who are not are under the control of the Jews," said Nimri. "This is why it is important to target these leaders, one by one."

Later that morning, after rush hour but before lunch, Nimri and al-Sharif left the house for a drive. Nimri drove Joseph Oan's Lincoln Continental. Al-Sharif drove the Toyota Camry they'd stolen in Lexington, Virginia. They abandoned the Camry at a Manassas shopping center. Al-Sharif went inside the supermarket while Nimri read a newspaper that covered his face.

Al-Sharif returned with soft drinks, boxes of microwave meals, potato chips, pretzels, and ice cream. "They are all halal," he said.

Nimri was curious how he could tell that the food conformed to Islamic dietary law. There had been nothing like that the last time he was in the United States. "You know this from the labels?"

"No," said al-Sharif, visibly embarrassed. He took out a box and showed Nimri the symbol. "Kosher."

Nimri only laughed. "Don't worry, brother. One day, before God, it will *all* be halal."

"We won't see the end of that fight, brother."

"It is 511 years since the expulsion, my friend, and Europe is now ten percent Muslim. God's time is his own. His warriors need not worry—he has promised them their reward."

"God is great," said al-Sharif.

"I must apologize to you," Nimri said. "You have done

such great work, made such sacrifices. It is beneath you to run these errands."

"I didn't complain."

"All the more reason for me to apologize."

"I have to do it, brother. I know why. Every Arab is a suspect."

A Prince William County Sheriff's cruiser pulled in behind them on the way out of the shopping center. Nimri's eyes kept moving from the speedometer to the rearview mirror. "If we are stopped, it will not be for a traffic violation. We kill the policeman immediately and leave the area."

"There's malls all over the place. We can get another car easy."

Nimri did not even go through the yellow light at the next intersection. The cruiser changed lanes and turned left.

Nimri took the Jack Herrity Parkway to Springfield, and found the fuel company. From Springfield they circled the entire Beltway, Nimri carefully checking out all the truck stops and al-Sharif taking notes.

On to the Route 66 exit, and into Arlington. Circling the National Cemetery, avoiding the Pentagon. Making no stops around there, always on the alert for counter-surveillance.

Al-Sharif kept his eyes on the screen of the Global Positioning receiver in his palm. "Fifty yards," he said.

Nimri put on the turn signal and glided into the break-down lane.

"A little more," said al-Sharif. "Get ready . . . stop!"

Nimri halted beside the concrete barrier, and put on his four-way flashers. He grabbed a cell phone off the dash and dialed a number. "Omar? Call the first number." A moment later the phone in his hand rang. "Good. Call the second." Another phone on the dash began to ring. "Good." He wanted to be sure they were not in a cellular dead spot.

A rattling sound. Al-Sharif was shaking a can of spray

paint. He stuck his arm out the window and, masked by the car, sprayed a vertical blue line on the concrete barrier. The can was capped and tossed into the backseat.

As soon as the road was clear Nimri pulled back into traffic.

"It looks good," said al-Sharif. And then, "If Dawood doesn't screw anything up."

"Will he?" Nimri asked. The meaning was clear: you are the one who chose him.

"He gets excited," said al-Sharif. "He feels bad about screwing up in Ohio. I'm worried about him trying too hard to make it right with you."

"No one else knows how to drive the truck well enough," said Nimri. "All of us could drive it. But one turn too tight; a blown tire; an accident. I cannot risk it. Dawood is in God's hands, and we are in God's—and Dawood's."

They drove back to Manassas. But keeping the conversation in mind, Nimri took Dawood out that afternoon. They drove over every inch of the route they would take Thursday. Twice.

After dinner the Oan family was again banished to the upstairs bedroom. Al-Sharif opened up his duffel bags and emptied the contents onto the living room carpet. Out came rolls of insulated copper electrical wire. A soldering iron. A tube of superglue. Electrician's tape. A large can of rubber cement. A box of condoms. And cartons of model rocket engines.

Nimri put the others to measuring and cutting the lengths of wire he would need. He concentrated on the model rocket engines. They were cardboard cylinders the size of a cigar, to be inserted in the base of a model rocket and fired by battery, the burning solid propellant shooting it into the air. In the base of each engine there was a hole for the igniter, a wire strip coated with pyrotechnic material, trailing two wire leads from its end. This would electrically fire the engine, like a blasting cap.

Nimri slid the initiators into the engines, seating them

with dabs of superglue so any jarring wouldn't dislodge them. A model rocketeer attached his firing wire to the igniter terminals with a pair of alligator clips so they would come off when the rocket fired and he could use the wire over and over again. Nimri soldered the copper wire to the initiator terminals. Then he taped the wire to the engines, again so any impact wouldn't yank them out.

The engines would have to swim in gasoline. Nimri rolled a condom over each engine, sucked the air out, and taped it closed over the wire. Then he dipped each of the sheathed engines into the can of rubber cement. He made them in bunches, not trusting enough to have only one engine in each tank of the trailer.

His final step was to open up the bodies of the two cell phones and solder two foot-long lengths of wire to the two contacts that led to the cell phone ringers. The cell phone batteries would put enough current through the wires.

They taped the engines together like bunches of bananas. The wire was coiled and tied with wire twist-ties for easy deployment.

Nimri had saved one of the prepared engines. They took it down to the basement and secured it in the vise on Oan's workbench. Nimri twisted the engine wires onto the wires of one of the cell phones. He moved anything flammable out of the way. "Fill a bucket with water," he ordered Dawood. Just in case. He felt he was forgetting something, and kept looking around. Ah. "Disable the smoke alarms," he said to Omar.

When all was done, Nimri flicked open his own cell phone and dialed the number of the one on the bench. From the moment he pressed the Send button he was counting off the seconds in his head.

A click, a pop, and a foot of orange flame erupted from the end of the engine. It burned for only a second, but that was more than enough. The melting rubber cement began to drip onto the wooden bench, so Dawood threw the bucket of water on it.

The basement filled with the smell of burning rubber and acrid propellant.

"Perfect," Nimri declared.

Omar went to open the bulkhead door to the driveway, to ventilate the basement.

"What a smell," Dawood declared.

"It's beautiful," said al-Sharif.

Eventually the faint odor drifted up to the second floor. Along with the sound of jubilant voices.

Steven Oan said, "Dad, they're going to take your truck and blow it up."

"I know," Joseph Oan told his son.

"We have to do something," Steven said.

"Steven, quiet," Yasmin ordered.

"If anyone does anything, then we'll die," said Joseph. "I know men like these. Killing is nothing to them. They think God is with them, so everything they do is allowed."

"But they're going to blow up your truck. Maybe at the White House."

"Quiet, Steven," his mother ordered again.

"Steven," his father said, "you're a brave boy. Almost a man. Your great-grandfather and grandfather were brave men, and they were killed in Lebanon. Your uncle was a brave man, and he's dead. I lost them all. I won't lose you and your mother. You don't say anything to these men. You don't do anything unless I tell you."

"Listen to your father," Yasmin added quickly, making her husband sigh.

Steven retreated into sullen silence. That moment in every boy's life when he finds out his father really isn't a hero is a hard thing to take.

23

Nimri held up his cell phone. "I will receive a call every fifteen minutes. If I do not answer, my men will call back immediately. If I do not answer again your wife and son will die. So the police stopping the call will do no good. If anyone other than me answers the phone your wife and son will die. If the police arrive at this house your wife and son will die immediately. Do you understand?"

"I understand," said Joseph Oan. He knew he was defeated. The youngest gunman and the leader were both dressed in the old work uniforms he kept for gardening. They'd thought of everything.

"You have no choice," said Nimri. "Deliver the truck to us, and you will be safe. Your family will be safe. You know nothing else—you have no responsibility. Do you understand?"

"I understand," Joseph Oan repeated. He watched his wife and son being tied to chairs again.

"We have no wish to harm believers," said Nimri.

"What about all the other believers you'll kill today?" Steven demanded from his chair.

"Steven!" his mother and father both said sharply.

"God directs all events," Nimri replied. "If they believe in Him and the Last Day, they will find Paradise."

* * *

Dawood drove Oan's Lincoln, with Oan in the front seat and Nimri sitting behind him. Al-Sharif followed them in Yasmin Oan's Chevy Blazer. Omar remained with the family.

As they entered Springfield, Nimri asked, "Will you have a full load of fuel today?"

"I usually do," said Oan. He thought about begging them to stop. But he knew they'd only laugh at him. He also knew that whenever what they were going to do happened, he'd be blamed for it. He'd probably have to go back to Lebanon. But at least they would all be alive.

Nimri was watching Oan thinking. "When I was in Tora Prison, they would shock me with an electric prod, much like the kind they use on cattle. The guards loved to do that, and they loved to show me that it was made in America. They did not even have to pay for it— it was given as aid. And while you have your good job, your grand car, your house with the garden I have seen in the yard, and you lose your faith pretending to be an American—you pay for the tyrants and their electric shocks. So remember, Youssif al-Oan, I will keep my promises. The promise of life, and the promise of death. It is up to you."

The car stopped. As Oan unsnapped his seat belt, Nimri tapped him on the shoulder. Oan turned to look over the seat. Nimri was holding up his cell phone.

Oan watched his Continental drive off. A couple of coworkers were just parking their cars. "Hey, Joe."

Oan waved.

"Who was that in your car?"

"Relatives," said Oan.

"Staying over, huh? When mine fly in I always have to give them my car for the day, too."

Oan nodded.

Inside, the dispatcher said, "Joe, you sure you're all right? You still look sick."

"I'm okay," said Oan.

"You want to take an easier route today? Ernie's out for the week, you can take his."

"No, I'm fine," said Oan, chilled at the thought of what would happen if he drove out in a smaller tanker filled with diesel instead of gasoline.

"Whatever you say," the dispatcher replied, handing him his delivery printout.

Nimri, Dawood, and al-Sharif waited at the Springfield Mall. Every fifteen minutes Omar called.

The constant ringing was making al-Sharif edgy. "I'm worried about this guy."

"I knew his brother in Afghanistan," said Nimri. "His brother was a hero. He is a coward. He will do anything to hang on to his life."

"I hope so," said al-Sharif. "You never know when a punk is going to decide he's not a punk anymore."

"God's will, brother," Nimri said soothingly. "God's will."

"God's will," al-Sharif repeated dutifully.

"There's the truck," said Dawood.

"Be calm," Nimri counseled him for the umpteenth time. "Drive carefully until you regain the feel of the vehicle. There is no rush."

"Yes, brother."

Then to al-Sharif, Nimri said, "Take him home. Wait with Omar for my call. Keep him safe, unless there is an emergency."

"I don't like leaving witnesses, brother."

"Witnesses to what? What can they do, show artists how to draw pictures of our faces? They know nothing else. Not our names, not our plans."

"I hate that kid," said al-Sharif.

"He is annoying," Nimri conceded. "But he knows the

Book. He is not apostate. I do not want his blood on my head, unless I cannot avoid it."

"You're our leader," said al-Sharif.

Nimri patted him on the back. He and Dawood got out and approached the tanker. In the fuel company uniform, no one should notice.

Joseph Oan climbed down from his cab.

"How many gallons?" Nimri demanded.

"Eight thousand, eight hundred," Oan replied.

Nimri was jubilant. "Go with the man who is in your wife's vehicle. He will take you home to your family." He held up his phone again. "Remember, I will be calling him also."

Oan nodded and trudged off toward the Blazer.

Nimri climbed into the cab and deactivated the GPS locator so the fuel company would not be able to track the location of the truck. Al-Sharif had al-Oan's work cell phone. If his company called, Oan would tell them it had to be an equipment failure. If anyone called the company to complain that their day's fuel delivery had not arrived, and the company called Oan, then Oan would have his excuses ready and al-Sharif's pistol to his head.

"Drive a bit in the parking lot until you feel comfortable," Nimri urged Dawood. "You will follow me, but the traffic may split us up. If that happens, you know where to go next."

Nimri embraced him. "I have faith in you."

"Thank you, brother," Dawood said emotionally.

Nimri watched him carefully. Dawood seemed to handle the truck well. Finally it could be put off no longer—he signaled the boy to follow him out of the mall.

Watching in his rearview mirror, Nimri cringed as the trailer wheels went over the curb.

They turned onto Interstate 95, and from there it was only a short drive to Interstate 495, the western half of the Capital Beltway. As always on the Beltway, at any time of the day, the traffic was chaotic. As he'd predicted, it did split them up. Nimri proceeded to their first destination, resolving to trust in God. He would not call Dawood's cell phone and distract him from driving unless it was absolutely necessary.

Just as he was thinking it had become necessary, Dawood pulled into the truck stop near Tysons Corner. As instructed, he went into the store and bought himself a soft drink and a snack.

They had the whole day to kill. Nimri's plan was to spend it circling the Beltway. But only once. Dawood would pull into a truck stop, buy something, and remain there for exactly one hour. Then move on to the next truck stop Nimri had chosen the previous day, repeating the routine. Not long enough for anyone to begin to wonder why the tanker was parked and not on the road. And long enough to keep Dawood's driving to a minimum. No one paid any attention to trucks coming and going at truck stops. Just as at the club in Bangkok, Nimri believed firmly in hiding in plain sight.

At every stop he called Dawood on the phone and chatted to keep his spirits up. Dawood felt obligated to report everything he did anyway, including his trips to the bathroom.

By 4:00 P.M. they had gone almost completely around, and were near the Maryland side of the Potomac River. Nimri had made allowances for rush hour. It was time to rig the vehicle.

They did it right at the truck stop. In plain sight. Dawood raised the truck hood, and he and Nimri in their uniforms looked like employees dealing with a problem. Nimri had the model rocket engines and wire in a canvas tool bag.

He had consulted knowledgeable people in Pakistan, and knew what to do. He made sure he was completely grounded, no trace of static electricity. It didn't take much of a spark to ignite gasoline fumes. Climbing up the ladder to the top of the trailer, he walked to the back and opened the first loading hatch just enough to get the cluster of engines in, keeping his head away from the fumes. He let the wire run through his fingers until he heard the splash, then shut the hatch quickly and secured it. The wire was secured with duct tape and uncoiled from the bag as he backed down the walkway on his knees.

Nimri followed the same procedure with the other three compartments, taping the wire down along the side of the walkway.

The job went very quickly. The wiring was run alongside the other truck wires and cables, and fed into the cab.

Nimri taped the two cell phones to the wall of the cab near Dawood's head. Very carefully, he spliced the cell phone wires to the loop leading out to the trailer, painstakingly wrapping each splice with electric tape.

Dawood sat in the cab with him while he worked.

"Brother Abdullah?"

"Yes, Dawood?"

"I have a request."

Engrossed in what he was doing, Nimri almost erupted with a *what now?* And would have, except he was afraid of making the boy jumpy. Inwardly, he chastised himself for his temper. "What is it, Dawood?"

"I want to stay with the truck. I want to be a martyr."

Nimri had not planned it as a martyrdom operation. There had been so many problems with the jihadis of the Blessed Tuesday dropping in and out of the operation. It had only been God's grace that the attack had come off so well. He had also not wanted to travel with a martyr who might back away at the last moment. It was safer to go alone. His plan was that the truck would sit by the side of the highway with the hood open, but locked. Unable to be moved unless by a special tow truck, and everything would be finished before one arrived.

Having someone in the truck would change the plan.

It would ensure the detonation, though, and lessen the time of exposure on the highway.

Yet again the emotions built up and made him feel like shouting. A year of meticulous planning, and now, with time so short, forced to consider a new set of consequences. "Are you sure you wish to do this, Dawood? I am pleased with your performance. You do not need to do this."

"I've thought about it, brother Abdullah. I want to be remembered like the mujahideen of the Blessed Tuesday. I want to taste Paradise as a martyr."

Nimri still worried about his plan, but he did not feel he could deny martyrdom to one of the Faithful who desired it. "Very well." He reached into his bag and took out a mushroom switch and a battery pack. Any pressure on the oversize plunger head of the switch, like a slap, would close the circuit. "I was going to prepare this only if you were stopped before you reached your destination, and were faced with capture."

He mounted the switch on the dashboard, wiring it and the battery pack into the two spare connections in his firing system.

Nimri would have preferred to rig one of the hatches to explode when opened, and perhaps a mercury-switch booby trap to explode the trailer if all failed and the Americans tried to move it. But these would take time to rig, and more important, Dawood would have to arm them properly after he stopped for the last time. Too much complication—too many chances for mistakes. Nimri could easily visualize Dawood blowing up the trailer prematurely. This way he only had to turn on the two cell phones.

They were ready. "Tell me once more," he said to Dawood.

Dawood repeated his instructions perfectly.

Now Nimri was emotional. "Then instead of me following and picking you up, brother, I will leave you now. You will fly directly to Paradise. God willing, one day I will join you. Prepare the way for me."

They embraced. "I will, brother," said Dawood.

"Remember your final words," Nimri said into his ear. "Activate the switch only if the convoy has passed you and nothing has happened. I will call you once you have stopped and are prepared. I promise you, you will never be forgotten." He broke the embrace, touching Dawood's head gently.

The big diesel rumbled to life. Dawood released the brakes with a blast of air and left the truck stop, waving good-bye.

24

Beth Royale and Paul Moody paused at the front door of the house in Reston, Virginia, to shake hands with the owners.

Ed Storey was waiting out at the curb. He gripped the walkie-talkie radio on his belt and squeezed the Transmit bar four times, breaking squelch. A few seconds later Lee Troy appeared around the side of the house and came down the driveway.

"Another nothing," Beth said.

"What's next?" Troy asked.

Storey shot him a look that failed to take effect.

Beth leaned in the car and plucked the next file from the stack. The FBI computer system was state-of-the-art, for 1990. "Manassas. Joseph Oan. Used to be Youssif al-Oan, changed it when he naturalized. Pronounces the last name like Owen now. Drives a tanker truck for a fuel company. He and his brother were orphaned in Lebanon. Came here to live with an uncle. The brother went the radical route, killed in Afghanistan. But he thinks we don't know about the brother. Scheduled to be interviewed by the Washington field office every quarter. No record of any kind. Pillar of the community, attends a moderate mosque. Wife and a twelve-year-old son."

"Sounds like good cover," said Storey.

"That's the third time you said that today," Moody mentioned.

"That's the third time I've meant it," Storey replied. "If I was running sleeper agents I'd want them flying under the radar just like that. Being good citizens, not attracting any attention."

Beth kept out of the conversation, skimming the file reproduction. "Gentlemen?" They all turned to look at her. "Let's go to Manassas." She gave Storey the address.

Storey and Troy were driving another Grand Cherokee. Black, but with tinted windows this time. Also armored. Part of the office motor pool, usually staged for deployment overseas.

"I'm definitely reenlisting," Troy announced.

"You don't say?" said Storey.

"Hell yeah. I'm sure as shit not getting out and joining the FBI. What could be more boring than driving around all day *talking* to people? Wait . . . no, there's *nothing* more boring than that."

"The FBI's loss is the navy's gain," said Storey.

Troy was pretty sure Storey was fucking with him. Problem with Storey was that the fucker was so dry you could never be 100 percent sure of anything. "Traffic around here drives me crazy."

"Good thing you're not driving."

"I mean it. How can these people take it? At least I got *ordered* here."

"This is where the money is, my friend. I think we're going to have to PT your ass after work. You need to blow off some steam."

"You're right about that. At least lying in that stinking cane field I was doing something."

Meanwhile, Paul and Beth were talking. "It's insane to have these military cowboys working cases with us,"

Paul Moody complained to Beth. "If they start shooting we'll all hang."

"We don't have enough people working the case as it is," Beth replied. "And have you ever seen them shoot? They're the best in the world, and that's no joke."

"I still don't like it."

"Next street, turn right."

"This one?"

"That's it."

Moody was going slow so Beth could read the house numbers. "Another Pleasant Valley Sun-day-ay," she sang.

"God," said Moody. "If your musical tastes were just a little less lame they'd have a chance of being funny. There's the house."

"Keep going," Beth said quickly.

"Wha—?"

"Don't slow down, Paul. Keep going."

"They missed the house," Troy said to Storey. He picked up his radio.

"Don't make that call," said Storey.

"Why not?"

"They know how to read house numbers. Let's see what's going on."

They followed the FBI sedan to the end of the street and made the right turn with it. The sedan pulled over and Storey slid in behind.

"What's up?" Troy said to Moody.

"Don't ask me," Moody replied.

"Didn't anyone see that?" Beth demanded. "Every blind shut tight, every curtain drawn. Every single window. The only house on the street like that. And with a car in the driveway."

The men all looked at each other.

"Attention to detail," Storey said to Troy.

"Glad someone around here has it," Troy said.

Storey then asked Beth, "What do you want to do?"

"I'm going to call it in first. They'll probably just laugh at me."

Beth disappeared into the sedan.

"Did you notice those windows?" Troy asked Storey.

"No. You're the sniper. Why didn't *you* observe it?"

Beth was out of the car. "They didn't laugh at me, but they're not calling out the cavalry unless we give them something more. We can stake the house out if we want to."

Moody shrugged.

"You really think we've got something?" Storey asked Beth.

"Just a feeling that something's not right," she said.

"Fine with me," said Storey.

"I've got nothing else planned," said Troy.

Moody shrugged again.

25

The rows of white stones stretched out over the hill-sides. Abdallah Karim Nimri's first thought was that there were not nearly enough of them. He carefully positioned the tripod and faced the camera to the west, as if to capture the setting sun. He did not need the telephoto lens—he could see the Pentagon and surrounding roads very clearly from the Arlington National Cemetery hillside.

Nimri checked his watch. This was a crucial decision. He did not know exactly when Rumsfeld would leave the Pentagon. The truck had to be in position beforehand, but every minute sitting on the highway was more risk. He flicked open the cell phone and dialed. "Go, Dawood."

From where he was Nimri couldn't see the paint mark. Dawood had to stop far enough away from the Pentagon so as not to attract the building security. Far less attention would be paid to a broken-down truck heading *away* from the Pentagon.

There was the truck. It looked like Dawood was stopping in the right place. Nimri could not see him get out of the truck. Then the hood tilted down. Dawood should be under the trailer now. Nimri smiled as he watched the truck rock to one side as the air left the slashed tires.

Nimri dialed again. "Excellent, Dawood. Have you activated the phones? No?" Nimri gritted his teeth to keep himself from shouting into the phone. "Go back into the cab and turn on the two phones. You have now. They are on? You are sure? Very good. No, they have not left. Patience now." Nimri realized that he could not stay on the phone with Dawood. Not only could he think of nothing to say, he did not want to be distracted. "Dawood, I will call you back when I see them getting ready to leave. No, everything is fine."

Nimri broke the connection with relief. The traffic was inching along the highway. Gridlock. Lights were coming on as the sun dropped to the horizon.

Then flashing lights appearing around the highway curve caught his attention. A police car moving fast in the breakdown lane.

Nimri got back on the phone. "Dawood, there is a policeman approaching you. No, do not activate the switch. If it stops behind you, get out and speak to him. Tell him your company is sending a repair vehicle. Stay on the phone with me. If he asks, tell him you are talking to your company. Remain calm and persuade him. You can do it."

Nimri took a second cell phone from his pocket. The first two numbers in the phone book were the two phones taped up in the cab of the truck. He had hope, though. Dawood's English had no accent, and he could be mistaken for a Latin. But Dawood had no Virginia driver's license. If the policeman asked to see it, he would have to blow up the truck.

The blue and gray Virginia State Police cruiser stopped behind the trailer, where Dawood was already standing. Afraid he'd get hit by the traffic, the trooper vigorously directed Dawood to come around to the passenger side of the cruiser.

Dawood said a short prayer beseeching God's help. He knees were twitching beyond his control.

The trooper ran the plate through his computer. It was clean, and registered to Legacy Fuel of Springfield, the company on the logo. He brought the passenger window down, and the truck driver leaned his head in.

"Blow a tire?" the trooper asked.

"Two, sir," said Dawood. He gestured with the phone. "My company has a wrecker on the way."

"You're not too far from home. But it'll still take them a while to get here in this traffic."

Dawood shrugged.

"Looks like you're full."

"Yes, sir."

"Got your paperwork?"

"In the cab." As Dawood gestured toward the truck he forgot all about the cell phone, and the hand holding it dropped to his side.

The trooper looked at the traffic. "That's okay, you don't have to go get it."

But the last thing Nimri heard was, "In the cab." Then nothing. He thought the policeman was taking Dawood to the cab. The policeman would see the firing system and the two phones. Nimri scrolled to the first number in the phone book of his other cell. All that work, and to be thwarted at the last minute.

"You need anything?" the trooper asked Dawood.

"No, thank you, sir."

Nimri put his thumb on the Send button.

"Okay," said the trooper. "Look, do me a favor, buddy . . ."

Someone farther down the line of traffic was leaning on their horn. Dawood had to lean farther into the cruiser to hear, and propped his elbow on the edge of the window frame to brace himself. Which brought his arm, and the phone, inside.

Nimri pushed the Send button.

"Wait in your cab until your wrecker gets here," the trooper continued.

Cursing, Nimri fumbled to turn the phone off, almost dropping it. He instinctively stuck it under his armpit, as if that would block the signal from going out. His eyes were on the truck, waiting for it to blow up.

"This traffic's murder, and I don't want you to get hurt," said the trooper. "When I pull out, walk up with my car for protection, and stay in the cab."

"Thank you, sir," said Dawood.

"Take it easy, buddy," the trooper replied.

The truck didn't blow up. Nimri looked down at the phone in his left hand, which was gripping it so tightly the blood had left his fingers. He jammed the phone into his pocket, irrationally feeling that if he even held it, it might transmit by accident.

The trooper bulled out into traffic with a blast of his siren. Of course the traffic stopped for him. Dawood walked alongside the cruiser, which stayed with him until he boarded the cab. The trooper waved, and Dawood waved back. The cruiser's flashing lights switched off.

"Brother Abdallah," Dawood blurted excitedly into his cell phone. "Did you hear?"

The temperature was only in the low sixties, but the steady breeze coming over the hillside made the sweat on Nimri's face feel cold. "Yes, Dawood, I heard. You did very well." He suddenly realized that he hadn't checked the Pentagon in all this time. He squinted into the twilight, heedlessly swinging the camera around for a better look through the telephoto lens. The black limousine and two black SUVs were formed up at their usual spot in front of the Mall entrance. "Dawood, it will be very soon now. I must make another call. I will call you back shortly."

"I understand, brother."

Nimri dialed al-Sharif at the house. "It is almost time. Bind them securely and leave the house. You have not forgotten to destroy the planning materials? Good. God willing, I will meet you at the rendezvous."

Nimri called Dawood again. The limousine doors were open.

26

"Time to go," al-Sharif told Omar. "Make sure they're tied up good."

"It's a mistake to leave them alive," said Omar.

"I know."

"Then why don't we take care of it ourselves?"

"Orders," said al-Sharif.

Omar was plainly unconvinced.

"If we kill them it's going to be on the news," said al-Sharif. "When Nimri sees it, we're out. You know what that means? We have to leave the country, because we're going to be on the Ten Most Wanted List. You try living somewhere else, without the organization. Not me."

Omar seemed to be reappraising his position.

"I thought so," said al-Sharif. On their way through the dining room he grabbed the maps and papers off the table and stuffed them into his jacket pocket.

"You were supposed to burn those," said Omar.

"I didn't have time," al-Sharif said defensively. "I'll get rid of them later. You just go make sure they're tied up."

* * *

"Vehicle pulling out of the driveway," Troy said to Storey. "Red Chevy Blazer."

"Red Chevy Blazer pulling out of the driveway," Storey said into his radio.

"The wife's car," Beth said to Moody. Then into her radio, "Copy."

Troy had the Kowa spotting scope braced on top of the backseat. He cackled with glee. "Jackpot! Al-Sharif and Omar. Al-Sharif's driving."

"You sure?" said Storey, not really believing their luck.

"Of course I'm fucking sure."

Storey ignored the display of sniper temperament—they were such divas. "Anyone else in the car?"

"Not in sight. They could have someone on the floor."

"Well, do they?"

The excitement made Troy testy. "I didn't bring my X-ray spotting scope."

Beth's hunch really paid off, Storey thought. "You got it, Beth," he radioed. "Al-Sharif and Omar in the Blazer. Al-Sharif's driving. No one else in sight."

Beth's voice crackled over the radio. "You sure?"

"You sure you're not related?" said Troy.

"No one else we can see," Storey said into the radio.

Beth picked up the car radio handset and called it all in.

"You are absolutely the luckiest—" said Moody.

"They're coming down the street toward us," said Troy. "How are we going to play it?"

"That's up to Beth," said Storey. He called her. She was on the other radio, and Moody told him to stand by.

"We could take 'em right when they drive past," said Troy.

"Hold on to your ass," said Storey. "It's not our party."

"Fine. What happens when they pass us before the FBI decides what they're going to do?"

"Duck down out of sight and let them pass."

Beth's voice came up on the radio. "Hostage Rescue

Team's going to take down the house. We follow the car and take no action until backup gets here."

"Cavalry's on the way," said Storey.

"Cavalry never had to ride through northern Virginia traffic," Troy replied.

"I'm not worried about taking them down," said Storey. "I'm worried about staying with them. It's getting dark and they could be heading into traffic. And the FBI won't notify the local cops. That's their pathology."

"Local cops probably aren't ready for these boys," said Troy.

Storey said into the radio, "Beth, how do you want to work the tail?"

"We'll come in behind, you fall back," said Beth. "If they get suspicious, we'll switch off."

"Here they come," said Troy. "Hit the deck."

The Blazer passed the Grand Cherokee at the end of the street, stopped, and turned right. The FBI sedan went by a few moments later.

Storey turned on the ignition.

"I'm staying back here in case I need to shoot," said Troy, remembering Pakistan.

"Don't get your hopes up," said Storey. "We're just backup. If there's any shooting to be done, I'd just as soon let the FBI do all of it."

"I'm with you," said Troy. "But the tangos might have other ideas."

"They usually do," said Storey.

"Looks like they're headed for Ninety-five," Beth said to Moody.

"They get on Ninety-five we've got real problems," said Moody. "They get on Ninety-five heading into D.C. and all those problems get even worse."

"What's the ETA on our backup?" Beth said into the car radio.

"Fifteen minutes," same the answer from Quantico.

"They'll be on Ninety-five by then," said Beth.

"If we try and stop them and they get a chance to make a phone call to that house, especially before HRT gets there, we've got a potential disaster on our hands," said Moody. "If they've got hostages on the floor of that Blazer . . ." He let the rest hang out in the air.

"It might be better to have a standoff in a car where we can contain the scene," said Beth, thinking out loud.

"Unless they blow up the car as soon as we try to pull them over," said Moody.

Beth was becoming impatient with the way the dialogue was going. "Well, what do you say, Paul? Take them down or take the risk of losing contact?"

"I don't know—it's your call."

With undisguised contempt, Beth said, "Okay, Paul, I'll be sure to make a note of that for the record." Then on the radio to Storey, "Ed, our backup's fifteen minutes out. We can't risk losing them in the dark. We may have to take them down before they can get on Ninety-five."

"Told you," said Troy.

"Whatever you want to do is okay with us," Storey said into the radio. "There's a park about a quarter of a mile ahead." He'd been checking the map while they were staking out the house.

"Better there than on a residential street," Beth radioed back.

"You might want to remind them we're the ones with the bulletproof vehicle," said Troy.

"Good point," said Storey. Then into the radio, "Beth, remember our vehicle's armored."

"I'm keeping it in mind," Beth replied into the walkie-talkie. Aware of the kind of groupthink that took place when the boys were standing around the radio watching each other and their own backs, she took out her cell phone and called Timmins directly. "Ben? Yeah, I didn't want to use the radio. What do *you* want to do? Look, Ben, if you want me to let them onto the highway, I'll let them onto the highway. Then at least get the local police to seal off the streets around the house. You're right, Ben, that's your call. You've got about a minute before they're on a busy road that accesses Ninety-five. I do not want to try and take them down there. Okay, then call me on the radio and clear me to take them down." Beth knew Timmins was going to hate doing that, but she also knew that if everything worked out right he'd remember being in charge, and if things went wrong his memory of the call was going to become really fuzzy.

Timmins's deputy came over the radio, clearing them to apprehend the suspects.

Beth smiled and went back to the walkie-talkie. "Ed, we just got clearance to take them down." And she told him what she wanted to do.

"Roger," said Storey. And then to Troy, "We're taking them down. Buckle up."

"Hold your arm out," said Troy, threading on Storey's body armor vest. Then he donned his shooting glasses. "How's my hair look?"

"Perfect," Storey replied, without taking his eyes off the road.

Beth put on her SWAT tactical vest. "Lean forward," she said, sliding Moody's body armor behind his back. Alternating hands on the wheel, he slipped his arms in and she secured the front.

Beth tripped the lights and siren.

"I'm going to have to get used to the concept of giving them fair warning," Troy remarked to Storey.

"What the fuck?" al-Sharif exclaimed. He looked down at the speedometer. It wasn't speed. "Did I run a red light?"

"No," said Omar.

Al-Sharif took a closer look in the rearview mirror. "That's an unmarked car. This is no traffic stop. They must've gotten Nimri or Dawood."

"What are we doing?" said Omar.

"You can do what you like," said al-Sharif. "I'm not going back to prison."

"I killed a cop," said Omar.

"Then get that duffel bag open."

Omar climbed into the backseat.

"They're not running, and they're not stopping," said Moody.

Omar pushed the open vest over al-Sharif's head, connecting the front and back panels with the Velcro straps. He jammed the metal cylinders in between the seat cushions. Pipe bombs, foot-long sections of steel pipe filled with gunpowder and capped at both ends. He rocked thirty-round magazines into the two folding stock AK-47s and cocked the actions.

Beth retrieved the 10mm MP-5/10 submachine gun from under her seat.

"Brace your feet and keep a good grip on the rifles," al-Sharif said to Omar. He told him what he was going to do.

Omar make sure his seat belt was tight. Al-Sharif pushed the gas pedal to the floorboard.

"There he goes," said Moody, speeding up and closing the distance.

"Will it work?" said Omar.

"They talked about it in prison," said al-Sharif. "I practiced it a few times on the street, but never for real."

There was an unmoving line of taillights up ahead at an intersection. Al-Sharif wasn't sure he could get around them. Alternating brake and gas, he made a skidding high-speed turn onto the next side street.

"Son of a bitch can drive," Moody exclaimed.

In between calling in their location on the radio, Beth said, "He's a car thief. Been running from cops all his life."

"Get ready," al-Sharif said to Omar. He took his foot off the gas to slow them down without showing brake lights. The flashing blue lights had closed to almost behind them. He hit the brake hard, cut the wheel, and yanked on the emergency brake.

"Shit!" Moody yelled. He tried to drive around, but the Blazer was turning broadside in the street. They hit it at nearly full speed.

Beth's eyes instinctively closed at the impact. A thunderous bang and air bag deployment; then eyes open, and the side of the Blazer point-blank in the cracked windshield. They hadn't stopped moving yet, and she'd lost her grip on both the radio and the submachine gun.

"Give me the rifle!" al-Sharif screamed to Omar.

Omar pushed it over the seat to him. He couldn't get the safety on his off—the AK's was awkward. Finally it slid down and he fired through the now-glassless side window.

The cracked windshield exploded, and Moody shouted in pain. Beth ducked down below the dash, glass showering her like rain. She tried to get lower, but was hung up on her seat belt. She had to twist around to find the button. It wouldn't unlock. Bullets were breaking the sound barrier an inch over her head. She yanked at the belt with all her might and when it finally came free the momentum threw her under the dash.

Beth started feeling around on the floor for the submachine gun before she realized how stupid that was. Still wedged under the dash, she grabbed the door lever and kicked the door. It was jammed too. No, it wasn't. It was locked. She leaned forward, flipped the latch, and kicked the door again. It creaked open, taking another kick to make enough room for her to get out.

Somehow her hair was stuck to her face and she couldn't see. Beth raked it out of the way and swept the Glock 22 pistol off her hip. The stress had dilated her pupils and she had to blink hard to focus on the pistol front sight. She opened fire on the yellow muzzle flashes inside the Blazer. Metallic screaming as bullets began to punch through the door beside her.

"Motherfucker!" Storey exclaimed when he saw the Blazer spin out and hit the sedan. Troy had already switched his radio to the FBI command frequency and was calling it in.

Al-Sharif dropped his rifle on the seat and grabbed the wheel. They were leaving, and even if they weren't dead those cops were not going to be following.

"Hold on!" said Storey, stepping on the gas. Muzzle flashes were blossoming inside the Blazer. The FBI sedan was under fire at point-blank range.

Storey spun the wheel, making a looping half circle to line the front of his ram bumper up with the front of the Blazer.

Al-Sharif saw the approaching headlights and groped for the shift, trying to get moving and out of the way. Not fast enough. When the other car hit, it felt as if his neck had snapped in half. Rebounding from the impact, he hit his head on the steering wheel.

Storey stayed on the gas, ramming the Blazer right up over the sidewalk.

For a second Beth hadn't been sure what happened. Another huge bang in front of her, and the sedan spinning sideways, knocking her out of her kneeling position and onto the street. Then from the ground, the sight of the Blazer sailing by under the power of the Cherokee.

When the Blazer hit the curb, al-Sharif's seat collapsed, throwing him into the backseat.

Storey kept his right foot down, the Cherokee swerving as the tires threw up dirt, aiming the Blazer into a line of trees. He braked just before that happened, to put a little separation between the two vehicles. The Blazer continued on and hit the trees.

As soon as they stopped Troy was out the door. But as he brought up his M-14 he realized it was too dark for his telescopic sight. He could see the red luminous crosshairs perfectly, but nothing else in the dark circle to aim them at. With no time to rip off the scope to uncover the iron sights, he fired instinctively, hammering rounds into the windshield and hood.

Omar opened his door and rolled out. He rose up on his knees, trying to get the AK into the V-shaped notch between the car body and the door window.

Storey saw the door open. Then he noticed the shadow of a leg beneath it. Extrapolating upward, he settled his sight on where he imagined the body would be behind the door. Just as he was about to fire, something appeared above the door. Storey shifted, and the red dot of his Aimpoint sight floated upward. As soon as the dot stopped, Storey slapped the trigger.

The 7.62mm armor-piercing round caught Omar at the tip of the shoulder and took his entire left arm off. The force spun him completely around and dropped him on the grass.

It took al-Sharif a moment to realize that he was in the back of the Blazer. His vision was fuzzy, but he knew the vehicle was being shot to pieces. He thrashed around like a drowning man trying to find the surface, and his arm hit his AK-47. Grabbing it, he scrambled over the seat, falling into the cargo area. He landed on something metal. One of the pipe bombs. He stuck it into his belt.

Storey saw Omar go down. He threw himself flat on the ground so he could fire under his door. He saw what looked like a leg first, and knew a lot could happen while you waited around for a better target.

Omar was bleeding out from his severed brachial artery, but at least for the moment pumping adrenaline was counterbalancing dropping blood pressure. He tried to tug the pistol from his belt with his right hand.

Until Storey's next round hit him above the knee and shattered his femur. Omar let out a howling scream.

Now Storey could make out the body and fired five more rounds in rapid succession. The 7.62mm went right through Omar's vest. He was dead after the second round, though since each impact kept jerking his body, Storey kept firing.

The scream had driven al-Sharif into motion. He dug around in his pocket for the butane lighter. With one hand on the latch of the rear hatch, it took three spins of the wheel to get the lighter to ignite. He pushed the flame into the fuse of the pipe bomb in his belt. The fuse ignited.

Al-Sharif twisted the latch, and as the hatch sprang up he threw first his rifle and them himself out onto the ground.

Troy saw the hatch go up but didn't have an angle for a good shot. That didn't stop him from emptying his magazine into the back of the Blazer.

Beth saw al-Sharif spill out the back of the Blazer, and she had the angle. Bracing herself against the car door, she settled the three glowing tritium dots of her pistol sight onto the form. As it sprang up she fired.

As al-Sharif threw the pipe bomb he felt as if he'd taken an incredibly hard punch to the chest. It knocked his wind out and sat him back down on the ground.

Storey saw the sputtering fuse spinning in the air, not the pipe bomb. He'd been in the process of getting to his feet, but instead yelled, "Grenade!" and threw himself back down.

Troy didn't see the throw but he heard the warning. And whether that grenade was incoming or outgoing made no difference—grenades tended not to discriminate. He dove face-first onto the grass.

The FBI training curriculum skimmed over immediate actions to grenade attack, so Beth hadn't developed the same instinct. She was still upright when the pipe bomb blew. The blast did what the warning hadn't—knocked her down.

Regaining his breath, al-Sharif grasped the rifle. Though he didn't know it, his vest had stopped both of

Beth's .40-caliber pistol rounds. At the sound of the explosion he was off and running.

Troy saw al-Sharif disappear into the trees. "One tango moving!" he shouted.

As he advanced on the Blazer, Storey cautiously circled around until he got a good look at Omar. "Other one's down," he called back. "Let's go!"

Beth was already back up on her feet. She ran up to Troy. "I'll stay behind him—you go wide to the right."

Troy recognized the wisdom. Storey was already out on the left. If there was an ambush, spread out they were less of a target. And one of them might just be able to cut him off.

Storey caught sight of al-Sharif running through the park, but a 7.62mm round flew a long way and he wasn't going to be sending any out into the darkness until he knew just what was behind his target. He tried the radio, but only Troy was on the net with him. Beth must have lost or broken hers. He thought about putting in a call to the FBI command center, but this was no time to change frequencies and lose contact with Troy.

Al-Sharif was running flat out, and so were they. The park wasn't large, and they soon crossed it. There was some kind of nonresidential building up ahead, all lit up. At this time of the evening? "What's that building?" Storey said over the radio. Al-Sharif was heading right for it.

"Looks like a school," Troy called back. "Parking lot's full of cars."

From the sound of his voice you could hardly tell he was running. Now Storey saw it better. It was a school, and there were people walking all around. What the hell were they doing at a school at this hour? Parents' night? Damn it.

Al-Sharif crossed the street and sprinted for the parking lot. A pair of headlights popped on in front of him, the sign of a car starting up.

The driver just stared at the man with the rifle running up to his car, as if he couldn't believe it because it was the suburbs.

Al-Sharif had done this before. He yanked the unlocked door open, grabbed the driver by the hair, and dragged him out of the car. In the prison yard they always said it was easier to drag a live motherfucker who wanted out anyway than a dead body. The woman in the passenger seat was screaming. He'd get rid of her later, when he had time.

Al-Sharif gunned the car into reverse to get out of the parking space. With a ride under him he was as good as gone.

Beth draped herself over the hood of a nearby car to make a stable shooting platform. But the woman passenger was right in her line of fire. All she could do was shout, "FBI! Shut off the engine!"

A command al-Sharif had no intention of complying with. He shifted into drive.

Storey fired a whole twenty-round magazine so fast that, even though he wasn't, it sounded as if he were on full auto. But not at al-Sharif—the woman passenger was in *his* line of fire too. Storey shot out the front and back side tires with his first two rounds, then put the rest right into the engine block. The engine blew and smoke began pouring from the hood.

As soon as the first rounds hit, al-Sharif crawled over the woman and out her door. He got his left arm around her neck and dragged her, still screaming, behind him. He fired a couple of rounds one-handed to discourage pursuit.

"Get around to the back of the building," Storey radioed Troy. He and Beth followed al-Sharif, moving from cover to cover. He knew he'd have to get a head shot, but the light was variable and the opportunities were fleeting.

Al-Sharif pulled the woman up the walkway to the

door, staying crouched down behind her. The door was locked. Someone inside had heard the shooting and locked it. Al-Sharif fired one-handed at the long glass window beside the door. After three rounds the firing pin clicked on an empty chamber. He was out of ammunition. He let go of the woman and frantically swung the rifle to smash the glass.

Storey edged around the corner and got his first view of the door alcove, which was recessed into the building. He snapped off a quick shot just as al-Sharif swung the rifle again.

The bullet skimmed past al-Sharif's head, struck the brick wall, and peppered him with masonry. He dropped the rifle and crashed through the window.

Storey made a radio call to Troy. "He's inside the school, but he lost his rifle."

Al-Sharif pulled the pistol from his holster and ran down the hallway, screaming parents scattering before him.

Beth covered Storey as he went through the window. The woman hostage was sitting on the concrete walkway, still wailing. Storey was halfway down the hall when Beth got inside, and she sprinted to catch up.

Storey was crouched down low, exposing only one eyeball before he went around the corner. As Beth came up behind him he pointed to the floor. Al-Sharif had cut himself on the window, and was leaving tiny, almost unnoticeable blood drops on the linoleum. Not that they couldn't track his passage from all the screams they were hearing.

Al-Sharif knew he had to get out of the building before they surrounded it. He was almost at the back. There had to be a door somewhere. As he turned the corner he ran into a knot of people. They were scared, bunching together in a herd instinct without ever realizing what they were doing.

Al-Sharif screamed, "On the floor, all of you!" As they

dropped he grabbed a woman by the arm. Women didn't try to be heroes.

"Please, not me!" she begged.

Al-Sharif ground the pistol barrel into her cheek. "Shut up or I'll blow your head off." Then to the others, "The rest of you stay down there." He looked around. There was a fire door. Finally. He dragged her to the door and pushed it open.

Troy heard the fire door first, then saw the flash of light as it opened. Al-Sharif with a woman in front of him. This would have been a great time to take a shot with the ACOG scope. Too bad he'd already taken it off the rifle. Putting it back on would be useless. He wouldn't dare take that kind of shot without rezeroing the sights. And he wouldn't try a head shot behind a hostage barrier with iron sights. At least not at that distance.

If al-Sharif didn't have a hostage, Troy wanted him outside. But with a hostage he had to be inside the building and contained. Troy fired a shot into the wall right above al-Sharif's head.

The woman screamed and al-Sharif pulled her back inside. He'd been hearing those big booming rifles all night. He didn't know who they were, but that wasn't the usual cop firepower. He had to find another way out. But he couldn't move dragging the bitch along with him. He threw her back onto the pile of people on the floor.

Troy checked the compass on his Suunto wristwatch. "Tango tried to come out a fire door on the north side," he radioed Storey. "I drove him back in. He has a hostage. White female."

"Roger," Storey replied curtly. He checked the next corner. There was a bunch of civilians huddled on the floor, but they were all white. "You people all right?"

"He went that way," one of the men blurted out, pointing.

"Get up, get out that door, and get away from the building," Beth ordered.

"Civilians coming out," Storey radioed Troy.

"Roger," Troy replied. Through the windows lining that outside hallway, he caught sight of al-Sharif running. "Got a visual. Tango's heading for the west side of the building. Just turned the corner. No hostage, I say again, no hostage."

"Roger," Storey replied. Now he and Beth could move a little faster.

Al-Sharif saw two wooden swinging doors and crashed through them. The lights were all out, but enough outside lighting was coming through the windows for him to easily make out the cafeteria. There had to be a door to the outside near the windows.

When Storey heard the thump of the doors he went around the corner without his usual caution. He signaled Beth that he was going right, and she should stay low.

Keeping both hands on his rifle, Storey hit the door with his shoulder, darting across the fatal funnel of the doorway.

Just like Troy, al-Sharif saw the flash of hallway light as the door opened. He turned and snapped off two quick shots, ducking down below the tables.

Beth was coming through the door at a crouch, and the rounds hit the wood over her head.

Storey fired at the muzzle flashes but didn't hear anything to indicate a hit.

Al-Sharif felt as much as heard the two bullets going by. By God, this bastard was good. And he had just a pistol against that rifle. He had to get out of there. He looked down the even line of tables and saw another side door. Not daring to show himself, he moved down the aisle on his hands and knees. By God, every time he stopped moving and started again, his body hurt worse. His head was aching something terrible.

Storey edged along the wall, scanning the cavernous room. Nothing was visible above the tables. He dropped down on one knee, but there were too many chair and table legs to see well underneath them in the darkness. He tried to listen carefully, but after shooting a high-velocity rifle one's hearing wasn't at its best.

Al-Sharif reached the end of the row of tables. He had to cross maybe twenty feet of open space before reaching the short hallway that funneled into the door. Rising up into a crouch, he said a prayer for help, hoping he had another sprint in him. Then he burst from the blocks.

Storey saw the movement and swung his rifle around. Not fast enough—the figure disappeared, and Storey didn't shoot just to make noise. The echoing boom of another door opening, and he and Beth were in pursuit again.

Al-Sharif found himself in the middle of a totally empty hallway. He knew he'd never reach either end in time. Instead he dashed right across the hallway and into a classroom. The lights were off in all of these, and it took a moment for his eyes to adjust.

Storey shouldered his way through the door, staying low. He bobbed his head out into the hallway, drawing it back immediately. Empty. He couldn't have gotten down it that fast. Then Storey looked down and saw a blood drop that had been smeared along by a shoe, pointing right across the hall.

He gestured to Beth, then got on the radio. "Move to the south side, he may be coming out a window."

"Roger," Troy replied while he was already moving.

Storey prepared a flash-bang, motioning toward the door.

But Beth shook her head, making a wide gesture with both arms.

Storey realized he'd forgotten his school days. All the classrooms along that side of the hall probably had interconnecting interior doorways.

He also got his first good look at Beth in the light. The hair on one side of her head was matted down with blood; there was a cut across the bridge of her nose and red scratches across her cheek. Her normally rosy face was pure white. The body draws all available blood inward to the torso under the stress of combat.

Beth grabbed the flash-bang from his hand and pointed down at the floor—*stay here.* Then she was running down the hallway, disappearing into a classroom at the end.

Storey got it—she was going to flush al-Sharif out so he only had two choices: go out a window to Troy or come out into the hallway to him. Except he would have preferred to do the flushing. Or maybe wait until some help arrived so they could at least do it in pairs. Alone anything could happen. He fretted about it but he was stuck. He had to sit tight.

The classroom windows didn't open—the school had central air. Al-Sharif picked up a desk, and just as he was about to heave it through the window he heard sirens and saw flashing blue and red lights. He couldn't go back out into the hallway. He was trapped.

Then, amazed that he hadn't noticed it before, he saw that there were doors to the classrooms on either side. And they were open. Probably by the janitor emptying wastebaskets. He could go all the way down to the end, and maybe find a way out.

Beth hadn't missed Storey's technique for checking around corners. He made a quick peek down low. You always expected a head to appear at head height.

She hooked the spoon of the flash-bang over her belt, keeping a good two-handed grip on her Glock.

The doors were all in a line. If she'd been standing up she could have seen all the way to the end. But down low there were desks in the way.

Storey heard the sirens and called Troy on the radio. "You in position?"

"Roger," Troy replied.

"Then I'm going off the net to talk to the FBI."

"Roger," Troy repeated.

Storey changed frequencies, calling the FBI command center to tell them the situation, that they were in the school, and to tell the local cops not to shoot them by mistake. Of course all the suits had a million questions and wanted to hear everything in detail. He switched them off and went back to the frequency Troy was on.

The reflection of the outside lights on the windows made it impossible for Troy to see inside the darkened classrooms. He'd just have to wait until someone bailed out a window.

Al-Sharif paused at each doorway for a quick look before he went through. He usually had to dodge around a row of desks in order to reach the next one. More sirens outside. More lights. He picked up his pace.

Beth moved very slowly, afraid the soles of her shoes would squeak on the linoleum. She walked with her head turned slightly so she could hear better. Not that the sirens outside were making that any easier.

Entering another classroom, al-Sharif thought he heard something along one wall. He stopped and listened. A metal squeak. He swung about and almost fired. There was an animal in a cage on a counter. A gerbil or something, running on its wheel. That was the squeaking—the wheel. His heart pounding, al-Sharif turned back toward the doorway. As he did, he nudged a desk and the metal leg scraped on the linoleum.

Beth heard it and froze. It sounded like the next classroom. She dropped down on one knee and took aim at the doorway.

Al-Sharif cursed the noise, but it really wasn't much louder than the animal wheel. He was wasting time.

Beth saw the shadow first. Her front sight was dancing—she pulled harder with her weak side hand to steady it. Then a figure appeared in the doorway. She waited until he took a step inside the room. "Freeze!"

The gun came up and she fired.

Al-Sharif felt that same punch in the chest. He charged forward, firing one-handed, screaming, "*Allahu Akbar!*"

Beth kept firing but he kept coming. Then a thought stabbed into her mind—*vest*—and she raised her aim point above center mass. He dropped right in front of her. Beth had fired her Glock dry, seventeen rounds in about five seconds. She dropped the empty pistol and snatched her backup piece, a snub-nosed Smith and Wesson Model 340 .357 magnum revolver, from her ankle holster. Realizing what was going to happen next, she shouted, "Clear!"

Storey crashed through the door, advancing on al-Sharif in that rock-steady left-foot-forward glide all the operators used.

Beth winced as he poked his rifle barrel into al-Sharif's open eye.

"He's dead," said Storey. "Don't move, he may be wired."

Storey switched on the classroom lights, momentarily blinding Beth. Very carefully, he searched al-Sharif for explosives.

Beth leaned forward to take a closer look. Al-Sharif *was* wearing a vest. There was a cluster of bullet holes in it, along with one in the throat and several in the face—she didn't feel like counting. "Did you hear what he was yelling?"

"No."

"Allah something."

"*Allahu Akbar?*"

"That sounds like it."

"God is great," said Storey. "If you're a holy warrior, those are supposed to be your last words."

"They were," said Beth.

Storey felt something bulky in the inside pocket of al-Sharif's jacket. "Hold on." It felt like paper, not explosives. Not wanting to move the zipper, Storey flicked out his knife and gingerly sliced the pocket open. It was papers. When he was satisfied that was all there was, he drew them out.

"What is it?" Beth asked.

"Don't know," said Storey, unfolding them on the floor. A Washington, D.C., and neighboring communities map, with routes marked in colored highlighter and a mark in Arlington. Storey flipped through the papers a little faster. "Rumsfeld? . . . Beth, you said the guy back at that house drove a tanker truck?"

"That's right."

The connection was instant. "They're going to blow it up in Arlington and try to take out Rumsfeld's limo." He went back to the map. The mark was within range of the Pentagon City shopping center, apartment buildings, schools, and a hospital. Storey thrust the radio into her hands. "Call it in, Beth. If they see any marked police cars or lights or sirens they'll blow the tanker right then and there."

Beth took the radio, and before she could switch frequencies Storey was gone.

Troy had seen the muzzle flashes but hadn't made any radio calls while everyone was busy.

Storey found him with hands outstretched, trying to talk down a bunch of jumpy Manassas cops with guns drawn.

"I told you, I'm with the FBI task force," Troy was saying. "Here's my military credentials and ATF card."

Running up on the scene, Storey was thankful that Beth had given them white-on-black FBI tags to velcro onto their vests. "We *are* with the FBI. We've got an agent inside who needs help. The gunman is down."

The Manassas 911 had received about thirty hysterical cell phone calls from parents about a black man with a rifle shooting at the school. They were somewhat mollified by the sight of a white man wearing the exact same equipment as the black man with the rifle.

"We've got a terrorist incident about to go down," said

Storey, flashing his ID. "Talk with Special Agent Beth Royale inside. We're leaving."

"Wait a minute," said a sergeant.

Troy watched him hit the cops with his stone-killer Green Beret Master Sergeant look.

"Son," said Storey, "you don't get out of my way, a lot of people are going to die tonight. Y'all will be the first." He grabbed Troy by the arm. "We need to get to the Cherokee."

They ran off, leaving the cops standing there.

"I hope they were real," the sergeant said.

"They had to be," another replied. "You see the shit they were carrying?"

27

Abdallah Karim Nimri had been deceived by the open limousine doors. Time passed and still it did not move from the entrance. He regretted telling al-Sharif and Omar to leave the house. It had been a mistake. What if one of the Oans managed to untie himself? Everything would be ruined.

He flicked open the phone to call al-Sharif and send him back. No. It was too late. They were miles away, and it would probably all be over before they could get back to the house.

After all, the whole point was for them to be miles away when it happened. It was all in God's hands.

As the twilight faded Nimri replaced the camera tele-photo lens with a starlight night scope.

The limousine and SUVs were still there. It was taking too long. The policeman who had talked to Dawood would come back, or another would stop to investigate the truck on the highway. Or someone would notice how long the photographer had been on this hillside, now too dark to take pictures.

Nimri felt as if he couldn't sit still, and yet he couldn't move. He forced himself to sit on the grass and look through the camera.

There was activity at the entrance. But this had happened before.

More of them now, coming out the doors. Then even more, gathering around. Men saluting. And two getting into the *back* of the limousine. All the vehicle headlights came on.

Nimri dialed the phone. "Dawood, they are preparing to move. Yes, finally. Be alert."

The convoy was moving now, and disappeared from Nimri's sight. He quickly swiveled the camera to the place where he would first see them on the highway. Not more than a minute. If they did not take an entirely different route tonight. *Please, God, not that.*

The seconds ticked away. It was agonizing. Nimri had never felt more frustrated.

More than a minute had passed. They had gone some other way. Because of the dinner they had gone another way. Nimri was resigned. His muscles uncoiled. He was defeated. He looked at the glowing screen of his phone. Time to finish it.

He went to move the camera onto the truck. By God, there was the convoy! Delayed somehow. He asked God's forgiveness for his lack of faith.

Nimri spoke into the phone. "Dawood, they are coming toward you. Be ready, my brother."

28

"The white man shows up and everything's all right," Lee Troy sputtered. "But can a brother get any love? No. No way. You weren't there—my ass'd be lynched right now."

Storey was topping out the Cherokee at around a hundred miles an hour, hoping the engine wouldn't blow. The vehicle was equipped with lights and a siren that only showed when they were turned on. "Ordinarily, you know I'd love to hear this. . . ."

It had taken them almost as much effort to get the Cherokee moving as it had to get away from the cops at the school. By the time they got to the vehicle it was already taped up as part of a crime scene, and the Manassas cops were none too accommodating. Troy had watched Storey turn into the barking drill sergeant, threatening them all with a command appearance in front of the next 9/11 commission.

"You really think we're going to get there ahead of the FBI?" said Troy.

"They have to get told. Then they have to get unfucked. Then they have to move. We're already moving."

"I still doubt it."

"While you're doubting, we need to keep the secretary

inside the Pentagon. Since I just thought of it, I reckon it's going to slip the FBI's mind."

"No problem," said Troy. "I've got Don's cell on my speed-dial."

"If that doesn't work, call the Pentagon ops center and have them pass the word on to him."

Feeling both stupid and punked, Troy got to work on his cell phone.

At least it kept his eyes off the road. Storey had started off in the car pool lane and was now weaving through all of them when the traffic didn't pull over fast enough.

Troy gave the duty officer his authentication code, and told him what was going down. Then was put on hold while the duty checked on the secretary's whereabouts.

They were getting close. "Switch off the lights and siren," Storey ordered, unwilling to take a hand off the wheel even for a second. He had to hit three exits to get off 395 and into the proper lane going in the right direction. A line of cars was stopped at the last exit.

Storey hit the brakes to slow down, the speed and weight of the Cherokee making it fishtail. Almost hitting the crash barrier, he swerved and hit the gap between two cars, knocking them both out of the way.

"Shit," said Troy.

Horns were blaring. Storey bulled through the opening he'd made. A grinding of metal car bodies; Storey hoping they wouldn't blow a tire.

"Get off the phone," he said. "Turn on the Warlock."

Troy switched on the black box plugged into the cigarette lighter. Really, really hoping it would work.

They made the exit, in the breakdown lane, at about fifty miles an hour. Troy was hoping there wasn't an actual breakdown anywhere up ahead.

Abdallah Karim Nimri was watching the convoy's progress in the shimmering green field of his night scope. He shifted the camera once again to take in both the truck and the length of highway approaching it. Nimri briefly took his eyes off the scope to make sure the first number in his phone book was entered. Placing his finger lightly over the Send button, he turned back to the scope.

Troy was making sure his magazine did indeed contain armor-piercing ammo, and locked it back into the M-14.

Storey was out of the breakdown lane and back up to speed. As he rounded a slight curve they both saw the four-way emergency flashers of the truck.

"Watch your angle," said Storey.

Troy was now making sure he had a round in the chamber. "Get me even with the cab."

Dawood gently touched the smooth plastic head of the mushroom switch. He shifted in his seat so he wouldn't have to stretch to reach it.

Storey gauged his stopping distance. Only one shot to do it right. At the center of the trailer he hit the brakes.

Dawood heard the tires and, startled, twisted his head to see the lights in the rear view mirror. He froze in a second of indecision and then raised his hand to slap the switch.

Troy was half out the window before the Cherokee even stopped. He fired through the driver's door, letting the recoil push his point of aim upward.

Dawood was watching his hand come down as the terrible burning blows knocked him over into the passenger seat.

In disbelief, Nimri pushed the Send button on his phone.

Storey's door was open and he was out, traffic swerving away from both the stopped Cherokee and the gunfire. He sprinted across the front of the vehicle with his .45 in his hand.

Lying flat across the passenger seat, Dawood could see the glowing screens of the two cell phones. Things were flying over his head. He tried to lift himself off the seat but couldn't. He couldn't feel his arm but imagined he saw it moving, so he swung it toward the switch.

Storey leaped up on the running board as Troy ceased fire. He pulled himself into the open window and emptied all eight rounds into Dawood, reloading in a blur.

Nimri kept pushing the Send button, waiting for the truck to blow up. He finally looked down at his phone. The screen said: *call failed.* He scrolled down to the second number and drove his thumb into the Send button again. Dialing. A ring tone. He looked over at the truck, waiting for the flash that would light up the night. The phone in his hand clicked, and a robotic voice announced that he'd reached the voice mail. Nimri threw the phone down and tried the other one.

The Warlock Green jammer continuously flashed through the entire radio frequency spectrum, transmitting enough power to drown out every incoming or outgoing signal within its range. Which, due to the power available from a car electrical system, was very short.

Storey leaned in the open window and clicked on the flashlight from his vest. Two cell phones taped to the cab meant there was someone within visual observation distance with another phone. Which meant he couldn't wait around for a bomb disposal technician. Who knew how long the Warlock was going to continue to work?

Storey climbed in through the open window, concerned about a booby-trapped door. He followed the phone wires to the larger bunch that led out to the trailer. Two from each phone, two from the switch on the dash. No others, which made him feel better about antihandling devices.

Storey knew more than a little about things that went bang, and it looked like Bomb-making 101 to him. Even so, he gave the problem the kind of intense consideration that's always justified when your life depends on your next move. He would have left little surprises all over the truck, just in case this exact thing happened.

Storey unfolded his multitool to expose the wire cutters. And clipped the pair leading from one cell phone, twisting them together to shunt the circuit. Still alive, he clipped the other pair.

"What's up?" Troy called through the window.

"Check the trailer for another cell phone initiator," said Storey. "Follow the wiring. Whatever you do, *leave the Cherokee running*. I'm thinking the Warlock is all that's keeping us away from the pearly gates right now."

"I'm all over it," said Troy.

Once more in a place where he could not scream, Abdallah Karim Nimri, tears running down his face, beat his fists in frustration on the grass of a Virginia hillside covered with the gravestones of American war dead.

29

The Cherokee hatch was up. Storey and Troy were sitting with their legs dangling over the bumper. One of the FBI agents had gotten them coffee.

The highway was blocked off at the nearest two exits, and explosive ordnance disposal technicians were crawling over the trailer. A tow truck was awaiting their clearance to drive it away.

After only a very few fast crime scene photos, Dawood had been zipped up in a body bag, tossed into an ambulance, and removed from the scene immediately.

"Well," said Troy, "looks like you won't get busted down to sergeant first class and end up a platoon sergeant in some straight-leg infantry division."

"And you won't get busted to second-class petty officer and end up on the next replenishment ship leaving Norfolk," said Storey.

"FBI guy told me Rumsfeld's convoy drove right by while we were shooting," said Troy.

"I'll bet the head of the security detail dropped a log right in his pants," said Storey, chuckling.

"Here comes Timmins," said Troy.

"He's going to start off by telling us all the rules we broke," said Storey. "For a lot of reasons, but mainly because we got here before his FBI boys did. Then he'll give us a grudging attaboy at the end, so we don't think we're getting over on him."

Timmins stopped in front of them as if he was expecting them to spring to attention and salute. Storey and Troy remained seated.

"Okay," said Timmins, "let's sum this up. When the FBI agents you were supporting lost their radios during the vehicle stop, you failed to pick up the slack and maintain communications with us. We didn't have a clue where you were and what you were doing until people at that school started calling 911. Only then do we get a radio call from you. Then, despite the fact that you'd discharged your firearms, you left that crime scene." He gestured toward the Cherokee. "You removed evidence from another crime scene before it could be processed. We might have lost a case because of it."

Timmins stopped for a moment, as if expecting them to either argue or defend themselves. But they had plenty of experience with officers in the military getting all wound up, and were only waiting patiently for him to finish. Troy was thinking: what case? Both the motherfuckers were dead.

"Despite all that questionable judgment," Timmins continued, "you two saved a lot of lives tonight. You did a good job."

He said that just as Troy was in the middle of a sip of coffee. He choked on it and had to cough it out. "Sorry, sir, coffee's too hot."

"How's Special Agent Moody, sir?" Storey asked, as if he hadn't been listening to any of it.

"He's on a ventilator," said Timmins. "Critical."

"You want to talk about good jobs, sir," said Storey, gigging him again, "every decision Beth Royale made tonight was the real key to the outcome."

Timmins only nodded at that, so Storey went on. "Anything on our fourth man, sir?"

"Nimri?" said Timmins.

"Yes, sir."

"There aren't too many vantage points of this spot," said Timmins. "Out of range of the potential blast area of this truck, that is." He pointed to the northwest. "We found a camera on a tripod and a camera bag on a hill in the cemetery. No prints on anything. There was a note in the bag—this is confidential, by the way."

"We understand, sir," said Storey.

"The note said 'next time.'"

"Fucker's got style," Troy remarked.

"How's this going to be handled, sir?" Troy asked.

"Tanker truck driver had a heart attack," said Timmins. "Two cop killers died in a shootout with FBI agents in Manassas."

"I see, sir," said Storey.

"Good job, guys," said Timmins.

As soon as he was out of earshot, Troy started mimicking him. "Good job, guys. Good job, guys. Better believe it was a good fucking job. Fuck you, if it wasn't for us a third of Arlington and probably a good piece of Alexandria would still be burning. And the president would be looking for a new boss for us."

"We were lucky," said Storey.

"Fuck yes."

"We only have to be lucky once—you have to be lucky every time."

"Sounds like a quote to me," said Troy.

"That's what the IRA said after they missed blowing up Margaret Thatcher at a Conservative Party Conference in England."

"Fuckers were right," said Troy. "That's the equation. They only have to be lucky once."

"We certainly can't expect to be this lucky every time," said Storey.

30

"Okay, who's next?" the operator yelled.

"Here you go," Karen the Spook shouted back. "Right here."

"I can't believe you're making me do this," said Beth Royale.

Karen's smile was dazzling. "Redskins twenty, Patriots seventeen. Time to pay up."

"You're such a bitch," said Beth.

"Did I mention you look simply adorable in your little red cowboy boots?" said Karen. She handed over the red cowboy hat Beth had conveniently forgotten at their table. "Your hat, my dear. A cowgirl isn't a cowgirl without her hat."

"A total bitch," said Beth, jamming the hat onto her head.

"You up or not?" the operator yelled over the noise of the crowd.

Beth shot him a murderous look.

"She's up," Karen assured him. "She's definitely up." She handed Beth a tequila shooter. "For the pain."

"An absolute, utter bitch," said Beth, tossing down the shot. "Aaagh. Where's my lime?"

"Only men need limes," Karen informed her.

"*Bitch.* Okay, let's get this over with." Beth stalked out into the padded circle and swung herself onto the mechanical bull.

The bar crowd, whooping it up, gave her a big hand.

Softening somewhat, instead of giving them the finger, Beth tipped her hat. Then she pointed an accusatory forefinger at the bull operator, as if to say: *I've got my eye on you.*

No doubt having seen it all, he responded with his own look of *yeah, yeah, whatever.* "You ready?"

Beth got a good grip on the loop and nodded.

The mechanism began to whir, and it gave a little jump as it started to move. A smooth buck, and the bull swung around. This wasn't so bad. Beth felt a little like Debra Winger in *Urban Cowboy.* Oh, shit. It was bouncing up and down, slamming her into the seat over and over again. Beth locked her thighs in a death grip on the leather seat. Her arm felt as if it were coming out of its socket. Her hat flew off. A roar came up from the crowd. Beth was hanging half off the bull. Then a roll and a snap, and she was in the air, landing face-first on the mats, with her butt sticking up in the air. A round of applause from the audience.

Beth rolled over, and there was an outstretched male hand being offered to her. She looked up, and the hand belonged to Ed Storey.

"Oh my God," Beth groaned. "If there's anyone from my office here Karen better be on her way to Mexico right now."

"Don't come up shooting," said Storey. "I don't see anyone."

Beth accepted the hand up. Her crotch felt as if it had been beaten with a baton. "Now I know why cowboys walk bowlegged."

Outside the padded circle Storey handed Beth her hat. Which she never, ever wanted to see again. "Thanks." Then she turned on him. "How did you get here?"

"Oh, I just stopped in for a beer," Storey said innocently. "And there you were on the bull."

Beth detected the evil hand of Karen the Spook. "A likely story." Her face was a particularly deep shade of scarlet. "My humiliation is now complete."

"I wouldn't say that," said Storey. "I wasn't watching the clock, but it had to have been over eight seconds."

"That's not really what I meant, Ed."

Storey took in the boots and jeans, and western snap-button shirt. "You look great," he said.

"Did I say anything out loud while I was bucking on that thing?"

"Nothing in English," Storey replied.

"There better not be any video."

Storey held out his arms in the universal gesture of *not me.*

Every step Beth took revealed a new pain in a different part of her lower body. "God, my riding days are definitely over."

"That's sad news," said Storey. "You should probably let me buy you a drink."

Beth looked up again, and his face was as red as hers. "All right."

BOOK YOUR PLACE ON OUR WEBSITE AND MAKE THE READING CONNECTION!

We've created a customized website just for our very special readers, where you can get the inside scoop on everything that's going on with Zebra, Pinnacle and Kensington books.

When you come online, you'll have the exciting opportunity to:

- View covers of upcoming books
- Read sample chapters
- Learn about our future publishing schedule (listed by publication month *and author*)
- Find out when your favorite authors will be visiting a city near you
- Search for and order backlist books from our online catalog
- Check out author bios and background information
- Send e-mail to your favorite authors
- Meet the Kensington staff online
- Join us in weekly chats with authors, readers and other guests
- Get writing guidelines
- AND MUCH MORE!

**Visit our website at
http://www.kensingtonbooks.com**